The True Measure

Terran Armor Corps Book 3

Richard Fox

PROLOGUE

Howling winds whipped snow across the mountain range as a single Mule transport descended from orbit. The gale swayed the ship from side to side as it sank beneath the side of a mountain range, the white caps of blown snow stretching like grasping hands toward the Mule.

It set down in a valley, running lights on and idling engines melting the snow pack.

In the cargo compartment, a woman unbuckled herself from an acceleration seat and shrugged off a coat. She pulled her long blonde hair into a ponytail and touched a bulge in a thigh pocket.

"This is the place." A burly man unsnapped a gauss carbine from the side of his chair and slapped in a magazine.

"Put that away, Medvedev. You'll make them nervous," she said.

"They want to meet on some no-name world in a no-name system for the exchange. They're already nervous. Having this means we don't trust, because you should never trust nervous people. You taught me that, Masha," he said.

"I can't wait for you to go back to the legions, you know that?" She walked down the empty cargo bay. She leaned close to the closed ramp, listening to the wind outside.

"Don't get captured by Haesh gangsters. The agency won't assign you a bodyguard." Medvedev rolled his shoulders forward and tapped the carbine against a meaty palm.

"I hardly need—"

Three knocks sounded at the ramp.

"Punctual," she said. "They are nervous."

Medvedev raised the carbine to his shoulder

as the ramp lowered. Snow broke against the weak force field separating the wintry world beyond and the cargo bay. A Vishrakath marched up the ramp; the ant-like alien walked upright on four limbs and wore nothing to protect its bare flesh from the elements. Two more Vishrakath came behind it, carrying a large metal case.

"The item." The lead alien extended a hand toward Masha.

"That's not how this works," she said. "I verify what you've brought, make sure you didn't kill it in the cold, then you can examine what I've got."

"We have what you want. Make the trade and conclude our business," the alien said.

"Take off your coat, stay awhile." Masha took a hand scanner off her belt and shook it at the two Vishrakath between her and the case.

Medvedev took two steps forward before the aliens got out of the way.

Masha ran the scanner over the lock and the lid popped open. Inside were several bags of green fluid in a chiller. She gave one bag a squeeze, then touched the scanner to it.

"Grade A green blood cells." She touched the scanner to another bag. "Just what the doctor ordered to combat infectious diseases the galaxy over. Where did you guys get this?"

"The security apparatus on New Bastion is less than efficient," the lead Vishrakath said. "We intercepted it in customs en route to your embassy."

"Not *our* embassy." She took a small box out of her thigh pocket and tossed it to the alien.

The Vishrakath removed a small plate from its utility belt and set the box on top. A hologram of a spacecraft modeled after a conch shell appeared over the box. Reams of data flashed up and down the sides of the holo.

"Why would you part with such knowledge?" the alien asked. "This artifact is far more priceless than a few liters of green blood cells."

"Well, no one's found it yet." Masha brushed the scanner along the inside of the case.

"And we have a colony full of people dying because their immune system encountered a virus we didn't find when we scouted the planet. Do Vishrakath understand that a bird in hand is worth more than two in the bush?"

"We do not." The alien slipped the box into a pouch.

"Horiek hiltzeko bigarren batean," she said to Medvedev.

"What?" The skin around the Vishrakath's eyes darkened.

"Another old saying. The trade was green blood cells for our data on the Qa'Resh Ark that's hidden somewhere in the galaxy. Not for green blood cells in a case with a tracking device. I was going to kill you and feel bad about it. Now I'm just going to kill you out of principle." She aimed her thumb and forefinger at the Vishrakath.

"Earth humor is not appreciated. The case—" The alien's head exploded with one shot from Medvedev's carbine. He cut down the other two a heartbeat later.

"Amateurs!" Masha lifted up a seat and pulled out a cooler with biohazard labels on it. She transferred the blood pouches as Medvedev removed the data box from the dead alien, then kicked the alien corpses down the ramp.

Masha let her bodyguard get rid of the case with the tracking device as she tapped in a command on her forearm computer.

"*Warsaw,* we've got the jackpot. Send the fighter strike to destroy their lander and take out whatever rock they came in. Send word back to Lady Ibarra that Balmaseda will have their green blood cells soon. We'll take the rest back to Navarre for processing as soon as we can."

Medvedev raised the ramp.

"See," she said, "I didn't even need you."

"I don't find you funny. I would be angrier, but I got to kill aliens. Today is a good day."

"Oh, by the Saint, how long do I have to deal with you?" she said, almost pouting.

****

Soon after the exchange ended on the unnamed and unclaimed ice planet, the *Warsaw* passed through the system's Crucible jump gate. Inside a bag of green blood cells, inert nanites were roused to life by the graviton disturbance. They melded into a small machine and sent a single transmission through the Crucible network.

Then, once the graviton field faded away as the *Warsaw* transited through the wormhole, the nano-machine broke apart and returned to slumber.

CHAPTER 1

Frost grew around the bars of Roland's cell. His breath fogged with each exhalation and his soaked body glove stiffened against him as the amniosis fluid from his armor's womb thickened in the frigid air.

In the next cell over, a metal man cocked his head to one side and stepped closer to the bars between them. His head was a perfect sculpture of middle-aged man of European heritage, but the skin and widow's peaked hair were silver, his every feature marked out by slight lines in the metal. Covering his body was a simple jumpsuit of the same silver color, like he was an incomplete drawing of a man, the lines inked but the rest uncolored.

"Like I said, I'm Marc Ibarra," the man said. His mouth didn't move when he spoke, but a slight ripple emanated across his face. "You have heard of me, haven't you? It's not like I was gone from Earth *that* long."

The chill air stung the edges of Roland's ears and his fingers ached. He stepped back, his heel cracking a thin sheen of ice on the floor of his cell.

"What the hell are you?" Roland asked, nearly slipping as he retreated to a bunk bolted to the wall.

"Inventor, entrepreneur, bold explorer…savior." Ibarra leaned his forearms against the bars as hoarfrost crept away from where his metal limbs met the bars. "I've been called much worse too. Now I'm a prisoner, one so unique—or utterly irrelevant—I don't even rate a number. Maybe now that you're down here, the guards will have to do something to tell us apart, though I doubt they'll ever confuse us."

He pulled back, and his arms caught against the bars, frozen in place.

"What the—?" His brow furrowed and he pulled his forearms free with a snap. "Ah...that's right, keep forgetting. They keep my cell's temperature and humidity regulated to stop this sort of thing. That I was throwing snowballs at the Tweedles after I was thrown in here probably had something to do with that...and why they took my sink and crapper away. Not that I needed them."

"Is...is everyone here like you?" Roland wrapped a blanket around his shoulders, and frost in his body glove cracked as he huddled against his mattress for warmth. "S-S-Stacey Ibarra..." He spat the name out as his teeth chattered. "She was—"

Marc Ibarra looked up at the ceiling and shouted, "Help the kid out! He's turning blue and I don't want a popsicle in my cell block." He stepped back from the bars. Roland didn't feel any warmer, but at least the air around him seemed to stabilize.

A vent behind thin crisscrossing bars blew

hot, wet air that turned to mist in Roland's cell. After a few minutes, Roland flung his blanket aside and squeezed the last of the amniosis from his body glove.

"The guards are listening to us…and watching us too would be a fair guess," Roland said, glancing around the cell. The jail was comprised of only two cells and a narrow hallway that ended at a vault door.

"That they answered me just means they assume you're not an idiot. Don't underestimate Stacey, kiddo," Marc Ibarra said. "I made that mistake and you can see where it landed me. All those decades of scheming and manipulating…I taught her too well. Most grandfathers I know would want their future generations to surpass them, but with Stacey…I would have been happy for her to live a normal, humdrum life. You know, a career, a pudgy husband with a decent office job, two kids and change. Not in the cards for her. Or anyone on Earth."

"You said we're in Navarre, capital of the

Ibarra Nation. Where exactly is that? How do I get back to Earth?" Roland asked.

"Ooh, you're an optimistic one. Well, to get home, all you need to do is break out of this cell, get past the many, many humorless guards in this building, commandeer a spacecraft, get to the Crucible gate, and enter in the code for Ceres or some other Earth solar system—all the while being chased by Stacey's forces. And I've got news for you, kid," Ibarra said, tapping the back of his head where Roland's plugs were, "you're not going to blend in."

"Guess I won't. Not if everyone's as...solid as you are."

"What? This old thing?" Ibarra slapped his palms against his chest and thighs, each hit ringing like a bell through their cells. "I'm afraid Stacey and I are the only ones sporting a Qa'Resh ambassador body. Everyone else is just as fleshy as you are. Though your hardware is something special. How long have you been armor? Dr. Eeks still kicking around Mars?"

Roland bit his lip and looked up, wondering where all the monitoring equipment was hidden throughout the cell block.

"Come on now." Ibarra pointed to a data slate on the end of his bunk. "I've been down here with nothing but a bricked e-reader for months. Getting caught up on my reading is nice and all, but it gets dull after a while. Been months since I've spoken to anyone. The Tweedles aren't that talkative."

"Maybe your granddaughter threw me in here to get me to reveal military secrets during idle conversation. I have a duty to resist any interrogation. How about we just keep quiet?"

Ibarra shook his head.

"You're how old? Twenty? I bet you were armor no more than a year or so before Stacey snagged you off a battlefield. I was a major power behind Earth's government for the last eighty years…though I've had something of a setback these past few months. If you knew something particularly useful, my protégé would have put you someplace far less comfortable than our little slice of paradise."

"So you're not that big of a deal anymore?" Roland picked up a tube of nutrient paste from the floor and squeezed the grainy, tomato-flavored meal into his mouth. Stacey Ibarra and her bodyguard— an armor soldier named Nicodemus—had captured him on Oricon days ago, ripped him out of his armor, and carted him away still sealed in his suit's womb. Time was difficult to gauge while in the abyss of an unpowered metal pod. The amniosis had kept him alive, but it had been so long since he'd eaten real food, the paste tasted like the ambrosia of legend.

"Walked right into that one, didn't I?" Ibarra shrugged. "Oh, how the mighty have fallen. I bet President Garret and his cronies in the senate would be just tickled pink to know where I'm at—though they should have some clue I'm in trouble as I've not been around to feed them information for quite a while."

"You were spying for Earth?" Roland

grabbed a water bottle on the end of his bed. Bits of half-formed ice swirled around in the liquid, and the cold plastic stung his palm. He took a small sip, spilling plenty of it down his chin. Using his own body after so long in armor took some getting used to.

"Mediating," Ibarra said, raising a finger. "Trying to keep Earth from coming after us. Trying to get Earth to see the errors of their ways in approving the Hale Treaty. Trying to keep Stacey from losing all hope…She just used that time to build up the nation, keep after her little pet projects. Now I realize she was playing me—brilliant move on her part. I'm almost proud. Earth never felt threatened by us so long as I was around to rein her in. Stacey kept me in play until I was on the verge of telling Earth exactly how many proccies we had and where to find Navarre."

"Wait." Roland set the water bottle against his knee. "I know you've got your own procedurally generated soldiers. I met some on Oricon. You were Earth's spy and you didn't tell them how many you were making?"

"I may have…lied. I've been known to do that and am of the opinion that one should not tell the truth when a lie will do. Old habit. Born out of necessity and practice. But when Stacey decided it was time to leave Earth along with a few like-minded individuals—"

"Like Nicodemus."

"You've met him? Isn't he fun? We skipped town with a fleet Earth wasn't even using…and some technology that I kept off the books for a rainy day: a small omnium reactor, construction droids, automated foundries and a number of procedural-generation tubes with psych compilers."

"How did you keep all that hidden?"

"I'm Marc Ibarra. I kept an impending Xaros invasion secret for sixty years and laid the groundwork to take Earth back with no one the wiser. You think keeping a secret stash was a challenge? Granted, I had help along the way." He looked over at the only drawer in a small desk by his bed.

"So President Garret thought you got away with only a fleet of ghost ships and a few armor soldiers. But the whole time, you were making your own army and navy."

"It was a matter of prudence at first—help crew the ships and build up Navarre. Then Stacey had more militant aims."

"How many?" Roland asked.

Marc Ibarra's head shook slightly from side to side, then he smiled.

"Now you're going to clam up?" Roland shifted back and leaned against the wall.

"I don't actually know," Ibarra said. "She started a rather aggressive expansion plan after she found some information on Barada. I found the crèches by accident—a power drain in the lower caverns, so many new people coming into the world—that's when I signaled Earth for a meet to finally spill the beans and that's when Nicodemus ripped me out of my air car and almost crushed my head. He's many things. Subtle isn't one of them."

"I noticed." Roland worked his shoulder

around. The Ibarran armor soldier had demolished Roland's own armor in their brief and one-sided fight. The phantom pain from those "injuries" still nagged at him.

"It takes nine days for a procedural tube and psych compilers to make a fully grown, fully trained adult," Ibarra said. "The technology was our saving grace against the Xaros…I wanted to phase out the program after the war. Let humanity do things the way nature intended. Stacey had other goals. Other needs, shall we say."

"What happened to her? To you?" Roland asked.

"I couldn't stand around and watch her die." Ibarra's face fell. "I was there, you know, when the Xaros scoured the Earth clean of every last human being. Billions dead to the drones. I heard the screams, saw the cities burn…but when I saw my granddaughter bleeding to death in front of me, I could not let her go."

He tapped the side of his head.

"I wasn't exactly corporeal when Stacey

needed me the most, but there was a Qa'Resh ambassador unit just lying around that I appropriated. I got her body into stasis and her mind into the shell you've already met."

Roland squeezed out the last of his nutrient paste and gave Ibarra a sidelong look.

"'Ambassador unit'?"

Ibarra waved his hands up his body.

"Obviously," he said. "The Qa'Resh had a good system going on Bastion, before the Xaros destroyed it. Bringing ambassadors from across the galaxy to one place was difficult without the Crucible gates we have now. So the Qa'Resh sent probes to planets with species that could fight the Xaros, put their bodies into stasis, and transported the consciousness of the ambassadors to Bastion, where they got one of these numbers to walk around in. This made the ambassadors effectively immortal. No aging. No risk of spreading disease. Through some advanced holo technology and translation programs, all the ambassadors saw the other races as species that looked like them. Spoke like them.

But Bastion could never make any of the ambassadors *think* like each other. Which is still a problem."

"And you just happened to have two of these ambassador bodies handy?"

"Pa'lon, the longtime Dotari rep to Bastion, wasn't using his. Stacey had hers. I got attached to this one and Pa'lon decided to retire after the war ended and the Dotari went back to their home world. It's a hassle around anyone not prepped for arctic temperatures, but it sure beats living inside a Qa'Resh probe. No more genie in a bottle routine for me."

Roland got to his feet and rubbed soreness out of his neck and jaw.

"Is this why you two dropped off the edge of the world after the Ember War was over? Because you were…that?"

Ibarra crossed his arms over his chest and paced up and down his cell.

"Most of humanity was wiped out by the Xaros. You were in the fleet that sidestepped the invasion, so you know what that mess was like. Reconstruction. The Toth show up. Everyone realizes that I've snuck proccies into the population. The Xaros arrive in that hollowed-out moon. More fighting…then the war's over and now it's time to let the immortal Marc and Stacey Ibarra run the show. My plan was never for me to control humanity forever. Just long enough to get through what would have been an extinction event. I thought I'd stay in that probe forever, but staying out of the limelight after the war seemed natural. Stacey, though, her trauma was never part of the plan."

"What exactly happened to her?"

Ripples spread across Ibarra's face…but there was no sound. The metal man's face contorted in confusion. He looked up and shook a fist at the roof. The light dimmed in his cell and a privacy screen formed between his cell's bars.

"Hey!" Roland shouted. "I'm talking to him!" His words echoed off the stone walls of the prison.

"Damn it." He kicked his bunk, got a spike

of pain for his efforts, then sat down on the bunk and looked over his enclosure. A sink and toilet. Small drain in the floor. He went to the small metal desk and opened its single drawer. Empty.

I am a prisoner of war, he thought. *I am not a criminal. I am armor. I still have my duties.*

Roland sank to one knee and bowed his head in prayer.

"Sancti spiritus adsit nobis gratia…"

CHAPTER 2

Gideon leaned against the railing of the observation pod. A wide oval window in the Crucible offered a view to the center of the gigantic jump gate, Ceres' horizon, and to Earth beyond. He'd been there for almost an hour, watching silently as the white plains of wormholes— humanity's link to the stars—opened and shut.

The basalt walls of the Crucible and the twinkle of golden flecks in the material told of the Crucible's alien construction. The miles-long and - wide thorns that made up the Crucible shifted between each jump. He'd found no rhyme or reason to the station's movements but knew they were integral to manipulating the graviton fields between the countless thousands of other Crucibles the Xaros seeded throughout the galaxy.

He felt the vibration of approaching footsteps through the catwalk.

"Tongea," Gideon said without looking over.

"How did you know?" The other armor soldier stopped next to Gideon and put his hands on the railing.

"You walk like you're ready for a fight," Gideon said.

The Maori grunted as the flash of an opening wormhole lit across the tribal tattoos on his face.

"It's a struggle to keep the mind focused when out of armor," Tongea said. "My synch rating always suffers."

Gideon finally looked at the other armor soldier.

"And instead of going back to the *Ardennes* to plug in, you came up here to find me. When will my lance be reassigned to the fleets searching for the Ibarras?" he asked.

"Your request was denied," Tongea said curtly.

Gideon slammed a fist against the railing.

"Bullshit, Tongea. The Ibarras took Roland away from us—from me! He is my responsibility and I won't let another risk themselves when I'm the one at fault."

"No one blames you for what happened. The Ibarras overpowered Roland and Aignar, then took Roland's womb and—"

"*I* am to blame." Gideon tapped his own chest quickly. "*I* gave the order to split up the lance while we were on that Qa'Resh station. *I* refused to fire on Stacey Ibarra and her pack of traitors. That she got away with the alien tech and my soldier are on me. No one else."

"You split your lance to stop Cha'ril from redlining. If you'd tried to stop Ibarra from leaving, then Aignar and the rest of your company would have been lost when the station sank into Oricon

Prime. You made the right decision...don't let your history with Nicodemus cloud your judgment," Tongea said.

"You think I can ever forget or forgive what he did?" Gideon squeezed a hand into a fist so tight his knuckles went white. "They betrayed the Corps, Earth...me. And for what? Some sort of mysticism?" He reached out to touch the Templar Cross on Tongea's shoulder.

Tongea's hand snapped out and grabbed Gideon by the wrist. The two strained against each other for a moment, then Gideon let his arm go slack and Tongea released his grip.

"There were plenty of Templar that stayed behind," Tongea said. "No one believes Nicodemus and the others did the right thing by siding with the Ibarras."

"'No one'? I'm not part of your little brotherhood, but don't think I'm ignorant to what you Templar believe," Gideon said.

Tongea stiffened and turned back to the view port. "Those that went with the Ibarras have been expunged from the honor role. Cast out. They are no longer my brothers or sisters. Not Nicodemus. Not Morrigan. Not—"

"Don't. Don't say his name." Gideon leaned his hands against the railing and let his head droop between his shoulders.

"They were my friends too," Tongea said, laying his hand on Gideon's shoulder.

"I have to find them," Gideon said as he shrugged the touch away. "I have to find Roland."

"Colonel Martel needs you elsewhere, someplace where you'll do far more for Earth than bringing traitors to justice: New Bastion."

"Where all the old Alliance sits around doing nothing? What the hell am I going to do there?" Gideon's brow furrowed.

"The Ibarras have been busy. They've raided more than one alien planet and the Congress on New Bastion demands answers from Earth. You're going there as a witness, to try to keep the rest of the galaxy from dog-piling on us while we figure out what to do about the Ibarras," Tongea said. "But we have to find the Ibarras first, which is proving harder than we thought."

"A witness? No. Send Admiral Lettow or the Oricon governor. I can't add anything more than they already know. Let me bring the Ibarras back in chains. New Bastion can watch the video of their trial and execution for treason."

"Lettow's taking the *Ardennes* to New Bastion. You and your lance are going with him. Martel's orders. By the time you get back, the Keeper thinks she'll have a way to track the Ibarras' movement through the Crucible network. Then we'll be ready to enact justice."

Gideon shook his head.

"I don't do well around aliens," he said. "I saw what the Toth did to prisoners on Hawaii, saw the dead on Cygnus killed by the Vishrakath."

"The Toth are gone and you do well enough with your Dotari lancer. Our ambassador there will help keep you in line," Tongea said. "Cha'ril is on her way. She's recovering well from her near redline. I wanted her in my lance, but *someone* took her on a shoestring tackle of an operation against the Vish and there was no separating her from that lance."

"I regret nothing," Gideon said.

"Go to New Bastion. Tell the truth. Then hunt down the Ibarras after that."

"We're going to kill the Ibarras when we find them. Promise me that," Gideon said.

"President Garret could be forced to ask for a declaration of war in the next few days," Tongea said, his face falling as he spoke. "It takes time to get the public behind something like that, especially since we as a culture should have moved on from fighting each other after the Ember War."

"The Ibarras are to blame. And they're going to pay for what they've done," Gideon said.

****

A bright light passed over Cha'ril's left eye. She fought the urge to blink, but the slight numbness across her body made dealing with the discomfort easier. She ran the blunted talon on her thumb across the side of her index finger.

"Uh uh uh," Dr. Eeks said as she moved the light to Cha'ril's other eye. "No moving while the neurometer is attached." The human woman was older than most of her kind Cha'ril had encountered, with gray hair and lined skin typical of those well past what humans considered "middle age." The aroma of burnt herbs clung to her lab coat, a by-product of an addiction that seemed oddly prevalent among human medical workers.

Cha'ril flared her nostrils in annoyance. The device interfacing with her skull plugs was heavy and had sent tiny electrical jolts through her muscles for the last ten minutes of the exam.

"What do you think, Dr. Bar'gil?" Eeks asked over her shoulder to the Dotari staring intently at a holo screen displaying Cha'ril's nervous system.

"Her neural kinetics are well within normal," he said. "She experienced a minor system spike, not a true redline. My recommendation stands."

"I can't find any reason to keep her off active duty," Eeks said. "Though her hormone levels have certainly spiked."

"Then clear me for deployment," Cha'ril said. The neurometer punished her with tiny shocks to the muscles she dared to voluntarily control.

"Don't, dearie. Things have a tendency to bite." Eeks reached behind Cha'ril's head and removed the neurometer with a click, then she slipped the palm-sized device into her lab coat. "Our jogger will link up with the Crucible in a few more hours. You can join your lance then. I'll have the paperwork done up after my smoke break."

"Thank you, doctor." Cha'ril rubbed the skin around her plugs, noting it was more sensitive than usual.

"I'd tell you to stay away from any weird geometry in Qa'Resh artifact worlds, but I doubt that'll happen," she said, getting halfway out the door before looking back to Bar'gil. "Coming, doctor?"

"I need a few minutes with her," the Dotari said. "I'll catch up."

He waited until Eeks was gone before he took a data slate out of his coat pocket.

"Your hormone levels are indeed above normal," he said in the clicks and tweets of Dotari language.

"The home world removed all the contraceptives from our food and water. This is to be expected, yes?"

Bar'gil removed a pen-sized device and pressed the tip under her beak. He looked down at his data slate and clicked his tongue.

"Not to this extent. Your pheromone glands are swollen…have you been exposed to anything unusual? Eaten something not from the food processors?" the doctor asked.

Cha'ril worked her jaw slightly, then gripped her hands together over her lap.

"I've been eating coffee berries," she mumbled.

"Aha," he said, putting the device back in

his pocket. "We did note an uptick in the birthrate during our stay on Hawaii. I'll send word back to Dotari that raw coffee berries warrant further study."

"What's happening back home?" she asked. "My father sent word that there's some sort of illness and that's why we're barred from going back and that's why the Council of Firsts lifted the restrictions on...breeding."

"They're calling it the phage," Bar'gil said. "When our ancestors fled the Xaros on the generation ships, we lost so much of our history and culture. Turns out we also lost our immunity to certain diseases present on our home world. We spent so much time in the clean environment of spaceships, and our home on Takeni had little to nothing in the way of microbes that could threaten us. Every Dotari on the home world is at risk, the young and elderly especially. The fatality rate is over seventy percent. More and more healthy adults are succumbing too."

"The humans have their green blood cells to

protect them from such things. Why haven't they shared the technology with us?"

"The Qa'Resh devised the green blood cells as a by-product of the outlawed procedural-generation program." Bar'gil's quills shuddered in disgust. "The green blood cells only work for the humans, but they've sent medical teams and are working with our scientists for a cure. Unfortunately, our physiology is quite different. Humans will learn to fly by flapping their arms before one of them could function as a Dotari physician."

Cha'ril touched the plugs beneath her loose quills.

"Mechanical, not biological," Bar'gil snapped.

"What's going to happen to us? To the home world?" she asked.

"If the phage continues on its current disease vector…a few hundred Dotari will survive the next decade." Bar'gil delivered the prognosis clinically, ignoring Cha'ril's gasp. "Many more in our expeditionary fleet and those assigned to joint commands like you. After that, those who outlast the phage may develop new immunity and we could return—though the Council of Firsts gives that a low probability."

"We're doomed, aren't we?" Cha'ril wrung her hands together.

"We survived the Xaros through great effort and sacrifice...and with the humans' help. We will do the same again. You understand why your reproductive cycle has been restarted?" the doctor asked.

"I do. I just...I feel like I'm going through puberty all over again." The skin around her eyes flushed with embarrassment.

"You're not the first to share that observation. You're in a joint unit with the humans. Are they aware?"

"They are not...between the conflict with the Ibarra faction and my hospitalization, I've not had the chance to explain why my pheromones are in the air." She shifted uncomfortably on the exam table.

The doctor held out his hand.

"The coffee berries. I'll not have your system upset any further."

Cha'ril clicked her beak in annoyance and removed a small case from a thigh pocket and handed it over.

"What now?" she asked.

"Nature."

The doctor slid the case into his lab coat and left.

****

Aignar squeezed past a Marine guard in the corridor leading to his berthing on the *Ardennes*. The Marine gave him a nod as he passed, eyes lingering on Aignar's bare metal cybernetic hands and the speaker in his throat.

Always the looks, Aignar thought. He pressed a shoulder pocket holding his access card to a door panel and kicked the bottom of the doorframe as he went into his room. He stumbled forward and attempted to catch the bulkhead, but his hands didn't open in time to brace his fall. The backs of his hands slid off the bulkhead and his shoulder took the brunt of the impact.

He sat against the wall and looked at his feet, both clumsy cybernetics within boots fastened by straps. His shoulder throbbed for a moment, but the shame of being forced to toddle around in full view of everyone bothered him more.

He flexed his metal fingers open and closed with the whine of servos. The Vishrakath grenade had taken much from him on Cygnus. The pain had been brief; the long recovery filled with failed transplant surgeries and rehabilitation were much worse.

The hands bent back at the wrist and went flat, and he rolled over and pushed himself up with the grace of a drunk struggling out of an alley. He sat on a disheveled bunk and stared at the other, pristine bed. Roland's bed. Neither of them brought much in the way of personal gear, as most of their time and all their fighting would be spent in armor, but the pair of spit-shined boots and a duffle bag in the footlocker bolted to the floor were a constant reminder that Roland should have been there.

Aignar ran the fight with the Ibarran armor through his mind again. He and Roland had focused on Stacey Ibarra, her unnatural metal body standing in the Qa'Resh data center. She had called Nicodemus out of a portal to deal with the Terran armor. Nicodemus had cut Aignar's armor in half at the waist, rendering him useless in seconds, before he hacked away at Roland.

With Ibarra as a distraction, the ambush was perfect. Overwhelming force from an unexpected direction. Textbook and flawless. Aignar knew he was lucky to even be alive…but that hadn't tempered the shame he felt. Together, he and Roland might have stood a chance against Nicodemus. Instead, Aignar's swift defeat likely slowed Roland's response and now his friend was their prisoner.

That he just left an audience where he explained his failure to his entire chain of command—including President Garret—was a cherry on top of a worsening day.

A data slate beeped beneath his pillow. He opened one hand like a clamp, gripped the slate, and saw a flashing reminder that the *Ardennes* had fellowship for the embarked Templar armor. Roland would have been excited for this, even though it meant a good thrashing with a bamboo training sword from the full members of the order.

No one expected Aignar to learn the blade, not with him being a cripple.

The memory of Nicodemus, a Templar Cross emblazoned on his shoulder, standing over Roland's broken armor, came to him, and Aignar squeezed the data slate until the screen cracked. He bashed his metal hand against the bed frame again and again until the slate broke into pieces and went bouncing across the deck.

He pried his closed hand open with the other, then lay his forearms on his lap. Slowly, and with great concentration, he tapped the tips of his forefingers against their thumbs. Then the middle finger, then down to his pinkies and back up to the first digits.

Roland was gone. Aignar's faith in the Templar faded faster the more he thought about Nicodemus and the armor that rebelled with the Ibarras…and he was out of his armor. He leaned his head back against the bulkhead while his fingers tapped against each other.

CHAPTER 3

The clang of a metal door woke Roland from sleep. He shot up in bed and set his feet to the floor as a pair of beefy guards came through the open vault door, both in light power armor. The one in front carried a nightstick that crackled as he moved. The other held a tray of food. Both were baby-faced and thick-necked. Neither looked happy to see Roland.

The privacy screen around Ibarra's cell was still up.

The first guard rapped his nightstick against the bars and the static electricity snapped in the air. He pointed the tip at Roland.

"The prisoner will move to the rear of the cell. Face the wall. Go to his knees and interlace fingers behind his head."

"And if I don't?" Roland asked.

"Then you don't eat," the second guard said as he raised the tray slightly.

The rumble in Roland's stomach was motivation enough to comply. He got up slowly and shuffled toward the back of the cell. It would take time to learn the guards' routine, to spot errors that he could exploit. Just because he was outside his armor didn't mean he was done fighting.

He went to his knees and loosely laced his fingers together. He heard the cell door swing open, then two thumps on his bed. The door slammed shut.

"The prisoner will have thirty minutes to eat. Leave the tray to the left of the doorway and be prepared to repeat this process when we return," the first guard said.

Roland got back to his feet.

"Prisoners of war have rights," he said.

"Does Earth know I'm alive? What happened to the rest of my lance on Oricon?"

The first guard rattled the cell door, then stepped back.

"We don't know any of that, sir," the second guard said. "We're told to feed you three times a day and see to your needs. You step out of line and we're authorized to treat you like any other inmate."

The guard with the nightstick slapped it against his gloved palm, and electricity arced down his fingers. Roland wasn't sure what that would do to the cybernetics in his skull and spine, but the effect wouldn't be pleasant.

"Who told you this?" Roland asked.

"Thirty minutes," the first guard said. "Fail to comply, and the prisoner will be on paste and water until he complies with instructions."

The guards left. The vault door slammed behind them and the whir of pistons groaned through the metal.

On his bunk was a bottle of water, a plate of macaroni and cheese, a peanut butter and jelly sandwich, and two cut-up hot dogs. The utensils were light, made of pressed pulp and shrink-wrapped, useless as weapons.

Roland took a bite of the undercooked pasta and gritty cheese sauce. The quality was a few tiers below what he was used to in the army, and almost as bad as what he had at the orphanage, but it still tasted great. Hunger proved to be the best sauce.

"How is it?" Ibarra asked.

Where the metal man leaned against his cell bars, frost grew slowly around the metal. The privacy screen had come down as silently as it had gone up.

"They don't feed you?" Roland took a sniff of the stale sandwich and dipped a corner into the cheese goo.

"I don't eat," Ibarra said. "My body runs off ambient heat. Don't drink or sleep either. Who were the guards? Pair of big dummies with no necks?"

Roland nodded quickly and kept eating.

"Tweedle Dee and Tweedle Asshole," Ibarra said. "I had a number of other affectionate terms for them…then they stopped coming in to check on me."

"I can't imagine why," Roland deadpanned.

"Ha ha. Look who has jokes." Ibarra pointed to the ceiling. "I guess there are a few topics that are off-limits. That's why they cut me off. Tell me, did the baseball league ever get up and running?"

"Baseball?" Roland wiped his sleeve across his mouth.

"Sticks, bats," Ibarra said, tossing an imaginary ball up and then swinging at it. "America's pastime. Far superior sport than football—American and European. Do you know how much money I spent on stadiums and teams across the solar system?"

"Oh, that. President Garret threw out a first pitch a few years back at MacDougal Stadium. I never had money to go to a game. Could never find the live games online. Never got into it."

"Ha! Blackout days still work. Your father never took you to a game?"

"He died with 8th Fleet deep in the void.

Mom was on Luna when the Xaros smashed it. I was just a kid."

Ibarra looked away. "Sorry to hear that. I remember when Luna fell. Those were some dark days. You wouldn't believe how close we came to losing it all."

"I grew up hearing about you, even before the war with the Xaros. Your name was on everything. Then came the war and you were still all over the place, even though you were just a hologram. Couple kids at school thought you weren't real at all, that you were some sort of fake that Qa'Resh probe made to control all of us."

"Jimmy was talented in many things," Ibarra said. "Acting like a human being was not one of them. Even after all those years working with him, he could impersonate me about as well as you could infiltrate a flock of geese."

"The Qa'Resh probe was named 'Jimmy'?"

"He had a quantum-state designation—the Qa'Resh were like that—which was a pain in the ass to say, so I called him Jimmy. Sue me. You want to meet him?" Ibarra went to his desk and opened the drawer. He removed a needle of glass that caught the light.

"It was…over a hundred years ago that he plopped down in the Arizona desert and gave me a call. His spark went out after the war, but I kept him around. Hard to imagine being without him. That Stacey let me keep him tells me there's hope I might get out of here someday. Otherwise she'd have me at the engineer center being worked on to find out just how indestructible this body is or isn't. She let you keep something too, I see."

Ibarra set the needle in his palm and rolled it from side to side.

Roland looked down at his plate and frowned.

"Let me keep what?" the armor soldier asked.

"What's under your pillow."

Roland lifted up the corner of his threadbare pillow and found a small book. Strips of green tape reinforced the cover and masked the title. He opened it up and found it was a Templar study book—pages of prayers, instructions for wearing the cross, and handwritten annotations in the margins of the text. He flipped to the front page and at the bottom was written PROPERTY B.B.

"This isn't mine," Roland said. "I have one just like it, though."

Ibarra peered at the pages.

"You're a Templar?" he asked.

"I've not stood the vigil, but I've pledged myself to the order. Is it true that all the armor that left with you were Templars?" Roland asked.

"It is," Ibarra said, glancing up at the ceiling, as if that admission would get the privacy screens turned back on. "Convincing Hurson's squadron to come with us wasn't too difficult. As I'm sure you understand."

"No, actually, I don't understand." Roland took a bite of his sandwich and chewed slowly, forcing Ibarra to wait. "Templar swear to defend Earth. To sacrifice for the good of all, to live up to Saint Kallen's legacy, and be the iron that strengthens the hearts of others. We don't take off with a traitor that didn't get his way with a treaty."

"The original oath was to defend humanity, not Earth," Ibarra said.

"Wrong. I have to memorize all this before I can stand the vigil. I'll show you…page thirty-seven." Roland flipped pages and cleared his throat. "For I swear on my honor and my life that to serve humani—wait." He frowned and went back to the beginning of the book. "This was published ten years ago…"

"We didn't leave Earth because we were throwing a tantrum over the Hale Treaty," Ibarra said. "We left to save Earth. To keep our deadliest weapon from being tossed aside to please an enemy that never truly wanted peace. There were some in the Armor Corps that understood this and some that didn't."

"What about the civilian transport ship High Command said you destroyed, the *Hiawatha?* You were about to be indicted for murder. That seems like a better reason to run off than what you're going on about," Roland said.

"The *Hiawatha*?" Ibarra frowned, then recognition filled his face. "That? They tried to pin that on me? President Garret had all the details about that little blip right after it happened. He was all for it after I told him. I do him a favor and give him plausible deniability in case of blowback and what does he do? Hangs that albatross around my neck after I'm gone. That bastard."

"So you did blow up that ship and kill all those people?"

"It's not like I had a choice. The Xaros were days away and everyone on board was a—"

The privacy screens shot up and cut Ibarra off.

Roland sighed and looked up at the ceiling. He took a bite of his hot dog and shook his head.

"How about you just give us a list of what we can talk about?" he said through a half-full mouth before he turned his attention back to the study book and went to the chapter with the Poems of Remembrance.

CHAPTER 4

Aignar walked through the officers' mess, his nutrient shake in hand. The smell of everyone else's meal used to bother him when he left the hospital. Now the aromas seemed to give his daily goo a bit of flavor.

He went past a round table of Dotari officers, all sitting shoulder to shoulder and eating from communal bowls of the *gar'udda* nuts that they never seemed to tire of. Some were armor, the rest pilots from the *Ardennes'* joint squadron.

As he sat down at an empty table, he heard a high trill. The grates on the air-conditioning vents looked normal and recently cleaned, but the pitch warbled up and down as he dug a knuckle against the back of his jaw and debated scheduling a hearing test with the medics. It was bad enough that he had to speak through cybernetics; bad hearing would make his non-armored life even more difficult.

Cha'ril practically slapped her tray down across from Aignar as she sat down quickly, her head bowed, her gaze squarely on the small bowl of steaming *gar'udda*.

The noise stopped. Aignar's brow furrowed further and he touched the other side of his prosthetic jaw.

"Cha'ril? When did you come aboard? How you feeling?"

"Just docked. I'm fine. Totally fine." She snatched up a *gar'udda* and ate it quickly, still refusing to look at Aignar.

"You look different. Your skin is a few shades darker and your quills are..." He sniffed the air, then took a whiff from the end of his straw. "What is that smell? It's like cut grass and lemons. That some sort of new spice on your lunch?"

"By the ships of my ancestors, this is embarrassing." She pressed her hands against the side of her face, then flapped the back of her fingers against the bottom of her beak.

"What *is* that?" He glanced at the bottom of his boots. "Ah...it lingers."

"It's me. The smell is from me. Okay? Just drink your goo so we can leave." She munched on another nut, cracking it loudly.

"Were the showers out on your way back from Mars? Now—" He cocked an ear to the ceiling. "There's that sound again. You hear it?"

Cha'ril pushed her bowl to one side and folded her arms on the table.

"Aignar, I need you to do something for me. Bang your fist on the table and look agitated," she said, looking at him with a plea in her eyes.

"Now it's weird, Cha'ril. Very weird."

The keening grew louder and other human diners began to look around in confusion.

"I'll explain in a minute. Just...do it," she said.

Aignar shrugged, lifted his cup of nutrient paste off the table, and struck a hammer blow against the corner. The tip broke off and the entire mess hall went silent. The table full of Dotari males turned their attention back to their food, occasionally glancing back over at Cha'ril.

"What the hell?" Aignar asked.

"My pheromones are…eliciting a response from the men. They're preening for me. That's the sound you heard." Cha'ril flushed around her eyes and across her forehead.

"Back up," Aignar said. "I'm missing something."

"This is very normal Dotari mating behavior. During the season, entire villages will be filled with song." Cha'ril tilted her forearm up from the table and blocked her view of the table full of the males as she kept eating.

"Mating…season?" Aignar set his cup down and pushed it to one side.

"Those of us in the Dotari Expeditionary Force had our reproductive cycles put on hold while we served, but the Council of Firsts put an end to that. Ha ha. Now our biological impulses are coming to the fore. Don't make it weird."

"Wait…what? Why did I have to hit the table?"

"As my lance mate, you fill the role of *ushulra*, an older male relative that keeps suitors away…well, you shouldn't as you're not Dotari. In fact, I shouldn't have asked you to get involved. Feces. I'm only making things worse for us both." She rubbed her temple.

"So much for not making it weird," Aignar said. "How long does," he sniffed twice, "does all this last?"

"I don't actually know. I've not had to deal with any of this since I entered the academy years ago. There are some environmental factors at work that are making things worse."

Aignar shook his head.

"And I thought dealing with Roland's hormones were a problem."

There was a slam of fists against a table, and

a Dotari male stood up. He was larger than the others and wore a pilot's overalls. He glared at another Dotari across the table and his quills furled out as he hissed. The other Dotari—the plugs at the base of his skull marking him out as armor—rose to his feet slowly, then beat his hands against his chest.

The Dotari table suddenly burst into action as one half grabbed the pilot and the other manhandled the armor in opposite directions, the air alive with a cacophony of squawks and chirps. As quickly as the din erupted, it ended as the two factions left through opposite doors.

"What the hell was that?" a Ranger lieutenant asked from behind Aignar.

Cha'ril kept her head down and chewed through her bowl as fast as she could manage.

"Aignar," she said as she chewed, "what are your opinions of this? Please be honest."

"I'm starting to wish the Ibarras had captured me instead of Roland."

CHAPTER 5

The hood over Roland's head cut out all light and sound, but he felt his seat shudder as whatever transport he was in came to a stop. The half-mask over his mouth kept his jaw clenched tight and muzzled. Some armor soldiers used the seclusion hoods to fall asleep when out of armor, their bodies so used to the sensory deprivation that resting was almost impossible outside the wombs.

Roland noted the count of this newest transition—9,482—and added it to his running total. This was the fourth time he'd been put into an air car, tube transit, and elevator. Keeping him blind and deaf would hide most everything of value he could learn about his surroundings, but at least he could gauge time and distance with his count.

Naturally, he assumed the guards were walking him in circles a few times to defeat such a tactic, but Roland felt the need to do something constructive.

A rough hand gripped him by the elbow and pulled him up slightly. He stood, the heavy shackles around his hands and ankles limiting him to a shuffle as the second guard took him by the arm and led him forward.

Roland felt a slight breeze tug at the hood and moist air caress his bare hands. A few minutes—and several direction changes—later, the guards jerked him to a stop. His hood came off and Roland blinked hard as his eyes adjusted to harsh lights.

"Wait outside," a man said.

There was a snap of a closing door and the lights dimmed. Before Roland was a man in his mid-forties, bald but for a ring of hair over his ears and around the back of his head. He wore an army uniform, the ribbons and design the same as the Terran Army, but the badges were different and a gold braid ran from his left shoulder to beneath his armpit. He had five stars on his shoulder, a rank not used by Earth since the end of the Ember War: marshal.

"I will show you trust and respect," the marshal said. "You will keep that trust and respect so long as you return the courtesy. Understand?"

Roland tried to work his jaw, but the muzzle tightened in response. He nodded.

The marshal waved a hand over the gauntlet screen on his left arm and the muzzle and restraints fell to the floor. Roland rubbed his jaw and looked around. They were in a small antechamber with marble floors and lacquered walls. A simple wooden door was behind the marshal.

The Ibarran officer turned around, and Roland saw a pistol strapped to his thigh. The man handed Roland a long coat from where it hung over a leather and chrome stool.

"I am Davoust. You'll appreciate this later,"

the marshal said.

"What do you want with me?" Roland took the coat but didn't move to put it on.

"It's not me that wants you. Do us all a favor and don't play games with her," Davoust said.

"If you think I'm going to help you—be a pawn in your war with Earth—you should've kept me blind, deaf, and dumb. Less trouble," Roland handed the coat back to Davoust.

The marshal glanced down at the proffered coat, shook his head slightly, then touched his palm to the doorknob and the door swung open. Davoust motioned for Roland to follow him.

Inside was a circular room, the ceiling four stories tall and domed. Shelves made up the lower levels of the walls, discordant colored spines of books and journals belying the organization of the room. The upper walls were computer banks, humming and emitting cold mist from their cooling systems.

In the center of the room was a wide holo tank. A network of golden lattices enclosed the only other person in the room, a shadow inside the holo tank, arms moving about like a conductor leading a symphony.

When the door shut behind Roland, he noticed a pair of large and armored legionnaires holding gauss carbines, standing on either side of the doorway.

Roland had some confidence he could wrest the pistol away from the marshal, but trying to overpower the two legionnaires was a losing proposition—as long as he was out of his armor.

"He talks too much, doesn't he?" came from inside the holotank. Roland recognized the voice from the Qa'Resh artifact on Oricon where he'd been captured. Stacey Ibarra.

The golden lattice degraded, revealing more and more of the person inside. She was silver, just like Marc Ibarra, her hair frozen in place in a short cut that extended halfway down her neck. Her body was a simple jumpsuit, detailed but the same color as the rest of her body. The golden lattice collapsed into a glowing flake, then lowered into the side of the holo tank.

She made her way down the curved stairs of the dais, her feet beating against the stairs with a metal-on-metal ding.

Roland's breath fogged as she drew closer and a chill wrapped around his body. He gripped the coat in his hands tightly, feeling foolish for not heeding the marshal's counsel.

"Look at you," Stacey said. "Always a surprise to see the heart of an armor soldier in person. Only human inside those amazing suits." She stopped a few feet away, her doll-like face betraying no emotion, but Roland could feel the soul behind her blank eyes.

"I didn't think you'd be so young. I expected a few years on you at least. Your other armor friend didn't put up much of a fight against Nicodemus. You at least gave him some sport," she said.

"What happened to Aignar? To the rest of my lance?" Roland asked, shivering.

"They all left the Qa'Resh station before I

had Oricon's atmosphere crush it into dust. The Qa'Resh built things to last, but they didn't build them that tough."

"Why spare them? We're at war and—"

"I am not at war with Earth!" She jabbed a finger at Roland's chest, then bent her finger back into a fist and lowered her arm. "They are at war with me."

"I saw what you did to the *Cairo*. Raw footage doesn't lie," Roland said. "You ambushed that ship and murdered her crew, then dumped it into an ocean world, hoping we'd never find the evidence."

"Oh that," she said, tossing a hand next to her head. "Did your masters tell you that the ship, the *Leyte Gulf,* was part of a squadron attacked by Earth—an unprovoked attack, I might add—and that the *Leyte Gulf* was the only survivor? That it fled to the system where the *Cairo* was hunting for it? Earth started this fight. The *Leyte* had vital information to bring me. That she repaid a blood debt on her way home was something of a bonus."

"So you're the victim here." The side of Roland's mouth pulled into a brief sneer as stiffness crept into his fingers and toes and pain needled along the edges of his ears.

"Earth could have left us well enough alone. We have…mutual problems." Stacey backed up and turned to a holo screen along the walls.

Marshal Davoust nudged Roland's arm. Roland scowled and put the coat on. The fabric heated up and pushed the chill away.

Stacey put her palm up to the holo screen and pictures flowed across the projection so fast they were almost a blur.

"We worried you wouldn't be of much use to us," she said. "But then the colonists on Oricon simply would not stop talking about a team of armor that rescued children from the Kesaht. Then the wheels began turning…"

The holo screen stopped on a picture of a sword, longer than Roland was tall, Templar Crosses built into the hilt and pommel. Text boxes popped up along the blade's edge. Roland recognized it immediately as the sword given to him by Ibarran legionnaires, one that originally belonged to an armor soldier named Morrigan. Stacey's bodyguard, Nicodemus, had taken it after crushing Roland in a fight on the Qa'Resh station.

Stacey touched one of the text boxes, and a double helix of DNA appeared on the screen.

"Plenty of blood on your sword," she said. "And this one here is different from any we've seen before. You came across the leadership caste of the Kesaht, didn't you? The ones called Ixio."

"I'm not going to help you." Roland straightened up. "You and your pack of traitors have done enough damage to Earth. You goaded us into a fight with the Kesaht and—"

Stacey raced toward Roland and grabbed him by the front of his coat, hefting him off the ground with ease and shaking him.

"You think they'll stop with us!" she screamed. "Do you know what they've done!"

The cold from her fists stung through the fabric and made Roland's breathing painful.

"My lady…" Davoust said.

Stacey dropped Roland to his feet and gave him a not-so-gentle push backwards, but the marshal stopped Roland from losing his footing.

Stacey's still features stared at Roland, and he could feel hatred burning inside her.

"You know what happened to the colony on New Caledonia?" she asked.

"Where?" Roland rubbed his chest, kneading warmth back into his flesh.

Stacey reached back to the holo screen and her fingers tapped out a code in the air. The dais changed, and the large field came to life and showed a burnt-out village, the streets littered with dead men, women, and children.

"Little over a year ago," Marshal Davoust said, "phase 1 colony from Earth in the Orion arm along the edge of Crucible space. Resupply convoy found it like this. Eight hundred sixty-three dead…two hundred and nine missing."

"No, never heard of this," Roland said.

"Of course not." Stacey walked into the holo

tank and knelt next to a dead woman clutching a bundle in her arms. She ran her hand along the woman's head, then set her other hand on the bundle. "It was just before the second Terra Nova expedition. President Garret couldn't have his good news story preempted by a story about human beings murdered in cold blood. Typical of him."

She stood and traced a circle with a fingertip. The holo sped ahead and stopped next to a partially collapsed building. In the rubble were black plates of armor, their edges stained with gray goo.

"Officially," she said, "the attack remains under investigation, with no clue as to the identity of the attackers. But you know now, don't you, Roland?"

"That's Rakka armor. They're the Kesaht's foot soldiers. They decompose rapidly after they're killed..."

"And Earth should have figured that out by now," the marshal said.

"Why would they attack us that long ago?"

Roland stepped away from Davoust. "Did you all kick that hornets' nest and lead them to the colony?"

"We encountered them only a few months ago," Stacey said. "And they were just as hostile. Willing to talk now?"

Roland hesitated. He'd fought the Kesaht, seen their fleet in action, and recognized them as a potent enemy on par with the Vishrakath and Kroar. If the Ibarrans had information that Earth could use...

"Only if you'll send me back," Roland said. "Send me back to Earth with everything you know about the Kesaht. Every bit of information. Promise that and I'll tell you what I know about the Ixio."

"Hardly a bargain for us." Stacey came down from the dais and extinguished the holo with a metallic snap of her fingers. "We'd get that information eventually."

"Not without risk to our agents on Earth," Davoust said.

"But is he worth keeping?" she asked the

marshal.

"Détente behar dugu. Lurra gehiegi behar da. Armadura hau besterik ez izatea zer behar dugu," Davoust said.

"English, please," Roland said.

"I accept your terms," Stacey said. "Tell me about the Ixio and we'll return you to Earth with everything we know. Their tactics. Fleets we've encountered." She extended a hand to him.

Roland grit his teeth and shook her hand. It was like pressing his hand to a glacier. His flesh flared with pain before going numb. He pulled back and gripped his stiff fingers.

"Their home world," Roland said.

"See," Stacey said, wagging a finger at him, "that's a good question. We don't know where it is. The Kesaht were never part of the old Alliance. How a new race managed to access the Crucible network is something of a mystery. There, I just gave you something. Now tell me about the Ixio."

Roland took a deep breath and wondered just how big of a mistake he was about to make. He told them how he and Cha'ril first learned of a third Kesaht species during a hasty autopsy of a Sanheel, then about encountering one of the tall biomechanical aliens named Tomenakai aboard their battleship.

"It wanted the children," Roland said. "Human children. Said they were important for whatever kind of 'unity' the Kesaht provide with their skull implants. The children weren't aberrant like the adults, who he said were 'false minds in weed bodies.' Then I—"

"Stop," Stacey said, giving Davoust a quick glance. "He said those words, 'false minds in weed bodies' exactly?"

"That's right. Then he went off about how we must be 'redeemed' for our crimes or we must be purged. Then I cut his head off and crushed his skull." Roland shrugged slightly.

"It fits the theory," Davoust said. "The shield tech. The cloaks."

Stacey half-raised her arms, then let them fall to her sides. She turned to the holo tank, then back to the marshal. Pressing her hands over her face, she then drummed her fingertips against her metal body, making high-pitched *tings* like the toll of small bells.

"No…no, no, no, this isn't my fault." Stacey looked around, as if she didn't know where she was.

Roland stiffened, his instincts sensing a threat.

"We didn't have a choice!" Stacey screamed, the words echoing around the room and the force of her words stinging Roland's ears. "I had to do it! We kept it from the rest because we knew they'd try and stop us. But when it was over, Valdar…Valdar blamed me. Me!"

She grabbed Roland by the back of the neck and jaw. He grunted in pain and tried to pull away, but her grip was like his armor's.

"Ken didn't judge me." She shook her head from side to side as Roland beat at her arms. "Ken understood. Is he gone? Did he stay for me like I asked?"

Roland tasted ice in his mouth as his spit

froze.

"Guards!" Davoust grabbed Stacey by the forearms and tried to pull her off Roland. A power-armored guard lifted her hand off Roland's neck and yanked Roland back, tossing him against the wall.

Roland touched his ice-cold jaw and watched as the two guards pinned Stacey's arms and legs and held her against the floor.

She wailed, a cry caught somewhere between grief and madness. She pulled an arm free and struck one of the guards in the chest, blasting him back and sliding across the floor.

"I had no choice!" Stacey struck at the other guard, who caught her by the wrist, the power armor's servos and pseudo-muscles straining against her raw power.

Davoust grabbed Roland by the back of his jacket and dragged him out of the room. The door closed, and Roland heard Stacey screaming…followed by the crash of metal being bludgeoned into scrap. Roland lay on the floor, staring at the vaulted ceilings as pain pulsed through his face and neck.

The marshal knelt near Roland, keeping a hand to the soldier's chest.

"Are you hurt...badly?" Davoust asked.

Roland tried to open his mouth, but it was locked in place. He managed a pitiful grunt.

Davoust looked at the flesh on his palms, stained white with frostbite.

"She has her moments," Davoust said. "When they tell Earth about this, know it doesn't matter to us. She is our lady. She loves us. She will save us. And we will die for her."

****

Stacey sat against a broken computer bank, sparks falling against her skin, leaving tiny black smudges that faded away seconds later. She stared at the dais in the middle of the room, her unblinking eyes locked on the flickering holo tank.

Hunks of broken machinery were strewn

across the floor, like the aftermath of a hurricane.

Her two guards huddled against the door, blocking it with their bodies. One was on a knee, a broken arm clutched against his side. The other stood up, his helm broken and blood dripping from a broken nose.

"Hamish. Tyrel…I'm sorry," Stacey said.

"Are you well, my lady?" asked the one with the broken nose.

"I am now. Would you…would you take Hamish to the infirmary? I need a minute." She got to her feet and brushed herself off.

"We cannot leave you," Hamish said.

"I shouldn't have made you so well." She went to Hamish and reached out to touch him, then pulled her hand back. "Look what I've done to you both. Just go. Leave."

"We cannot—"

"Then summon the doctor!" Stacey stamped a foot against the ground, cracking the marble.

Tyrel nodded and touched the screen on his forearm.

Stacey walked slowly to the dais. She ran her fingertips along the edge and tapped out a code against the side. There was a hiss of hydraulics and the dais rose out of the ground. A clear cylinder came up, its contents hidden momentarily by steam that faded away.

Inside, a young woman was frozen in stasis, her chest covered in blood from a bullet wound. Blood stained a hand reaching for help, spilled down the sides of her mouth and hung frozen in time within the chamber. Stacey, her mind and soul trapped inside the metal shell, looked at her true body, her mortally wounded flesh and blood.

"Should I go back?" she asked her guards. "Go back for that last moment of true life?"

"We need you," Hamish said.

"We are lost without you," Tyrel added.

"I fought the monsters," she said. "I stared into the abyss. And this is what I have become."

She ran her fingers down the seam of the stasis pod and it sank back into the floor.

"Why do I do it?" she asked.

"Every soul cries out to live," Hamish said, wiping blood off his lip. "You will save us. You will save all of us."

"Just like you did during the Ember War," Tyrel added.

"There are dark days ahead of us," Stacey said. "But who better than an Ibarra to bear the torch?"

CHAPTER 6

Sitting on his bunk, Roland rubbed his aching jaw and poked at a plate of rubbery potatoes. He looked up at Marc Ibarra through the cell bars and shrugged.

"A pair of medics looked me over, then I got the hood and muzzle and they brought me back here," Roland said.

"This is worse than I thought," Ibarra said. "But things are beginning to make sense now."

"Really? I got the impression that she's had meltdowns like that before." Roland mashed his fork into a potato and took a bite. The pain of chewing spoiled his meal.

"Not that—the Toth, you nitwit." Ibarra

shook his head. "We thought they were extinct, but some of them must have been away from their home world and had a ship with a Qa'Resh jump engine. The overlord must have…" He paced across his cell, one hand on his hip, the other tapping against his lips in thought.

"They must have feared we'd hunt them all down," Ibarra said. "This was before the Xaros were defeated. They jumped to a system beyond the Crucible network, in Alliance space where the Xaros hadn't made it to. Then they must have gone to the Kesaht system and…it fits."

"What fits?"

"Fits that the Toth would masquerade as divine beings to a less advanced culture. They've used the glamour of high technology to enthrall others. How did I miss this?"

Roland waited as Ibarra kept pacing, occasionally raising a hand mid-revelation, then dropping it again to continue wearing a rut into the floor.

"Why would the Toth be afraid of us killing

them off?" Roland asked. "Wasn't it the Xaros? They were the ones bent on xenocide across the whole galaxy."

Ibarra stopped, then clasped his hands behind his back.

"It wasn't the Xaros that annihilated the Toth home world…it was us," Ibarra said. "Do you know what the Xaros masters were? Energy beings. Nigh immortal, with an infinite supply of drones and technology that we still don't fully understand. By the end, they'd destroyed Bastion and the Alliance. There were drone armadas several-trillion strong closing in on Earth before we launched the final attack on the Key Hole gate and the Xaros' Dyson sphere. Things were desperate, you understand?"

"I know about the last battle," Roland said. "What I don't understand is what any of this has to do with the Toth. We killed off the Toth? I don't believe it."

"What you believe is irrelevant." Ibarra's surface shimmered. "We had one real weapon at the end of the war: a Qa'Resh named Malal. The last Qa'Resh in the galaxy. He was left behind and imprisoned after the rest of his kind…ascended, shall we say. Malal was willing to help us fight the Xaros, but he had a price. And when you make a deal with the devil, you end up losing your soul. So Stacey and I agreed to Malal's terms once the Xaros were gone. And the Toth paid the price."

Roland set his fork down, his appetite gone. He looked at Ibarra, a man he knew had traded billions of human lives so that a few—Roland included—might survive and reconquer Earth. What Ibarra told him made a certain horrific sense.

"What did you do to the Toth?" Roland asked.

"Malal wanted to follow the rest of his kind into paradise, some other dimension where death was impossible," Ibarra spoke quickly. "To do that, he needed the gate, which the Qa'Resh had, and he needed the strength to open it. Malal fed off the minds of sentient beings, their souls. And the number of souls he needed was in the billions."

"That's why the *Breitenfeld* vanished right after the last battle with the Xaros," Roland said.

"Smart lad. Stacey and I commandeered the *Breitenfeld* and jumped to the Toth home world...and we let Malal loose. The Toth were in the middle of a civil war after I helped assassinate their last tyrant. All their fleets had been called back to the home world; their one colony on Nibiru had been destroyed during the in-fighting. You should have seen it. A white pulse of light spreading across the planet, devouring every Toth in existence...well, almost every Toth."

"This was after the Xaros masters were dead," Roland said. "Why? Why keep your deal with this Malal? It was genocide."

"The Masters were dead, but the drones were still out there. Drones with programming and reproduction protocols good enough to wipe out most of the galaxy without a Master directing them. Just because the Masters were gone didn't mean we were safe. But Malal had the means to get rid of the drones, change their programming and make them fly into the nearest star. He wasn't going to trust that we'd deliver the power he needed. Again, you deal with the devil…"

"And then the devil won? Malal went to that paradise of his? Did you wave goodbye or try to go with him?"

Ibarra stopped and looked away from Roland.

"We took Malal to the dimension gate after we dealt with the Toth," Ibarra said quietly. "The Qa'Resh had the door ready for him. He used his power to open it and…well, the Qa'Resh put some fine print into the devil's contract because they gave him a door all right. But it wasn't to where the Qa'Resh exist, but to some nightmare. Whatever lived in there tore Malal to pieces and devoured him. The screams were…impressive. He didn't get what he wanted, but he got what he deserved."

"If Malal could have been tricked, why didn't you, Stacey, and the Qa'Resh do it before an entire alien race was wiped out?"

"I've run more than one long con in my day,

kid. You want to do that, you'd better be smarter than your mark. Malal was evil, the purest evil I've ever come across. No, I didn't think I could pull one over on what the Average Joe might consider to be a malevolent space god that would eat my soul out of spite. So I acted in good faith, which is what you do when you've got a knife to your throat. Thankfully, the Qa'Resh were that confident and knew Malal better than I did. I'm glad the Qa'Resh left the galaxy after they took care of their straggler. Anyone with that much power can never be trusted."

"And you don't think you did anything wrong?"

"Don't act like the Toth were innocent bystanders in all this. They betrayed the Alliance. They attacked Earth. They enslaved races and used them like cattle. As food! They were a hostile, evil species, and they were hell bent on gaining control of our proccie tech…until I poisoned that well for them. Removing the Toth from the galactic stage was a win-win for us, the Vishrakath, the whole galaxy."

"Then why was it kept secret? Why not proclaim what a hero you were for doing this?" Roland got off his cot, hands balled in anger. His visceral reaction to the story struggled with the analytical part of his mind that, in ways that terrified Roland, found reason in the Ibarras' actions.

"Imagine there's a wolf terrorizing your village," Ibarra said. "A smart wolf, an apex predator that no trap can catch. The wolf's threatening the children, snatching away sheep just before winter arrives. A hunter decides to end the threat, but the only way he can catch the wolf is to use a villager as bait. Even if the hunter uses an outcast…the village will always be a bit suspicious of the hunter after that."

"So you kept what happened to the Toth hidden from Earth and the rest of the galaxy."

"There weren't many eye witnesses. Those that saw what happened have been scattered to colony worlds, many sent off with Hale to Terra

Nova, never to be seen or heard from for a couple hundred years. Now Admiral Valdar may be a war hero, but when Valdar was captain of the *Breitenfeld*, he made a few errors in judgment that I leveraged to keep him quiet. That the ship had a sudden and total system failure that erased some of her logs and video files was a coincidence." Ibarra winked at Roland.

"Much easier to get along with everyone when they don't see you as the same genocidal enemy that was just defeated," continued Ibarra. "Also easier to move on to a glorious future if you're not soul-searching over the path. Stacey and I chose to be humanity's sin eaters."

"She's not dealing with it very well," Roland said as his anger subsided.

"No, that's not what's eating away at her." Ibarra leaned against the bars and motioned around him. "When I saved her, put her mind into one of these bodies, it was rushed—she was moments away from dying. It's not like I had a chance to consider the long-term implications—and the transfer was imperfect. Her mind's stabilized in the past year, but she's not whole. The trauma of being shot and that she can't go back to her old body has been an…issue for her. Among many, many other things."

"She had proccie tech. Why not just grow herself a new body?"

"Two reasons." Ibarra started pacing again. "First, we cannot grow a body without building the mind within it at the same time. Transferring her consciousness into a brain with a mind of its own would kill the host. That's the best-case scenario— I'll let you marinate on everything else that could happen—and killing the host would be murder."

"That's beyond the two of you? Simple murder?"

"There's killing and then there's murder. You're a soldier. I think you can draw a line between the two. At first, Stacey wasn't willing to do a transfer…but the longer she's stuck in that body, the more she slips away."

"And the second reason?"

"We need a Qa'Resh probe to do the transfer. They were the conduit from an ambassador's home world to Bastion. Want to see one?" Ibarra went to his desk and opened the drawer. He pulled out a thin glass needle and held it up to catch the light.

"This is Jimmy. About a century ago, he dropped into the Arizona desert and made a phone call. It's been quite a trip since then." Ibarra laid the needle on his palm and pushed it from side to side. "The Qa'Resh took his light away when they left. This is all I have to remember him by."

"That's what she was looking for on Oricon, wasn't it?" Roland asked. "A way to live again?"

"No, son." Ibarra placed the inert probe back in the drawer and slid it shut. "She's looking for something far more dangerous than the privilege to eat, feel, and grow old. She wants control, and for that, she needs power. If she finds the Qa'Resh ark, then she can remake this whole galaxy in whatever way she wants."

Ibarra sat on his bunk and leaned forward,

elbows on his knees.

"And it's my fault," he said. "I made her this way. I set her on a path before she was ever born, never gave her the chance to be her own woman. Now she's free. Free and in control of her own nation, armies, fleets. Free to choose her own path and she's chosen to never, ever let anyone control her again. And it is all my fault."

"Then how do we stop her?" Roland asked.

Ibarra lowered his head and remained silent.

CHAPTER 7

Aignar steadied himself against the railing of the *Ardennes'* observation deck as the ship translated through the wormholes connecting Crucible gates. He knew the science behind the event, knew that the travel was as instantaneous as science could detect, but every time he made a jump, he felt like his body was stretching.

Gideon seemed no worse for wear, same with Cha'ril. The other officers and sailors on the deck spoke amongst themselves and pointed out the tall windows. The points of the Crucible's gigantic thorns moved slowly, occluding the dense star field beyond the New Bastion system.

A spacecraft shaped like a silver corkscrew rotated slowly in the distance.

"Naroosha." Aignar's metal hands opened and shut with a snap, earning a look from Gideon. "Sorry, sir. Gets my blood up just seeing them. I'm used to 'see the alien, shoot the alien.'"

"I didn't know you felt that way," Cha'ril said.

"Not you. You're not an alien. You're Dotari. Which are alien but not the ones we shoot. Are you just being difficult?" Aignar asked.

Cha'ril made small clicks with her beak.

"This is neutral space," Gideon said. "No active weapon systems allowed, which is why Admiral Lettow didn't make this jump under combat conditions."

"Must be driving him nuts," Aignar said. "Where is New Bastion anyway?"

Cha'ril ran a finger down the smart glass and opened a menu. A window popped open and lines traced from the corners to a large pale dot halfway up the glass. A close-up of a desert world with extensive mountain ranges and small ice caps ringed by oceans appeared.

"Real garden spot," Aignar said. "Why'd they pick this place to have powwows?"

"It's located on the far side of the galaxy from the edge of the Xaros advance. Not close to any of the old Bastion worlds. The desert where they're building the Congress is in a dead zone, no risk of local microbes infecting anyone. The main reason they picked this place is that no one else wanted it," Gideon said. "Radiation levels are higher than most species can tolerate over the long-term, so they're building biomes for each member and calling them embassies."

Cha'ril double-tapped an icon on the planet and the holo zoomed in on an incomplete large dome with several smaller spokes connected by covered highways. She panned the camera around, pausing over construction equipment. The covered stadium looked like a cloud with even layers.

"They've still got some work to do," Aignar said.

"Anything done by committee is inherently inefficient," Cha'ril said, "and ugly. What architectural style are they going for?"

"It's modeled after the old Qa'Resh station that was the original Bastion," Gideon said. "Which the Xaros destroyed at the end of the war."

Cha'ril zoomed out and sent the camera to a line of alien vessels in orbit around the planet. She stopped over an asteroid with massive engines protruding from one end, its irregular surface broken by weapon emplacements and lit bays.

"The Vishrakath are here," she said.

"Vish…" Aignar held a prosthetic hand up in front of the glass, looking at the reflection. Seeing their ship and hearing the name of the insect-like aliens seemed to make him more self-conscious about his appearance than usual.

"They called this session," Gideon said. "Seems we aren't the only ones that have had run-ins with the Kesaht."

"The Kesaht are the reason we're here?" Aignar asked. "Not the Ibarras?"

"I doubt we'll leave here without a long, painful discussion over the Ibarras," Gideon said. "It's an eighteen-hour burn to the planet. Get some rest. You're both coming down as my bodyguards. There've been some security incidents in the past few months."

"Will I get to see Vish?" Aignar asked.

"Best behavior," Gideon said.

"Leave it to diplomacy to suck the fun out of anything," Aignar said.

****

Ding ding.

Aignar woke with a snort. He lifted the stump of an arm that ended just below his elbow and wiped sleep from his eyes, then he rolled over in his bunk and squinted at the blinking time on his new data slate. He had ten minutes to get to the cemetery and suit up and he had incoming calls from Cha'ril and Henrique, his chief armor tech.

"Balls," he said as he sat up, swung his legs

over the side of his bunk, and pushed the nub of his right leg into his boot. The cybernetics interface at the bottom of his calf clicked into the boot and he rolled the ankle of his prosthetic around.

"Balls, balls," he said as he connected his other foot, then leaned to one side where his hand and forearm waited in a holster. He snapped it on as he mentally kicked himself. He'd forgotten to set his alarm with the new data slate and now he was about to make a mortal sin as an armor officer: missing time to cross the line of departure for a mission.

He twisted his other arm on and bumped an elbow against the door control panel. On the other side of the sliding door hung two cylinders the width of a finger. Each was plastic, but carved with little totems of birds and Dotari language.

"Sure. Why not?" Aignar grabbed both totems and snapped them free of the string connecting them to his door frame.

"No, no, no!" Cha'ril shouted from the end of the passageway.

At the other end, the two aggressive Dotari pushed past the Marine guard, both calling out in their native language.

Aignar looked town at the two totem sticks, then to Cha'ril, then to the two males that didn't seem interested in each other, but were pointing at Aignar.

"A little help here!" Aignar yelled to Cha'ril.

She ran up to Aignar, twisted him toward the oncoming Dotari, and ducked behind him. She then began singing in Dotari, a soothing rhythm that only confused Aignar more as it seemed to make the two males even angrier.

The Dotari pilot snatched a totem away and broke it in half.

The Dotari armor grabbed the other and bit down on it, breaking it into thirds and spitting out a chunk at the other's feet.

The corridor was silent but for the constant beeping from all their forearm screens.

The pilot pointed at Aignar.

"I am Man'fred Vo and I demand the *ushulra* choose once the mission allows. I do not yield."

"I am Fal'tir, and I do not yield," the armor Dotari said.

"That's great, guys—really it is. But I— ow!" Aignar winced as Cha'ril pinched his back. She then shook him by his jumpsuit, and he continued. "Mission? Yes, after the mission. We all have someplace to be, right?"

Man'fred brushed his forearms off with an exaggerated gesture and Fal'tir mirrored him. The two turned and jogged away.

Cha'ril spun Aignar around.

"Why? Why didn't you answer your phone?" She buried her face in her palms.

"Walk and talk." Aignar nudged her toward the elevator at the end of the passageway. "I don't know what the hell is going on, but it can't be as bad as missing our call time."

"I didn't think they would offer dowries so quickly. Damn my pheromones!" Cha'ril said as they stepped into the elevator. "They put their lineage totems in my door overnight. I didn't choose one, so they went to you…and then you went and touched them both!"

"I have no idea what's happening right now," Aignar said, tossing his hands up.

"You—I—now I have to join with one of them." Cha'ril rubbed the bridge of her nose. "And you get to pick."

"Oh no," Aignar said, shaking his head. "You need to back that truck up. Tell them I'm just a clueless human that doesn't know the rules—true statement!—and you're not getting married to anyone. Will that fix this? We'll tell them once we've got our armor on. No one argues with armor."

"You don't understand." Cha'ril removed her hand, and small blue freckles appeared across the bridge of her nose and spread up her forehead. "This has to happen. I want this to happen."

"No. No you don't. You said this would pass, right? No one needs to get married. Let's stop all this crazy talk right now," Aignar said.

"The two of them will only get more aggressive," she said. "Other males will catch my scent and the threat of them killing each other over me will only get worse. You have no idea how many Dotari stories start like this, because an *ushulra* refused to act. There were wars, cities destroyed. Humans wouldn't understand."

"You think humans have never done something stupid because they were in love or especially hor—obsessed with the opposite sex? Let me tell you what happened in fair Verona sometime," Aignar said. "I don't have to choose, just delay," he continued. "We'll get the brass involved and then you all can go back on Dotari saltpeter and we'll have a nice laugh about this," Aignar said.

The elevator stopped and opened to the cemetery where Gideon stood on the catwalk in front of two waiting suits of armor, their chests and wombs already opened. The lieutenant, in his dress uniform and spit-shined strapped boots, looked at the clock on his forearm screen and then glared at Aignar and Cha'ril.

"The first person my suitors will hurt is probably you," she said. "That you're not even Dotari has raised my desirability in their eyes."

Aignar waved to Chief Henrique as he stomped a foot and pointed at Aignar's waiting armor.

"Cha'ril, you're explaining this to Gideon. Not me."

CHAPTER 8

Roland, his body braced in a push-up position against the floor, lowered his upper body. He hissed out a ten count, then kept his chest hovering just over the ground for another ten count. He pushed up slowly, his arms quivering with fatigue, sweat dripping from his forehead. He locked out his arms and collapsed.

"Fourteen," he said.

In the other cell, Marc Ibarra glanced up from his tablet and shook his head.

"Why bother?" Marc asked. "You armor types have no need for physical fitness. Back when I started the program before the Analog War, I recruited—"

The privacy screens snapped on and the vault door opened with a hiss of pneumatic locks. Roland grabbed the side of his bunk and struggled to his feet as the same two guards entered the cell block, an appearance off his normal mealtimes. The ever-scowling guard rapped his truncheon against the bars, electricity snapping between the club and the metal. The man behind him carried a hood and muzzle.

"The prisoner will prepare for transport," the lead guard said. He swiped a hand over the cell door and a panel fell open, large enough for Roland to stick both hands through and receive his restraints.

"Your queen want me again?" Roland asked.

The guard slammed his club against the bar and lightning flickered up and down the cell wall.

"Don't push it, kid," said the more genial guard. "You've been granted a small privilege. Keep the lip up and you can keep up your mushroom routine in your cell."

"What privilege? Maybe I'd prefer you come check out just how slippery it is in here," Roland said.

"You're not in your armor," said the guard with the club. His hand tightened around the handle.

"Prisoner gets marked up, you'll explain it to the colonel," the other guard said. He elbowed his fellow guard out of the way and rapped the handcuffs against the open window. "Exercise, kid. You're getting it one way or another."

Roland flexed his hands, feeling the blood flow through his arms. Any chance to leave the cell was an opportunity to devise an escape. He went to the door and let the guard cuff him. He accepted the muzzle and hood and let the friendlier guard lead him out of the cell.

"What's wrong?" he heard the guard say.

Roland seized up as the club struck his lower back and sent an excruciating bolt of pain from his knees to his shoulders. One of the guards caught him before he could fall and he felt flesh press against his ear through the hood.

"Speak against Lady Ibarra again," the angry guard said, his breath stinking of spicy food, "please."

Muscles along Roland's back and legs twitched, threatening to cramp up. A half-dozen retorts he'd been practicing stayed bottled up inside. The guards hauled Roland to his feet and dragged him away.

****

The hood came off and Roland found himself in a wide room with wooden beams running across the ceiling, and the walls were paper screens held within a thin grid of wooden rods. Mats of woven fabric made up the floor.

The guard removed his muzzle and the handcuffs and stepped back from his prisoner as Roland rubbed his aching back.

"Why the gag?" Roland asked.

"There are worse things you can say than insulting the Lady," the guard said. He looked over

Roland's shoulder and raised his chin slightly.

Behind him a set of full-body training padding and two longswords in scabbard belts hung from a wooden rack in the middle of the room. A few yards away along the wall, before a small shrine to Saint Kallen, a man in training gear knelt in prayer, a sword gripped in one hand. He looked well-built...and had plugs at the base of his skull.

Another armor soldier.

"...*aliisque insidiantibus sit pavor, terror et formido,*" the other man said.

Roland recognized the near end of a prayer for the blessing of a sword and drew one of the swords. It was dull, lightweight, but he could swing it with enough force to make it hurt.

The penitent man kissed his pommel and stood. He was dark of eyes and hair, his skin faintly olive. A hint of crow's feet around the eyes and a weariness to his countenance hinted at a life of war.

"I'll have your name," Roland said, testing the weight of his weapon.

The armor soldier motioned to the pads.

Roland watched the gesture and narrowed his eyes. The way the man moved…Roland recognized the body language. He moved like the Ibarran armor that ripped Aignar apart and laid Roland low on Oricon.

This was Nicodemus. Rage born of his humiliating defeat and days in a cell rose in Roland's heart and took over. He charged forward and swung his sword at the other man's neck.

Nicodemus raised his sword arm, the blade held flat against his forearm. Roland's strike careened off, sending a jarring shake up his arm. The Ibarran snapped out a kick that caught Roland on the thigh and caused a spasm in his quadriceps strong enough that Roland's leg buckled.

Nicodemus' sword struck Roland's wrist and sent his weapon flying. Roland tripped over his own feet and fell to the mats. History seemed to repeat itself as Nicodemus planted a boot on Roland's chest and raised his sword up, the tip pointed at Roland's heart.

The Ibarran slammed the sword down and

buried the tip into the mat next to Roland's head.

"You have a hole in your swing," Nicodemus said. "I see Gideon's hand in your training. I know you have been trained better than this." He ripped his sword from the mat and stepped back.

Roland shook pain out of his throbbing wrist and propped himself up on an elbow.

"What do you want with me?" Roland asked.

"I'm here to train you." Nicodemus planted the tip of his sword between his feet and rested his hands on the pommel.

"Train me? Why?"

"Your future hasn't been decided. Perhaps you'll be sent back to Earth. Then you'll fight again as armor. Put the pads on. It'll hurt less."

Roland rubbed a knot out of his leg and got up, wincing.

"I'm going home?"

"You may. You may not. But while you are here, you will be trained."

"If I go back to Earth, we may end up on the opposite side of a fight again. Why would you train me?"

Nicodemus tilted his head slightly to the side.

"You heard me pray. You've seen my armor." He touched his left shoulder, where the Templar Cross would be. "You are a supplicant, aren't you?"

Roland paused, his thoughts going to the primer he read that morning.

"'For the Order is never complete,'" Roland quoted, "'and the hands that bear the sword must forge the next.' That's why you're here? You think you have a duty to train me?"

"There's no question if I have that duty," Nicodemus said.

"I don't bel—I know the vows. The oaths. But you training me…"

"The Templar are the sword and shield of all humanity. The Kesaht are enemies to Earth and the Ibarra Nation. As are the Vishrakath. As are others.

If you go back, you may fight them. I'll not return a dull instrument."

Roland considered his options and decided he had little to lose. He took the padded jacket off the rack and slipped it on.

"What happened to my lance mate? To Aignar?" The jacket tightened around his body as he ran his fingers down the seam to seal it.

"We gave your squadron enough time to find him. They left the station long before we sank it into the gas giant. Sobieski and Gideon would never have left so soon unless they'd found him." Nicodemus lifted his sword off the ground and gave it a twirl.

Roland stepped into the pair of oversized pants and wiggled his foot into the loose mesh sock at the end. The bottom and top halves of the outfit attached around his waist, and Roland felt the suit adjust itself to his body.

The training gear was modeled off the pseudo-muscle layers of combat power armor. While this outfit wouldn't augment his strength, it would dampen the force of any hit he took…and the control systems would insulate against the shock batons the guards carried.

"Don't pretend that you know them."

Roland put on a pair of gloves and slapped on a full-face helmet. "They stayed loyal to Earth when you ran off with the Ibarras."

Nicodemus lunged forward with a fencer's strike and stabbed Roland in the solar plexus. Roland's armor stiffened, spreading the force of the impact across his chest, but the blow still hit like a punch. Roland twisted to one side and pushed the blade tip away with his upper arm. He snapped an elbow at Nicodemus' bare face.

The other fighter caught the elbow with his palm and dug fingers into the joint and then spun and pulled Roland off-balance. Roland tripped over Nicodemus' leg and fell to the ground with the grace of a dropped sack of potatoes, his sword bouncing against the mats.

Nicodemus kicked Roland's sword back to him.

"You know nothing, pledge. Get up, and I'll teach you to handle a blade with some skill," Nicodemus said.

****

Roland collapsed onto his cell floor. Bruises and welts pulsed on his arms and shoulders, but the cold concrete floor was oddly soothing to his battered body. He ran his tongue against the inside of a swollen lip, tasting blood that oozed from a cut down the side of his nose.

"Dear God, they tortured you!" Mark Ibarra shouted. "Which was it? Tweedle fat ass or Tweedle no neck?"

"No," Roland said as he scrubbed dried blood off his cheek and propped himself up. "It was Nicodemus, and I deserved every hit he landed."

"And they brainwashed you!"

"We were sword sparring." Roland worked his hands open and shut, feeling the pain of too many strikes against his training gear. "Even with pads…he's damn strong. I managed a number of insults that no amount of pain meds can cover up."

"Did what? You look like you got a good kicking from a football team."

"Just him." Roland turned to his bunk, where a covered tray sat next to his pillow. He lifted the lid, and steam from pork chops and peas mixed with carrots wafted out. He put the lid back on and became acutely aware of the ache in his jaw.

"Ibarra, why do they keep putting a muzzle on me?"

"Because of me," the metal man said. "I controlled the procedural crèches on Earth and when we first arrived here. You control the crèches, you can edit the consciousness that goes into the body. Stacey must be afraid that I snuck in voice commands that you could activate with a choice phrase."

"Did you?"

"What? I'm shocked. Shocked that you would even accuse me of such a thing." Ibarra raised his chin.

"So you did." Roland went to the sink and washed his face.

"Not just *me*, mind you. Stacey and I made a few adjustments to crèches in the home system before we took our leave of Earth—only to those still in the tubes. The code erased itself after that batch. Something of an insurance policy. I was against it after the last debacle," Ibarra said.

"When did you play mind games with other people? Or was that something you did since the first proccie walked out of the farms?"

"There was always one that…she doesn't matter anymore, but she's half the reason we're in this mess. What were you doing while the Ruhaald and the Naroosha occupied the Crucible? You were a kid, probably sitting in a bunker wondering why the Xaros hadn't killed you yet. What you missed was a rather daring jail break led by yours truly while under great duress. We kicked the aliens off the jump gate and sent them home with their tails between their legs, but in the few days they had control, they modified the proccies coming out of the tubes on the Crucible. One was a woman I've known for many years—a fixer, assassin, all around evil yet eminently useful woman named Shannon."

"The Naroosha made their own proccies?" Roland wiped a cloth across his face.

"They injected some rather ingenious behavior protocols, which turned a few hundred proccies into sleeper agents. I was so confident in my system that I never thought anyone else could hack codes…and I was so very wrong. Shannon's the one that hurt Stacey so badly. After that, I found what the Naroosha had done and decided to eliminate the rest of their assets."

"The *Hiawatha*," Roland said as he sat down and poked at his dinner, nibbling on a few peas at a time. "The ship they accused you of blowing up. All the evil proccies were aboard, weren't they?"

"Evil is a choice, Mr. Shaw. They were created to be weapons against humanity. I destroyed them to keep Earth safe. After what they did to Stacey, I wasn't willing to take risks with letting them stay active."

"Why not bring them in for treatment? Do something other than kill them?"

"And how would that have played out if I got on the vids and said, 'No need to panic! The following proccies, please report to your nearest security team. You may be subject to alien mind control at any time. Purely routine.' It would make everyone suspicious of every proccie in the system. All this was happening while a Xaros drone armada was advancing on the system, mind you."

"So you murdered them all."

"I didn't have time for a perfect solution. Not the first innocents to die because of me. Not the last."

"And what happened to the software the aliens used? Did you erase that along with the people on the *Hiawatha*?" Roland dropped his fork onto the plate, his appetite gone.

"Tools are tools."

"Do you think Stacey's using that 'tool' to keep her people under total control? Did she work in a fail-safe we could find? Use it to stop whatever she's planning?"

Ibarra walked up to the bars between their cells and looked hard at Roland.

"Son, if you could snap your fingers and kill every proccie in the Ibarra Nation, would you?" His head turned from side to side slowly, waiting for an answer.

"I...I don't know. They're not any different from the people on the *Hiawatha*, are they? Victims of circumstance. None of them chose to be what they are or where they are."

"I've had a long time to get used to making decisions like the *Hiawatha*. I hope you never find yourself in the places I've been. They leave black marks on your soul that grow with time...until the good man you once were is a memory."

He walked back to his bunk and sat down, hands linked behind his head, legs crossed.

"Eat your peas, Roland. A clear conscience isn't the only thing I envy about you."

****

The crèche was normally rather quiet. Rows upon rows of tanks filled with light green fluid and shadows of the people growing within generated little noise beyond the hum of generators and the very rare thump of an appendage against the glass as a procedural's body twitched as some memory was etched into its brain.

Today, the sound of footfalls and muffled conversation echoed between the tanks.

Stacey Ibarra walked down the narrow maintenance pathway bisecting the crèche. She wore a long quilted overcoat, not because her metal body needed the warmth, but to keep from upsetting the delicate balance within the tanks.

Keeping pace beside her was a bald man with a drooping mustache and a lab coat.

"What do you need, Dr. Cummings?" she asked. "Production is down ten percent across Navarre's crèches. We're building ships faster than we can crew them. This is unacceptable."

"My lady, I warned you…side projects

would impact our operations. Nine days is the standard for a trained adult in all manner of military specialties. The Legionnaires take two more days as their physical attributes are a bit more difficult to bring forth while they're in the tanks. Getting the growth hormones just right is difficult and there will be long term health repercussions."

"It's not like I'm demanding officers derived from Caesar, Attila, Napoleon and Alexander the Great," she said.

"My Lady, genetic stock is largely irrelevant given the amount of gene editing that goes into each unit and the procedural consciousness that—"

"I am aware of the process, doctor," she snapped. "Why has production slowed?"

"I told—forgive me. It's the special orders. Changing the procedural generation code so drastically takes time and a fair bit of trial and error. Making a change like this would have been easier during the war when Mr. Ibarra—" he shrank back slightly as she glared at him "—had the Qa'Resh drone to do all the heavy lifting. Of course, I doubt the drone would have made these changes."

"The project continues," Stacey said. "What do you need to make your quota, doctor?"

"More tubes, more computing power." Cummings shrugged. "We can't shorten the gestation period. You're aware of what happens if we do."

She removed a data slate and tapped at it, her fingers moving far faster than Cummings had ever seen before.

"There." She pressed the slate to his chest. "Fifty thousand new tubes and associated equipment will go into the south ranges. Once the project moves into phase two, you will supervise the transfer of those mainframes and a thousand tubes to the test planet. Understand?"

"Of course, my lady," Cummings raised an eyebrow at the order on the data slate. "This is my life's work. Anything for you."

"Meet the quota, Cummings. There will be casualties soon." She continued down the pathway and left the doctor alone in the crèche.

CHAPTER 9

The Destrier-class transports were the larger,
hardier cousin to the ubiquitous Mules used for
most personnel and cargo transports within the fleet.
The cargo bay could carry up to a hundred combat-
loaded Rangers for an orbital insertion and nearly a
dozen armor soldiers.

That this cargo bay held only Cha'ril,
Aignar, and the armor-less Gideon lent it an almost
eerie emptiness. The two armored soldiers stood
with their feet locked in deck clamps. Gideon was
between them, lights glinting off his medals and the
silver bars on his rank epaulets. He had his hands
clasped behind his back and his eyes were squeezed
shut.

"Then, Mr. Aignar, you volunteered to be Cha'ril's...*ushulra*?"

"No, sir." Aignar's helm shook quickly. "There was a lot of yelling in Dotari that I didn't understand and then Cha'ril was there and she started singing—"

Gideon held up a hand and cut him off. He looked up to his Dotari soldier.

"Cha'ril, is there any way to get Aignar out of this?" he asked.

"Yes. A male blood relative of mine can take his place. All of whom are on Dotari Prime and under quarantine. The role is one of great honor in my community. He should be proud."

"Helps to know what the hell I'm supposed to do before I can put on airs," Aignar said.

"Having one of my lancers play matchmaker for another is not a complication I anticipated for this mission," Gideon said, his voice full of frustration. "Aignar will choose who you marry? Is that it?"

"There are varying degrees of Dotari

marriage," she said.

Gideon pressed a palm to his face.

"Sir, are you well?" Cha'ril asked. "I can see your body temperature and blood pressure rising on my IR."

Gideon slammed a fist against his thigh and looked away from her.

"A joining under these circumstances is temporary. There are many conditions under which the joining may be annulled. A full marriage with clan transfers, inheritance rights—"

"So this may not last?" Gideon asked.

"Correct."

"And you're okay with that?" Aignar asked. "Human divorce is about as fun as a kick in the crotch."

"An unsuccessful joining is considered a positive," she said. "If a couple prove…incompatible, then they should search elsewhere. My parents were of different castes and married for love and experienced great social hardship until we resettled Dotari Prime. Had they joined during the season, their lives would have much easier."

"And I thought dating apps were complicated," Aignar said.

Gideon pinched the bridge of his nose.

"Is there a chance your suitors—by God, I never thought I'd have this conversation in the Armor Corps—will lose interest by the time we return to the *Ardennes?* It could be days or weeks."

"If my pheromones were absent…but I left both of them *yiliri*."

Gideon made a rolling forward motion with his hand.

"A *yiliri*, a small cloth that I dabbed against my pheromone glands," she said.

"They have the smell of your perfume to keep driving them crazy." Aignar tossed his hands up. "Why? Why make my life more difficult than it already is?"

"That's what you're supposed to do!" Cha'ril said, loud enough for the Destrier's cabin crew to perk up and notice. "I wasn't going to be rude. Do you want to read the poetry they sent me?"

"No," Gideon and Aignar said at the same time.

Gideon sighed. "Cha'ril. I understand this is a significant event for you. It's just frustrating for us."

"I'm experiencing frustration in other matters," she snipped.

The Destrier rumbled as it descended into New Bastion's atmosphere.

"Wheels down in five minutes!" a crew man shouted.

****

The Destrier's ramp lowered to a dust storm. From the edge of the cargo bay, the dry air and fine dust particles assaulted Gideon's eyes and nose. Of all the things he missed about his days as a grunt Marine, dealing with weather was not one of them.

Cha'ril and Aignar stood behind him, their rotary cannons panning across the landscape. The dust storm turned New Bastion into little more than an orange haze. Lights from distant buildings diffused through the sand like stars within nebulae.

Their rotary cannons snapped forward as a ground car emerged out of the gloom. It pulled parallel with the end of the ramp and a human woman in an overcoat hurried out of the backseat and up the ramp.

"Lieutenant Gideon, I presume," she said loudly over the storm. Her long black hair blew free in the storm. He nodded.

"Ambassador Ibanez," she said as she looked up at the two armor, then over Gideon's shoulder. "Where are your bodyguards?"

"What are we, chopped liver?" Aignar asked.

"No armor allowed on New Bastion," Ibanez said. "Didn't you get the memo? I specifically sent that almost three days ago. The Ruhaald delegation are terrified of you and they made an amendment to the security forces—"

"We've been under commo blackout for the

last week," Gideon said. "They're all I brought."

"They have to go back!" Ibanez waved a hand at the armor. "Things have gone from bad to worse since the Vishrakath emissary showed up and I can't deal with another security breach—especially not one as obvious as those two."

"Our effectiveness as bodyguards would be limited if we leave our armor," Cha'ril said.

"Go back," Gideon said as wind howled around them.

"Sir?" Aignar's rotary cannon popped back onto his shoulders as he looked down at his lieutenant.

"Return to the *Ardennes* and have them send another security element. This situation is delicate and I can take care of myself just fine," Gideon said.

"Great! Settled. Can we get out of this mess?" Ibanez asked.

"Stay safe, sir." Aignar backed away from the edge and Cha'ril followed.

Gideon stomped down the ramp and opened

the car door for Ibanez. He looked back at the Destrier and saw both his lance mates staring out at him as it buttoned up. He got into the car and slammed the door.

"To the embassy, Jerry," Ibanez said to the driver. She raised a privacy screen and shook sand from her hair. "I swear, this planet has two seasons: miserable and shitty." She opened a compartment next to her seat and fog rose from a small cooler with ice in it. She took out two glasses and a bottle of liquor.

"Drink?" she asked.

The ambassador was in her early forties, attractive, and lacked a wedding ring. Under normal circumstances, Gideon would have found nothing wrong with her offer.

"I'm on duty," he said.

"This is a Standish special reserve." She raised an eyebrow at him. "Prewar whiskey recreated in the omnium foundries. Tastes like the original because it is the original down to the molecule. Lots of speculation as to how some junior enlisted Marine got his hands on the booze and the reactor."

"Is the answer in that bottle?"

"No, but I can appreciate the taste and the mystery at the same time." She dropped two ice cubes into a glass and poured herself more than a finger's worth of the whiskey. "Do you know why you're here?"

"The surface reason is that I fought the Kesaht on Oricon. Then there's what the Ibarras were doing there…"

"It's a shit show." She swirled her drink around and took a sip. "The whole galaxy. We had a great framework going for us after the Hale Treaty: races could stake out territory across the galaxy, build up their own little enclaves. Plenty of room for everyone. Then the Ibarras emerged from hiding and moved our cheese."

"Did what?"

"Spanner in the works. Knocked over our tea cart. I know you're armor and tend to deal with problems by shooting them but work with me here.

The Ibarras raided alien worlds—looking for God knows what—and that raised questions back here on Bastion. 'Why is Earth doing this to us?'"

"It's not Earth. The Ibarras are traitors."

"See, you can make that distinction. The rest of the galaxy…not so much. To join the old Alliance, a species had to be unified. No squabbling nation-states or factions to upset the Qa'Resh's grand plans. The old members were unified for thousands of years before the war ended. Earth met that criteria…after the Xaros wiped out everyone but the Atlantic Union fleet Ibarra created 'to colonize Saturn.' So when we tell the rest of the galaxy that the Ibarras aren't us, they're skeptical." She took a longer sip and glanced at the bottle.

"Then we will make them understand," Gideon said.

Ibanez spit some of her drink out.

"Oh, I like you." She dabbed at her mouth with a napkin. "Four hundred and nineteen different species are here. All with different cultures and histories. All it'll take is a lecture or two and all our problems will go away."

"Then why did Phoenix send me here? Admiral Lettow dealt with the Ibarras on Oricon. He's here."

"Because you're armor." Ibanez sighed. "And armor's role in the end of the war carries weight with plenty of species. That, and I know for a fact that every single ambassador here has seen that stupid *Last Stand on Takeni* movie in an attempt to better understand human culture."

"That's a propaganda film," Gideon said. "How the armor in that movie, the Smoking Snakes, died on Takeni isn't at all how it happened in the movie."

"Don't spill that secret. That you're armor carries a good deal of weight in your testimony— which needs to focus on the Kesaht as much as possible. How dangerous they are, big scary teeth. All that."

"Why the Kesaht? I thought New Bastion called this meeting because of the Ibarras."

"They did, but we need to hijack this thing

and get the ambassadors concerned about the Kesaht, not the Ibarras." She pulled a data slate out of her coat pocket and handed it to Gideon. A map of the galaxy came up and attack icons dotted settled systems. At least a dozen different races had been affected.

"The Kesaht have been busy, much more so than the Ibarras," she said. "They raid settlements, take prisoners, and then vanish back into the Crucible network. We have no idea where their home world is or where they're staging from. The only one of our systems they've hit is Oricon."

"They've skipped over Vishrakath worlds," Gideon said.

"Yes…curious." Her eyebrows jumped up and she finished her drink.

"Anyone know why the Kesaht are using Toth technology?" he asked.

Ibanez slammed her drink down and blood drained from her face.

"You are forbidden from mentioning the Toth, you understand? You know nothing about them," she said forcefully.

Gideon turned his head so she could see the scars running down one side of his face.

"I know nothing?"

"Do not talk about the Toth. I will have your armor if you fuck with me on this."

"The lady doth protest too much." Gideon leaned back. "Why is this such a touchy subject?"

"I don't know what you're talking about. Now, let's go over how this session will play out…"

CHAPTER 10

Aignar waited as the ramp of the Destrier lowered. Being armor changed his demeanor, as being fifteen feet of killing machine will do to a man. Towering over the deck crew didn't make him feel superior to them; it made him feel protective of them.

"Let's see if your boyfriends are here," Aignar said to Cha'ril just behind him. "They'll learn what it means to mess with a man's little sister."

"Your attitude is not helping," she said.

"Well, waking up and learning that I'm in the middle of a Dotari love triangle was a bit more than I anticipated this morning. I'll cope however I want—ah, damn it." Admiral Lettow walked up the ramp before the edge could hit the deck. A Dotari officer, 2nd Circle and equivalent to a Terran navy captain, kept pace with him.

"Which of you is Cha'ril?" the admiral asked.

She raised a hand in a tentative wave.

"And you're Aignar," Lettow said. "I've just had a most informative briefing on the Dotari-Terran mutual-defense treaty. Chief Warrant Officer Aignar, are you aware of Addendum E, subsections 19-85?"

"It's been learn-as-I-go, sir," Aignar said.

"Same here, seems I didn't get the memo that my Dotari crew would start secreting pheromones and demanding honor duels with each other over possible mates." Lettow put his hands on his hips and frowned at the Dotari officer, who nodded emphatically. "I also didn't know that I would be required to host said duels, but there it was in black and white."

"Duels? Sir?" Aignar suddenly felt much smaller within his armor.

"Cargo bay 11." Lettow pointed a knife hand at Aignar's chest. "Both of you. Two hours."

"Appropriate dress is waiting in your berthing," the Dotari officer said.

"I can't have any more disruptions on my ship," Lettow said. "Bring this to whatever conclusion you need to. Just don't let anyone get so hurt they can't fight." He spun around and marched to the exit, muttering and cursing the whole way.

The Dotari officer bowed and spoke in his native language, then ran after Lettow.

"What did he say?" Aignar asked.

"He hopes you choose well for me and that my suitors remain as brave and committed after the joining," she said.

"Well…shit. Guess we better get dressed."

CHAPTER 11

As Ibanez faced away from Gideon, murmuring words to a prepared speech from her data slate, he looked over his uniform in the reflection of the small dome over their ambassador pod. The robot that met the car at the grand hall had done a remarkable job of cleaning New Bastion's dust from his coat and pants.

The dome was mostly opaque, but Gideon could see the faint outline of other domes around them and shadows of alien ambassadors filing in. The center of the stadium-sized hall was lost to darkness.

"This is what Bastion was like?" he asked.

"Before the war ended?"

"To a degree." Ibanez put her speech down and touched up her eyeshadow. "The ambassadors had their consciousness transferred to the station and put into shells. Brilliant idea. Solved most of the administrative problems we're dealing with now. The Eridinu are on their fourth ambassador; they keep dying of old age once they get here."

"How long have you been on this assignment?"

"Four years and counting. You know who should be here? Stacey Ibarra. She's dealt with these ambassadors before. President Garret *begged* her to take the position once New Bastion was announced, but she had a whole cornucopia of issues to deal with…which leads back to why you're here."

She opened a drawer and removed two small collars made of transparent plastic with a round nub in the middle.

"This is how we talk to each other around here," she said, snapping one around her neck and handing the other to Gideon. "We call them wielding modules, lets you wield your voice as a tool. The collar reads your vocal cords and the translations go straight to your inner ear."

Her fingers danced across a keypad and a circle of light lit up on the ceiling.

"Holo projector. Step inside and you'll be on the big stage," she said. "Which hopefully won't be necessary. You don't have a fear of public speaking, do you? Probably should have checked on that sooner."

"It takes more than a suit to be armor," Gideon said, tapping his chest.

The lights inside the pod dimmed and flared.

"And here we go." Ibanez popped open a small hand mirror and smoothed out an errant hair.

Gideon doubted any of the alien representatives cared about her appearance and decided that her attention to detail had more to do with her shifting her mind-set from idle conversation to her public persona.

Not that any of the aliens could appreciate

how striking he found her, but that was their loss.

The dome darkened for a moment, then the view changed to a dais made up of hexagonal rock beams, the surface mostly level. Gideon thought back to a childhood trip to Ireland and a day spent on the Giant's Causeway. Beyond the dais, hundreds of ambassador pods were arrayed along the walls of the conference center, some much larger than others.

The point of view of their pod hovered just over the edge of the dais. Gideon hadn't felt any movement from the pod and realized the view through the dome was a holographic trick.

"The old pods could move," Ibanez said. "No one has anti-grav-repulsor tech good enough to manage that. Or if they do, they're not sharing."

"What now?" he asked.

"The Vishrakath called this meeting. They'll open." She folded her hands on her lap, fingers fiddling with each other.

Why is she so nervous? he thought.

A Vishrakath materialized in the middle of

the dais. Its body was segmented like an ant's, four legs attached to the lower abdomen, the thorax and head upright. Its flesh was a deep purple with white around the edges of the maniples and along the edges of its upper arms. In true Vishrakath fashion, it wore no clothes but for a gold-embroidered sash across its thorax.

"Oh no, not Wexil." Ibanez ground her jaw. "He was their ambassador on old Bastion. If the Vish sent him, that means they're dead serious."

"Ambassadors." Wexil's mouth began moving quickly, the tip of a forked yellow tongue darting in and out. "Thank you for continuing the spirit of cooperation the Qa'Resh brought to the galaxy so many years ago."

"A 'spirit' he tried to wreck when he led a coup against the Qa'Resh. But that's beside the point," Ibanez muttered.

"After so many years of peace throughout the galaxy," Wexil continued as Gideon raised an eyebrow—he'd fought the Vishrakath on Cygnus, and if that wasn't a conflict, then Gideon was

141

curious as to what exactly constituted a war for the alien, "we are faced with a challenge to the very thing that provides the framework for our peaceful coexistence and colonization of the galaxy."

"Right to the point." Ibanez stood and smoothed out her coat.

"What I'm about to show you came at the cost of several Vishrakath lives," Wexil said. One arm moved to the side and a small tendril emerged from his palm and tapped at an unseen surface.

A starship appeared above him, floating in the void. Gideon thought it was a Terran corvette at first, but the paint was different—white and red versus the Navy's earth tones. Atmosphere leaked from blast holes in the hull. Damaged bits of the ship spun slowly in the expanding vapor cloud.

"This ship was brought to heel after a force illegally entered Vishrakath space," Wexil said. "The other ships managed to escape, but not before they raided an artifact site…a site they destroyed once they left. The construction is Terran, as you all can see. But it is the crew that is of great interest."

Ibanez began muttering a low string of profanity.

"None of the criminals were captured alive," the alien ambassador said, "and the ship's computer core was damaged beyond repair, but we were able to recover a number of bodies."

The hologram over his head switched to a line of human corpses suspended in midair, all badly injured and burned. Gideon knew they were Ibarran sailors, but their deaths still tugged at a small part of him.

"During our meticulous examination of the bodies, we discovered this." Wexil waved a hand in front of his face and the bodies were replaced by a double helix of DNA. Sections of the strands flashed white.

"The humans call this part of their makeup 'telomeres,'" Wexil said, "and the length of the telomeres are abnormally long in their procedurally generated members. By our analysis, these dead were mere months old."

He paused, and as he waited, pictures of

other alien races appeared around the dais, the borders of their pictures flashing on and off.

"They figured that out too fast," Ibanez said. "Wexil's engaging in theater, as always."

"I will remind you all," Wexil said, "that the key provision of the Hale Treaty—the agreement that governs the known sentient races in the galaxy and this body—is that the humans abandon their procedural-generation technology. They agreed," he said, turning toward Gideon and Ibanez's pod and pointing a six-clawed hand at them. "They agreed almost ten years ago. Earth has violated the Hale Treaty. There can be no denying this."

More and more ambassador posters appeared around the edge, all demanding to speak.

Ibanez stepped into the circle and appeared in front of Wexil on the dais.

"On behalf of the Terran Union, we thank the Vishrakath for bringing this to our attention," Ibanez said. "Any violation of Vishrakath territory is regrettable and was not carried out at the behest of *my* government." She swallowed hard and glanced at Gideon.

"As for this…evidence of yours," she said, "we must examine it ourselves. Our scientists are not as…astute when it comes to the biology of other members. I must assume that the Vishrakath suffer the same difficulties."

"DNA is the building block of life across the galaxy," Wexil said. "None here have ever encountered life composed of anything but these same components. All would reach the same conclusion."

"But only humans have ever utilized the procedural-generation system," Ibanez said. "Any anomalies you've detected could be the result of exposure to radiation, fire…any number of things. We must examine this evidence ourselves. The definitive answer can come only from Earth."

"An answer you wouldn't wish to share with the Congress," Wexil said. "The truth, and it will be laid bare, is that the Terrans have broken the treaty. As per the treaty, the charter for your colony worlds would be revoked…expulsion from this body may even be necessary."

"Only if the evidence you claim to have is legitimate," Ibanez said.

"I am confident in what we've recovered," Wexil said. "Stalling only makes your guilt more obvious."

"You have too much faith in your own conclusions," a new voice said. A long-limbed alien with coal-black scales and a wild mane of spikes around its long-snouted head appeared on the dais—a Haesh. The species always struck Gideon as the nightmare version of the Dotari.

"Ambassador Fengarra, you have not been recognized," Wexil said.

"The Haesh mission currently holds the premiership of this council," the ambassador said. "Given the…interest in this event, I'm exercising my authority. The ship you captured does not match any recorded Terran vessel. This begs a number of questions."

"Human aesthetics are of no concern to the Vishrakath," Wexil said.

"I have one with me who can speak to this," Ibanez said. Fengarra scratched at the ground and a text box appeared next to the ambassador reading PROCEED.

Ibanez stepped out of the circle and Gideon took her place. The view around him altered, changing his point of view to stand on the dais so close to Wexil that he could see the creases in the flesh around his black, oval-shaped eyes.

"I am First Lieutenant Jonas Gideon of the Terran Armored Corps," he said. The Haesh reached back and touched the base of its own skull, reacting to the implant on Gideon's body. "The ship you encountered is not of the Terran Union, but of another faction, one that rebelled against Earth and vanished almost five years ago. They operate beyond our control and our laws. They are traitors to their home world and they will be brought to justice."

"Another human convenience," Wexil said. "First, they call into question our findings, then they set themselves up to be apart from any responsibility once their culpability in violating the Hale Treaty becomes undeniable. Earth cannot go unpunished for this."

"Earth did not cause this. Earth is not responsible for this," Gideon said. He stood up a bit straighter, eyeing Wexil.

"Humans signed the Hale Treaty," Wexil said. "Your representative spoke on behalf of your entire species. There is no separation."

"Your narrow view is wrong," Gideon said. Wexil's back legs gripped at the ground while the fore legs lifted up and down rapidly. Gideon wasn't exactly familiar with Vishrakath body language, but if he had to guess, he'd say Wexil was growing agitated. "There was a rebellion. Honored soldiers and sailors abandoned their oaths and followed a pair of traitors into deep space. Since then, they have attacked Earth's ships, killed her soldiers and sailors, and taken captives. The Ibarras act on their own."

Gideon heard Ibanez breathe in through her teeth. They'd agreed to release the identity of the rebel leaders before the conference began. The Congress's reaction to the news would be telling. Around the dais, the number of ambassadors wishing to speak dropped off to only a handful. Gideon wasn't sure if that was a good or bad sign.

"The Ibarras?" Wexil asked. "You expect us to believe that the two chief leaders of Earth have gone rogue? Stacey Ibarra was once your ambassador to this body. She was Earth's strongest voice throughout what you call the Ember War, and you suggest that she is somehow acting against the Hale Treaty? This is ridiculous. That Earth would send one of their armored warriors here to lie to us is—"

"Silence!" Gideon shouted. The word echoed through the chamber. His face flushed red as anger roiled through him. He gripped his fists beside his waist and would have charged Wexil had the alien actually been mere yards away. The ambassador shrank against himself.

"She is a traitor," Gideon said. "I have seen her with my own eyes, leading her confederates after assaulting my own soldiers. What you knew of her is gone. She has either fallen to madness or a lust for power. Her actions are hers and hers alone. Not of Earth. Not of humanity. The Terran Union will find her and bring her to account. You have my word on that."

Gideon turned around, letting the entire chamber see his plugs.

"I am armor! And by my honor and my oath, I will not rest until the Ibarras are dead or in prison." Gideon turned his head back to Wexil. "No one will stop me. No one will stop the Armor Corps from bringing justice to the Ibarras. Do not get in our way."

Wexil's head stretched up, blood vessels visible beneath the almost-translucent skin of his neck.

"Then you will want to know where the Ibarras are hiding…won't you?" Wexil asked.

Ibanez tugged at Gideon's arm, but it was like trying to move a statue.

"Get out of the way," she hissed. "Let me

handle this."

Gideon stepped to one side and Ibanez took his place.

"Any information you have regarding the Ibarras will be appreciated," she said.

"No doubt…" Wexil's hand wavered up and down and a wall of text appeared overhead. "I remind you—I remind all signatories to the Hale Treaty—of the Omega Provision."

Ibanez froze, her eyes widening ever so slightly.

"I am aware of it," she said softly.

"The what?" Gideon asked. Ibanez raised the fingers of one hand toward him.

"Then you will act in full accord, naturally." Wexil glanced up and a star map of the galaxy formed. A single dot appeared in the Perseus arm, near the galaxy's edge. "Before this meeting, Vishrakath operatives tracked the Ibarras to here, a tertiary world barely habitable by any of our members and in the neutral zone between the Kroar and Mendesan spheres of influence."

"We'll need to examine—"

"You'll have no excuses this time," Wexil said. "The Crucible gate logs are quite clear. How long until Earth acts, proves that it will honor its agreements in the Hale Treaty—every word of the treaty?"

"I'll see that this information is returned to Earth immediately," she said. Gideon watched as sweat formed on her brow. "While the Ibarras are a priority to us, we must discuss a new, and far more concerning threat. The Kesaht."

Wexil's head bucked like an angry horse's.

"Raids by this new species are of little concern compared to the threat from humans using banned technology," Wexil said. "Earth is in violation of the Hale Treaty. As per the treaty, you have ninety of your days to come into full compliance. To include the Omega Provision."

"Earth does not accept responsibility for this." Ibanez's fists pressed against her hips. "The action of a rogue faction and unverified autopsies are not enough."

"The matter will be revisited," the Haesh said. "An examination by a neutral third party is in order. The Xin'Tik perhaps?"

"Earth will accept the Haesh's analysis," Ibanez said, somewhat relieved.

"Every moment this body refuses to act against the humans gives them more time to build up a fighting force with their illegal technology," Wexil said. "Bringing them into compliance later only makes the task harder."

"The Terran Union will adhere to the Hale Treaty," Ibanez said. "Every word."

The black claw tips on Wexil's fingers tapped against each other.

"Then there is the matter of the illegal colony," he said.

"We will remove it," Ibanez said, "with all force necessary."

"And you will accept observers to ensure your good faith is confirmed," Wexil said.

"We will welcome the Ruhaald to accompany our task force," Ibanez said.

"Unacceptable." Wexil's hands rose over his head and fell to his sides. "You have a military alliance with them. They are disinclined to provide this body the whole truth."

"What is unacceptable is your insult, Vishrakath," said an ambassador as it appeared on the dais. The Ruhaald was stoop-shouldered and its lower body ended in a fleshy tail. With the long feeder tentacles in place of the mouth and overly long fingers, it looked like a horrible cross between a manatee and a squid. The Ruhaald floated slightly off the dais, swimming in its ambassador pod. Gideon had never seen one in person, but he understood why those who'd been on maneuvers with the species called them Cthulhus.

"Ambassador Darcy," Wexil said, "I didn't know you'd be here."

"No doubt," Darcy said. "The Ruhaald will accompany the Terrans to the Ibarra colony. We have our own concerns over the Ibarras' actions."

"Will you concede the point?" Fengarra asked Wexil.

"I demand a roll-call vote," the Vishrakath said.

Ibanez stepped away from the projection circle and went to a holo panel that lit up on the wall. Text and pictures of Wexil and Darcy came up and she touched the Ruhaald and the border glowed blue.

"Bastard always wants a vote," Ibanez said.

"What is the Omega Provision?" Gideon asked.

"Hush." She moved to the front of the pod and tugged at her lip as red and blue tick marks appeared over the dais...and the great mass of blue for the Ruhaald brought a sigh from Ibanez. She tapped her forearm screen.

"Darcy, thank you for volunteering. I'll send you details once I have them." She swiped her hand over her screen and dropped into her chair. "Now we get to sit around for an hour while others bloviate their opinions. Our part's done."

She lifted an armrest and took out a small bottle of amber liquid.

"A nip? I won't tell." She unscrewed the cap and took a swig.

"Omega Provision," Gideon said.

Ibanez took a longer sip.

"Well, it's tricky," she said, "as that was something of an addendum to the Hale Treaty and was never ratified by the senate. The committee pigeonholed it very quietly, and it never got to a floor vote. You have to understand what was going on at the time. More and more species were coming online as they built their own Crucible gates. Sure, the solar system was a fortress by then, with all the macro cannons and the restored fleets. But our numbers weren't enough to fight off any of the member races that had billions and billions of fighters. We needed time to grab all the systems within jump distance of Earth, get us some breathing room."

"Answer me," Gideon said.

"I am answering you, you blunt instrument." She waved the bottle in the air. "It's not as simple as 'there's one, kill it.' So we sent our very own

Ember War hero Ken Hale off to negotiate a deal and we had the *Breitenfeld* take him. We laid on the 'Just beat the Xaros and you're welcome' pretty thick. Told him to work up a framework that would give us time to secure our own little corner of the galaxy. They treated Hale like he could walk on water," she said, taking a sip and wincing, "and he got us the deal...in exchange, we gave up procedural-generation tech."

"A stipulation the Ibarras fought against," Gideon said.

"Yeah, they didn't take that well. The Ibarras put their little rebellion in order pretty quick and vanished through the Crucible. We thought they got away with a few ships, an omnium reactor and..."

"Armor," Gideon said flatly. "A squadron of armor went with them."

She raised a toast to him.

"And we were certain that they didn't take any proccie tubes," she said. "There was something of a hiccup with the tubes at the end of the war, some Naroosha meddling—I never got more details than that—and we had every tube in the system on lockdown. Strict accountability." She let out a long sigh.

"Strict accountability we put on Marc Ibarra's shoulders. We never should have trusted him. Should have removed him from public life the minute the war ended, but here we are. He must have had a stash of proccie tubes and naissance computers in the fleet he escaped with."

"And?"

"And so, when the Vishrakath came up with the Omega Provision after most of the treaty had been ratified, we didn't object. We didn't see a problem—we had all the tubes. They were decommissioned. Anything to get Wexil and his clique to stop holding up the rest of the process." Ibanez screwed the cap on and walked to the edge of the pod, her back to Gideon.

"The Omega Provision was our promise that if any proccies were made after the treaty, they would be…destroyed. Destroyed by us or any other signatory that encountered them." Her shoulders slumped.

"Destroyed? You mean killed," Gideon said.

"Every proccie the Ibarras have will be...murdered."

"Don't put it that way," she said. "It's not diplomatic."

"Hale negotiated this? The same Hale that refused to give the proccies to the Toth when they came to Earth demanding them and the technology?" Gideon asked.

"No. The Omega Provision came up after he'd transitioned to the Terra Nova colony. Ugh, I bet he's having a great time right now, far beyond the galaxy's edge where none of this crap can follow him."

"Then who agreed to murder every new proccie?" Gideon asked.

"President Garret...a few others." She unscrewed the cap on her flask and took another sip.

"Do the Ibarras know about this?"

"Given the placement of spies we've

detected throughout the government, the intelligence types have 'high confidence' the Ibarras know about Omega," she said.

"Then you've pushed the Ibarras into a corner. They have the choice to die on their knees or die fighting...but Omega isn't law yet?"

"Not for us. Given the complexities of other races' governments, that the provision's been in limbo for a few years is not much of a concern. But when the Haesh come back and announce that, yes indeed, the Ibarras have illegal proccies, the issue will come to a head."

"And what do we do with the Ibarras then?"

"I don't know, Gideon. There's no easy way out of this mess."

CHAPTER 12

Aignar looked at the wide silk sleeves hanging from his raised arms. A Dotari crewman draped a sash over Aignar's head, fished a bit of white paste from the inside of his beak, and used it to fasten the sash against the fold over his chest.

"You can use a bobby pin, you know?" Aignar asked.

"Must be perfect. Gives good luck to the joined," the Dotari said as he tugged at the robes and continued to tut-tut the poor fit.

"There any way this ends without anyone being 'joined'?"

The Dotari froze, his eyes wide.

"If the two pledged die during combat," he said. "Such a tragedy when that happens. My mother took me to see the play *Yush'ura and Cin'mai* when I was a boy. I cried for days. But then someone else would pledge to Cha'ril. She's *so* beautiful. Like that one human—Orozco—on the videos advertising liquor."

The Dotari held a spray bottle up to the side of his face and said, "For the good times. For all the times. Standish Liquors." The Dotari made a phlegmy hiss, which passed for laughter.

"We wouldn't call Orozco 'beautiful,'" Aignar said.

"But he has many offspring? Over twenty." The Dotari stepped back, then retied the wide belt around Aignar's waist.

"With like twenty different women. That's not a good thing. You know what? Just finish what you're doing so I can get this over with before some Dotari decides to make this a shotgun wedding?"

"A what?"

Aignar swatted lazily at the Dotari, who

easily swayed out of the way. The alien held the spray bottle directly over Aignar's head and gave him a quick spritz.

"Good God, what is that? It smells like cat piss and hatred." Aignar buried his nose into the crook of his arm.

"It's to negate her pheromones, help the pledged think clearly," the Dotari said. He sprayed Aignar's cuffs several times.

"Will it wash out?"

The Dotari looked at the bottle and clicked his beak.

The door to the dressing room opened and another Dotari stuck his head into the room and squawked at them.

"You remember what to do?" the dresser asked.

"Pretty sure." Aignar pulled one sleeve back and looked over notes taped to the inside of his metal forearm. "No one's making a video of this, right? I don't want my son to see me dressed up like-like-like I don't know what the hell is going on."

The Dotari at the door motioned for Aignar to hurry.

"'Have a Dotari lance mate,' they said. 'It'll be fun,' they said," Aignar grumbled.

He walked out into a cargo bay with a raised platform and two seats atop of it. Poles with lanterns fixed to the ends—meant to approximate torches, Aignar figured—formed a semicircle around the platform. Dotari crowded beyond the perimeter. There wasn't another human in sight.

Aignar walked up the stairs and paced around the seats five times (not three, as Cha'ril emphasized several times) then brushed off one of the seats with the edge of his sleeves. He sat down in the other, then rapped against the armrest.

Cha'ril came through a door on the other side of the platform. She wore a blue-gray, formless gown and a veil that covered her face but left her quills exposed.

Aignar bent a metal finger and tapped a button on his wrist. The Dotari language came out of the speaker embedded in his throat and the aliens around the room joined in, repeating segments over and over again as the song spread through the crowd like a wave.

Although Cha'ril sat in the chair beside Aignar and he could see her face through the sheer veil, he couldn't gauge her expression.

"Now you must act disinterested," she said.

Man'fred Vo pushed through the crowd on one side of the torch-lined semicircle. He was bare-chested, and chalky-white runes were dabbed against his blue-green skin. He wore leather pants that ended at his knees and he carried a thin staff with a multicolored ribbon tied to one end.

Fal'tir emerged from the other side, similarly dressed and armed, though the runes were markedly different. Aignar leaned forward to gaze at Fal'tir and realized that neither of the Dotari had belly buttons.

"Disinterest," Cha'ril hissed. "You must recognize the winner. If you show any favoritism, their clans may not accept the outcome."

Aignar pulled back and looked at her.

"So we just chat while they—" Aignar winced as the two Dotari opened their beaks and bellowed a war cry, which changed to a song that they sang in tune with each other.

"Yes, best to ignore them," she said.

"They're done up like island savages about to go on a head hunt and I should ignore them. Sure. Easy." Aignar leaned toward her. "Which do you want?"

"Man'fred Vo is the son of a hero from the Ember War," Cha'ril said. "His father flew on the *Breitenfeld* and went on to train most of our fighter pilots. 'Vo' means 'son of,' an old-fashioned naming convention. He is ambitious and skilled. Scored nine kills during the fight with the Kesaht."

"So you want him?"

"Fal'tir is armor. He fought the Naroosha on Togrund."

"Fal'tir...his lance was human. They all redlined after the Naroosha hit them with some sort of ion pulse. He's the one that broke through the

Naroosha spike drones and killed the aliens in their nerve center."

"He is brave. The only Dotari to receive our Mark of Valor and your Armor Cross."

"So…him?"

"You are *ushulra*. You are to choose."

The Dotari abruptly ended their song and began twirling their staffs overhead, then striking the deck and hissing at each other.

"If you have a preference…help me help you, Cha'ril. I don't have to choose at all, do I? I'll delay, find a better solution for you than this business," Aignar said.

She reached over and gently put a hand on his.

"What do you mean? This is wonderful. This is how the Dotari survive," she said. "My parents will be so proud."

"All of you are—" *slaves to your hormones,* he didn't finish. Aignar's shoulders slumped. The Dotari were determined to play this out. He realized that the more he tried to overlay his own sense of what was right and wrong, the more friction he would cause.

"If this is what you want," he said.

"It's getting worse." Cha'ril looked back to the posturing males. Man'fred rammed one end of his staff against the deck and pointed at Fal'tir. Man'fred raised his face to the ceiling and made a choking sound, then he thrust his head at Aignar and spat.

A wad of phlegm hit Aignar in the chest. He froze in place, the feeling of warm goo seeping through his robes.

"Am I supposed to ignore that?" he asked.

Fal'tir raised his head up and made the same gagging noise.

"No!" Aignar held his hands out toward the Dotari armor solider. "No, don't you—" Fal'tir spat and hit Aignar in the shoulder.

"Son of a bitch," he fumed as he scraped the spit off his robes.

Fal'tir spun around and struck at Man'fred with his staff. Man'fred swept his weapon around to block and their staffs met with a crack of wood. The pilot turned the sweep into a full turn and whipped the other end around, striking Fal'tir in the ribs with a smack.

The Dotari armor retreated, one elbow clutched against his side.

"Cha'ril, what? What are they doing?" He looked at his cheat sheet on the inside of his arm and didn't see anything about combat.

"*Fuli ma thrish arra,*" she said. "'Until one yields.'"

Man'fred raised his staff overhead and slammed it down at Fal'tir, who dashed aside and snapped a blow at his opponent. Man'fred tried to parry and took the hit on his hand. Man'fred snarled in pain and pulled the hand back, two fingers obviously broken.

"Or *lax-i-dive log,*" Aignar read from the notes.

"No. This is not a cooking contest."

"*Fore es smog?*"

"That's indecent."

169

"Thrak azog?"

"Yes, with a 'k.'"

Aignar hit his hand against his chair.

"That means I can stop this if there's an obvious winner? Right?"

"Don't. One will yield and then you'll give me to the winner," she said.

Gripping the end of his staff, Man'fred spun it around into a wide arc and swept it at Fal'tir's knees. The armor jammed his staff against the deck and stopped Man'fred's swing. Man'fred moved forward with his momentum and took a jab to the stomach from Fal'tir.

Aignar squirmed in his seat, confused that neither had tried to strike each other with hands or feet, even though both had several openings for a punch or kick that could have ended the fight quickly.

Fal'tir swung the other end of his staff at Man'fred. The pilot yanked his staff back and blocked the strike, then planted his weight on his back foot and spun around, swinging his staff in a backhanded strike.

The blow hit Fal'tir on the side of his head, knocking him off-balance. Man'fred struck the armor soldier on the knee and sent him to the ground. Fal'tir's staff escaped his grasp and rolled toward Aignar and Cha'ril.

"Dentar!" Man'fred pointed his staff at Fal'tir. *Yield!*

The armor looked up at Cha'ril and crawled toward his weapon. Purple blood ran down his face and dripped from his beak.

The crowd broke into a chant. *Dentar! Dentar!*

Man'fred rammed the tip of his staff against Fal'tir's back, jabbing his already hurt ribs. Fal'tir cried out in pain but kept crawling toward his staff. Man'fred raised his staff over his head and let off a long trill. When he turned around, Aignar saw murder in the alien's eyes.

Man'fred faced the crowd, beat a hand against his chest, then whirled around and struck at Fal'tir with an overhand strike that would shatter his skull.

The staff hit Aignar's metal forearm and shattered. Aignar stood between the two fighters, arms bent at his side and ready to fight. The crowd had gone silent.

"Enough!" Aignar's fingers snapped open and he clamped down on the remnants of the staff still in Man'fred's grasp. He yanked the staff away and held the other end with Man'fred's cloth to Cha'ril.

She reached out, hesitated, then undid the knot on the cloth and held it to her chest. She stood and held out a hand to Man'fred. He jumped up on the stage and intertwined the fingers of his unbroken hand with hers.

The crowd began singing, the same tune she had sung in the passageway when Aignar held the two fighters' totems.

The main doors to the cargo bay slid open and Dotari carried in tables and giant bowls of steaming *gar'udda* and metal kegs. Cha'ril and Man'fred hurried away to an open side corridor.

The crowd's mood changed immediately and they swarmed around the food and drink.

"You made a mistake," Fal'tir said. The armor lay on his side, clutching broken ribs and bleeding freely from the cut on his face.

Aignar knelt next to him and looked over the cut.

"Buddy, you lost."

"No. I am armor, same as you. We cannot fail. We do not surrender." Fal'tir crawled toward his staff.

Aignar put his hand on the staff and pinned it in place.

"If you go after them, what'll happen?" Aignar looked the armor in the eye. "He'll kill you. You want to die for pride? We are armor. Save your fury for the enemy, a real enemy."

"You don't know what I'm feeling. Cha'ril is the most beautiful—"

Aignar grabbed the edge of his robe, the part doused with the foul-smelling spray, and rubbed it against Fal'tir's nose. The Dotari gagged before

173

falling on his back. Fal'tir looked up at the ceiling, then propped himself onto an elbow.

"Did that work?" Aignar asked.

Fal'tir wiped the back of his hand against his cut and looked at the blood coating his fingers.

"Can you...can you get me to sick bay?" the Dotari asked.

"Sure thing. Then we'll find a bottle of whatever'll get you drunk and I'll show you how humans handle a little heartache."

****

Gideon, still in his dress uniform, walked into the *Ardennes'* cemetery where a dozen suits of armor stood in coffin-shaped maintenance enclosures along the edge of the room. Gideon took steps up to the catwalk that ran at waist height to the armor.

Stopping at a suit, he typed in an access code at a small workstation and the breastplate on Gideon's armor came loose with a thump.

"I don't blame you, sir," came from the armor to Gideon's right. Aignar's helm turned toward his lance commander.

"Aignar? The ship's personnel tracker has you in your quarters." Gideon unsnapped his collar.

"My tracker's in my wrist." Aignar's hand rotated from side to side. "I left it behind. Couple advantages to being part man and part machine. Then I came down here, figured I deserved some quiet time."

Gideon leaned against the back railing.

"Admiral Lettow sent me a message explaining everything that happened," Gideon said. "The whole thing was...unexpected."

"At least it's over," Aignar said. "At least I hope it's over. Fal'tir seemed to chill out after the medics patched him up. I doubt any Dotty will come demanding satisfaction now that Cha'ril and Man'fred are joined. Did the admiral mention I got spit on? Was that in the memo?"

"He left that out."

"Part of the theme to being an *ushulra*, sir.

Lots they don't tell you. Good news is that the smell goes away after you burn the clothes and take a couple showers. Why the Dotties can't just get drunk and do the walk of shame the next morning…"

"But it's over now that Cha'ril is married." Gideon rubbed a hand against his cheek.

"Not married married, but joined married. They kept correcting me on that. The two lovebirds are on a special pass. We won't see them for another twenty-four hours. Which is fine by me."

"Honestly, what you had to deal with up here was better than what happened on New Bastion," Gideon said. "The Ibarras got greedy, made proccies that the galaxy can't accept. There will be a war…"

"That bothers you, sir? You don't have any love lost for the Ibarras."

"I don't. I'll tear down their cities brick by brick and smash their ships with my bare hands. But I'd rather this fight be one Earth wants, not one that we're forced into. Others—not me—will pull their punches, and that will get the entire galaxy against Earth."

"What about the Kesaht?" Aignar asked.

"They're more afraid of procedurals than the Kesaht," Gideon said. "I can't say I blame them. They all know the Ibarras, what they're capable of. As far as they can tell, the Kesaht may be nothing but a bunch of raiders."

"So now what?"

Gideon shrugged off his jacket and folded it neatly.

"We've got the location of an Ibarra world," he said. "We take that back to Earth and then Phoenix decides the next move. Pull up your VR sims and load a firing range. Ibarra targets."

CHAPTER 13

A sparkling white disk formed in the center of a Crucible gate and a single Vishrakath ship emerged through the wormhole. This ship was small; all that remained of the asteroid it had been built into was a crust of rock. It zoomed out of the jump gate and hooked around a lime-green moon, the atmosphere swirling with methane.

Kesaht claw ships tracked the Vishrakath ship, motes of glowing light at the apex of the ships' irregularly sized digits.

The craft sped past the Kesaht defenses, skirting a battleship and accompanying fleet. It came around the moon and shot toward a world made up of brown seas and deserts. Patches of brightness on the dark side marked domed cities. A patchy belt of light stretched around the equator, tracing to a massive construction project in orbit over the day side that would ring the planet once it was complete.

It angled away from the planet toward a star fort made up of the reddish-brown plates the Kesaht preferred for their void craft. Crescent-shaped fighters spilled out of the fort and swarmed the asteroid ship. The Vishrakath continued, barreling toward an open hangar as fighters maneuvered out of the way.

The ship came to rest in the dock as the Kesaht fighters roiled like a disturbed hive.

****

Three Vishrakath rode a lift through the Kesaht star fort. Two held stubby gauss rifles, their white skin cracked and covered with old battle scars. The third, its skin an aquamarine blue,

179

scratched at the deck with its four legs.

The lift slowed to a stop in front of metal doors. Hydraulics hissed and the doors opened. A Toth warrior, down on all six limbs, bared shark-like teeth at the Vishrakath and snorted at the two bodyguards.

Another warrior holding a crystalline pike leveled the weapon at one of the bodyguard's rifles and let out a dull battle ululation.

The head of the delegation sidestepped the hissing Toth. There, at the far end of the bay next to a large window, was a Toth overlord. Bale's nervous system twitched inside the glass tank mounted atop a mechanical body with four limbs. The metal was embossed in gold, images of Kesaht history carved into the limbs and the bulging metal beneath the tank filled with bubbling water.

"Enough posturing, Bale," said the head Vishrakath. "It grows tiresome."

"Let them have their fun, Tuchilin," Bale said. "The Kesaht are of no threat to me. You represent a bit of sport."

"We are not here for sport." Tuchilin walked forward, almost stepping on one of the warrior's hands. "We are here for a progress report."

"Come and see." Bale's forelimb tapped the glass in front of him. Tuchilin kept a wide berth as he went around the Toth.

Below, thousands of Rakka were in a hangar, all in lines to surgery stations where thin-limbed Ixion supervised as the bestial Rakka had cybernetics implanted into their skulls.

"The Rakka are primitive," Bale said, "a tribal species that can barely utilize fire, though their petroglyphs are rather ornate. Their cognitive abilities are perfect for adjustment into a mind-set far more useful."

"Cannon fodder is hardly useful," Tuchilin said. "Do the Ixion and Sanheel think so highly of themselves that they choose not to fight?"

"The duo that considers themselves true Kesaht are quite willing to do what is necessary to win. They merely recognize that if there will be causalities, the Rakka should bear them. The Ixio and Sanheel tried for centuries to bring the Rakka up to their level of 'perfection.' I succeeded where they failed."

"Your raids are getting out of hand," Tuchilin said. "You agreed to remain hidden until such time as the Kesaht were ready to destroy Earth and the Ibarras."

"While I am the Kesaht's savior, I still require sustenance," Bale said. "Feeding on my adoring subjects would be…problematic. It took Doctor Mentiq quite a while to train his gardens to appreciate the event."

"Eat your own kind." Tuchilin pointed at one of the Toth guards. "Eventually, you will provoke a response and Wexil won't be able to stop it."

"You are shortsighted. The Kesaht think it is their mission to bring their blessed unity to all the galaxy. We can hardly work toward that goal if we don't have subjects to experiment on."

"Our bargain was to destroy the humans, not engage in some quasi-religious nonsense. Stop your raids. That's an order," Tuchilin said.

"Order?" Bale spun in place, bringing the front of his tank to square off with the smaller Vishrakath. "You think you can order me to do anything? The Kesaht are my playthings, not yours. I will be the one that finally destroys the humans. I will burn Earth to cinders and force the survivors to watch, just as I saw my home world annihilated by them. Then I will savor their suffering as I feed on them and make the rest watch as I do it."

"You will have your revenge, Bale. Wexil and the rest of the Vishrakath want you to have it. But don't force us to choose between the situation we've created for you and New Bastion. You're not that important."

Bale's claws dug into the deck.

"Your armada's growing." Tuchilin moved closer to the glass, ignoring the angry Toth overlord. "Are you prepared to assault Earth? With the system's macro cannons, a head-on assault would be futile. Earth must be destroyed from within. That is why Wexil has Earth and the Ibarras at each other's throats. Let the enemy weaken itself, then strike. Simple."

"And how has Wexil managed this?" Bale asked. "The Ibarras are hidden."

"We found one of their worlds," Tuchilin said. "Not Navarre, as we hoped, but a decent-sized colony. Earth has no choice but to attack. Open warfare will follow and the Ibarras will be flushed out. If our projections on the Ibarras' strength is correct, they should deal significant damage to Earth before being destroyed."

"You would have Earth—not me—kill the Ibarras?"

"The end result is the same." Tuchilin clacked his claws in annoyance.

"The Ibarras were there. With that...*thing* they used to destroy my world. They are more responsible for the Toth being driven to the edge of extinction than anyone else, and you would deny me this?"

"Your ego is not our concern, only the forces you command. We estimate it will take less than two years to wipe out the Ibarras. By then, your armada will be of sufficient size to make taking Earth relatively easy. Then the Kesaht will be welcomed onto the galactic stage as heroes. Your involvement needs to remain hidden, for obvious reasons. I cannot say that anyone grieves the Toth's absence."

"I grieve, you fleshy little maggot," Bale said.

"Cease your raids and wait for our signal to attack Earth," the Vishrakath said. "There. My work here is done." He turned and marched back to the door, but a pair of Toth warriors blocked his path.

"One last thing before you go," Bale said. "Earth is about to attack an Ibarra colony?"

"That's right. We traced it through—" Tuchilin stopped. The skin around his eyes flushed purple. "It does not matter. We'll be on our way. Now."

Bale's neural pathways twitched.

A Toth guard lunged forward and chomped on the head of an armed Vishrakath, swinging the body from side to side and sending the rifle flying. The other ant-like alien barely raised its rifle before a Toth polearm sliced through its arms. The Toth leapt on the Vishrakath and began tearing at its flesh.

Tuchilin backed away, watching as the Toth devoured his bodyguards.

Bale's forelimbs snapped out, grabbed him by the shoulders, and twisted him around. The overlord lifted Tuchilin up, letting him see the brain and neural pathways wriggling inside the tank.

"I don't know where it is!" Tuchilin shouted. "Wexil didn't tell me!"

"We'll just have to find out." A spike-tipped arm rose up from the housing under Bale's tank. The spike popped open and thin tendrils danced across Tuchilin's skull.

"No! If you do this, the Vishrakath will—" He screamed as Bale broke his arms with a pinch from his claws.

"I don't need you!" Bale shouted. "The humans will suffer and die at my hand. Mine!"

The feeder wires stabbed into Tuchilin's skull and he began convulsing. He kicked and moaned for a moment, then Bale threw the body to his warriors.

"So...that's where I'll find the Ibarras," Bale said. He walked back to the window, his neural system alive with pleasure, his mind racing with possibilities.

CHAPTER 14

Roland flapped his arms across his chest, then pulled them open wide to warm up his shoulders as he entered the dojo. He caught himself mid-exercise and frowned. Nicodemus and the racks were missing.

A woman knelt in the middle of the room, her legs hidden beneath the folds of a wide-legged martial-arts uniform. A white canvas gi top clung to her shoulders and folded across her torso. Her head was bowed, hands in a lotus position over her naval.

Beside each knee was a Templar long sword lying parallel to her body.

She looked up at him. An ugly patch of scar

tissue made up the flesh around her right eye and stretched to her temple and hairline, where a shock of pale skin stood out from the light-brown hair pulled into a bun. Her right eye was pale, but still focused on him.

Without the scars, she looked to be in her late twenties, with delicate features. Even with the injury, Roland couldn't deny that she was beautiful.

She motioned to the mat just in front of her. Roland shrugged and sat down, mimicking her position but keeping his hands on his knees. His eyes flitted over the two swords and realized that they were sharp, not training mock-ups like he and Nicodemus had used the last time he was there.

She looked him over. Lenses in the pale eye twisted to focus on him. A cybernetic replacement.

"Nicodemus is right," she said, her voice soft and kind and faintly Irish. "You do remind me of him."

"And who would that be?" Roland raised an eyebrow. "And who would you be?"

"I am armor." She lowered and twisted her

head enough for him to glimpse the plugs at the base of her skull.

"You're…Morrigan, aren't you? I had your sword. That's where you were hurt, wasn't it? You lost your sword there and the legionnaires gave it to me."

"It was mine to give, not theirs," she said. "I saw iron in you during the fight with the Kesaht. I did not think you were so young. You fight with the fury of an older soul. Gideon has trained you well."

"You and Nicodemus knew him?"

"He never spoke of us? Of his old lance?"

"Never. Gideon focused on our mission, our training. It never occurred to me that there was more to know…"

Morrigan brushed a strand of pale hair away from her face.

"We knew he would take the three of us leaving badly. I wanted him to come with us, but he would never have accepted. I remember the look on his face during that last vid call. That man has no capacity for forgiveness, which serves him well in the armor."

"You said three of you. Who's the last?"

Morrigan's lips twitched. The skin around her milky eye crinkled.

"Does it bother you?" She brushed her fingertips across her scars.

"No, not at all." Roland shifted in his seat. "I know someone that can't get vat replacements. He's...stronger for it."

"The Ibarra Nation has the medical know-how to replace damaged tissue. I could have this taken away," she said. "But why would I? I earned my scars. To deny them is to deny myself."

"Like Gideon," Roland said as he traced his lance leader's scars down his own face.

"You are of Mars. You've been to Olympus...is Saint Kallen's tomb still there?" she asked.

"Of course." He frowned. "Why would you think otherwise? Because Templar defected with the Ibarras? That was before I ever got my plugs. Saint Kallen fought and died on Mars. She's buried there with the memento mori of all those who died on the Xaros world. Why would that ever change? Just because some of you—"

Morrigan grabbed his hand.

"You've seen her?" Her one green eye looked at him with hope.

"Once. Tongea took me to the tomb." Roland looked down at her hand on top of his and almost pulled away. "It was...was...you've been?"

She smiled and nodded slowly.

"I've never been religious," Roland said, "but Saint Kallen's statue made me feel something...different. I can't explain it. Then a drop of water from the ceiling ran down the statue's face and—"

Morrigan pulled her hand back and covered her mouth.

"What?" he asked.

"If the Saint wept for you...you know what that means." She frowned, her remaining eye full of emotion.

"That I'll die in my armor? That's just a

story."

"The last time we saw her," Morrigan said, brushing her hand across her eye, "she wept for him...and now he's with her." Morrigan snatched up a sword and rolled backwards. Momentum carried her to her feet and she stopped in a fighting stance, weapon level with her shoulder and pointed at Roland.

"Nicodemus says you fight ungrounded. That your footwork is atrocious. Get up. I'll not let one who'll bear the cross embarrass it by being sloppy. You're not leaving this dojo until you meet my standards."

CHAPTER 15

Admiral Lettow watched the force field over the entrance to his small shuttle bay. The Crucible and Ceres hung just beyond the edge, a thin crescent of Earth in the distance. He knew what was coming, knew—intellectually—that it wasn't a threat, but his heart was racing and his hands kept brushing past his hip where his sidearm should be.

A shadow flitted past the open bay. Lettow felt sweat drip down his face as he bent slightly at the knees.

A gray-black Xaros drone rose up and passed through the force field. The eight stalks bent forward and morphed together by twos. The oval-shaped body shrank and reformed into a human body, fractals swirling over the Keeper's shell as she stood up. A simple jumpsuit and boots formed over her shell as short blond hair framed a face riven with wrinkles.

"Hello, Admiral," Keeper said. "Still not used to this, I see."

"I get my orders from High Command through sealed and encrypted channels. That's what I'm used to," Lettow said.

The Keeper walked up to him, her bearing and pace of a much younger woman than her elderly face suggested. She held up a palm and a data chip emerged from it.

"I've got that," she said. "The *Ardennes* has been on commo blackout since New Bastion. Any reason to believe there's been a breach?"

"We've been back for an hour," Lettow said. "I've got the ship on a gunnery drill. If anyone's screwing around, my chiefs will notice. No breach."

"Good. Since your encounter on Oricon, we've been screening out anyone that may have been…tainted by the Ibarras. Your fleet was the first place to be cleared. You shouldn't have any other difficulties for what comes next."

"'Difficulties'? You mean when Ibarra activated sleeper agents and my artillery ships mutinied and opened fire on the Kesaht on Oricon? That kind of 'difficulty'?"

"After a thorough investigation, intelligence determined that the Ibarras altered up to fifty thousand procedurals while they were still in the tanks. They've been removed from key positions across the system. Your 14th fleet and the 30th are clean," Keeper said.

"Fifty thousand? Someone's going to raise questions. Some spring butt in an important career position gets reassigned to passing out basketballs…it'll come out."

"The president and I know that, but what should we do? Address the entire Terran Union and tell everyone that some of their fellow citizens are unwitting sleeper agents that might turn on them at any moment? I'm not saying we're French and have a Huguenot situation on our hands, but it won't be that far off."

"A what situation?"

"Sorry, I don't sleep and have been reading a lot of history looking for a solution to our situation," she said. "You and the 30th will lead the assault on the Ibarra colony. As Keeper, I've examined the activity through that Crucible gate—minimal. Only a few dozen ships have ever been in and out of there in months."

"You're certain my ships won't jump in on top of an Ibarra armada? We still don't know how they escaped us on Oricon," he said, taking the data chip from her.

"Your fleets will jump to DE-882, unoccupied space in the neutral zone. From there, you'll wait until we send a probe through the Crucible in the Ibarra system. It'll have a few seconds to gather data and get a message back to me. They'll button up the Crucible after that, but I'll know if you've got enough ships to present overwhelming force."

"What do you want done to the colony?"

The Keeper crossed her arms over her chest. "What do you think?"

"We show up with enough guns and Marines that they have no chance to beat us in a fight. Get them to surrender without a shot being fired or anyone killed. You're not sending me there to occupy the system, are you?"

"No. You're to detain every illegal settler and bring them back to Earth for internment on Mars. Destroy all critical infrastructure."

Lettow's jaw worked from side to side.

"This is an eviction followed by prison. You think they'll just run up the white flag and come along willingly? We're talking about possible civilian casualties, not a straight military engagement."

"You're to use all force you consider necessary," Keeper said. "There's no perfect solution, and yes, you're being rushed into this before the Ibarras' spies can get this news back and make our job even harder. Earth needs to show

Bastion that we're not in league with the Ibarras, that we're committed to the Hale Treaty."

"How committed are we, Keeper? I read Gideon's report. I know about the Omega Provision. Exactly how far does President Garret need to go to keep Bastion happy?"

Keeper's surface rippled.

"The Provision hasn't been ratified by the Senate. The procedurals on that planet are safe."

"For now." Lettow's face darkened. "How do I convince them to give up without a shot if they think they're boarding trains to a death camp? Tell me that! How did we ever agree to do this to our own kind?"

"Calm down, Admiral. I...you're not the only one that sees things that way. But Earth has her back against the wall. We don't know how strong or aggressive the Kesaht really are. The Vishrakath are on the verge of turning the rest of the galaxy against us and the Ibarras are not our friends. We need to buy time. Negotiate our way out of the Omega Provision, maybe have it become effective at some date in the future—a date *after* the Ibarras have been brought under control."

"You promise me that any civilians I capture will be safe," Lettow said. "Military defectors will get their justice through court martial."

"You're putting conditions on your orders?"

Lettow grabbed the admiral's stars sewn onto his collar.

"As an officer in the Terran Union, I swore to uphold the Constitution and the rights secured by that document. I will not deliver human beings to a summary execution nor will I command my ships to do the same," Lettow said.

"You have my word," Keeper said.

"And the president's?"

"Not mine to give. Listen to me, Admiral. If we drag our heels on this operation, then the Vishrakath and every other species that's terrified of the proccies will have all the ammunition they need to demand a full implementation of the Omega Provision. The Ibarras aren't just on that one small colony. There are many more lives at stake."

Lettow dropped his hand to his side.

"We had it," Lettow said. "A détente with Bastion. A whole galaxy to settle...then the Ibarras decided they knew better than everyone else and wrecked what could have been centuries of peace and prosperity. This is their fault. Any blood we have to spill is on their hands."

"No one ever said this would be easy...or fair," Keeper said. "You'll make your jump in two hours. Additional personnel transports and limpets to disable the Crucible are being delivered to your fleet."

"Hours. You're giving me hours to put this operation together."

"The Omega Provision is not final and is not common knowledge. Keep it that way. You're one of our best, Admiral. Don't let us down." Keeper backed away, then morphed into her drone shape and flew out of the hangar.

CHAPTER 16

A blade flashed through the air. Roland swung his own sword around and deflected the strike before it could hit his shoulder. He shoved Nicodemus' weapon away and lowered his shoulder. Roland ducked his head and lunged toward his opponent, intending to knock the larger man off-balance. Roland anticipated the impact…but felt nothing as he advanced.

He did feel his lead foot trip over Nicodemus' shin and then he pitched forward. He lowered his shoulder and turned his fall into a forward roll. He kept his head ducked and thrust his sword behind him as air whooshed over the back of his neck and his sword jammed against something solid.

"Touch!" Morrigan shouted.

Roland spun around and brought his sword up to high guard. Nicodemus backed away, a red line on his chest padding.

"Point for the left," Morrigan added from where she sat along the edge of the dueling square.

"Sorry, what did you say?" Roland asked, his blade still en garde.

"It was luck." Nicodemus removed his helmet and wiped sweat from his brow.

"You always press the attack after knocking him off-balance," Morrigan said. "He anticipated and used your aggression against you. Isn't that right, Roland?"

"It was more instinct and opportunity…I didn't plan on it," he said.

"Luck!" Nicodemus struck a hand against his padding and the red mark faded away.

"You're just mad he finally got a solid hit on

you," Morrigan said. "Which is something I struggle with, but after so long, I thought Roland would have scored a point before now...even by accident."

Nicodemus grumbled, brought his sword hilt up to the front of his face, and swiped downward in salute.

Roland relaxed and returned the courtesy. The pain of the many bruises and raw welts beneath his padding faded away as a warm feeling spread through his chest.

Morrigan rose to her feet.

"I'm due back at the Keep," she said. "The supplicants have the Feast of Saint Kallen and I'm to bless the wine."

Nicodemus gave her a nod and tucked his helmet beneath his arm.

"I forgot about that." Roland took his helmet off, the chill air of the dojo a relief from the damp protective gear.

"You forgot about one of our holidays?" Nicodemus asked.

"Forgot what day it is," Roland said. "I was in my womb for who knows how long before I was dumped in that cell. Then all I've had since then to tell the time are meals and these training sessions. Sleep. Exercise. Study the primer. I didn't think the calendar had flipped to April yet."

"To get you out of the cell took some doing," Nicodemus said. "If you weren't a supplicant, we would have never let you out."

"How long will I be here?" Roland tossed his helmet to one side. "What does Ibarra gain by keeping me around? She wanted information from me about the Kesaht. An exchange of information that I agreed to. When will I go back with what you know? That was the deal."

"When she decides to let you go," Nicodemus said.

Roland raised his sword to throw it but stopped himself.

"You should not spend the feast by yourself," Nicodemus said. "You can join me, if you choose."

Roland did a double take at the older man.

"Eat something other than processed nutrient paste outside my cell? Let me think…yes." Roland tapped his sword against the side of his leg. The Feast of Saint Kallen on Mars was a significant event. Every Templar in Mount Olympus attended. The only time Roland had gone, a bison had been harvested from the Dakota plains and served.

More important than the chance to eat real food, though, was the chance that Roland might glimpse the entire strength of the Ibarran armor force.

"I'll need your word that you will act as a proper guest," Nicodemus said. "Abuse this courtesy and every privilege we give you will vanish."

Roland bowed slightly.

"I will be honored."

****

Roland tugged at the collar of his fresh

utility coveralls as he followed a step behind Nicodemus, who led him down a narrow hallway.

That Roland could actually see where he was going, move his limbs without the weight of his restraints, almost made him skip with joy.

"How far is the Keep?" Roland asked as his stomach rumbled.

Nicodemus gave him a quick glance, then waved his palm over a sensor on a recessed door. The door slid open and a gust of cold, wet air passed into the hallway. Roland followed him into a small hangar, where an air car covered in a sheen of moisture waited. The gull-winged doors rose as the two men approached.

Roland cut to one side and looked to the front as he ducked inside. No driver, no auxiliary controls. He'd seen automated cars like this in Phoenix but had never been able to afford a ride in one. There was no chance of gaining control of the car if he had no way to fly it.

He sat on a seat that ran the length of the passenger compartment, catty-corner from

Nicodemus. The doors closed and locked with a *thunk* of metal pistons, not a far cry from the vault door to his cell block.

The windows went opaque and Roland hid his disappointment. So much for getting the lay of the land.

"Air-car tech...fancy," Roland said.

"Necessary." The other man tapped on a control screen built into his door and the hum of anti-grav repulsors in the wheel wells thrummed through the car. Roland felt the car lift off, then accelerate forward. The patter of rain beat against the windows.

Roland started an internal count.

"What does Earth tell you about us?" Nicodemus asked. "That we're traitors? Living like pirates on some forgotten world? Deviants creating some twisted society that worships the Ibarras?"

"Honestly? I didn't even know the Ibarras had gone rogue until after I found gun-camera footage on the *Cairo*," Roland said. "Before that, word was the Ibarras were off on some kind of science mission. Then her fleet showed up on Oricon and the details came out. The brass pinned Marc Ibarra and the *Hiawatha* as why he ran off. They never told us about Stacey's…condition. Or about you and the other armor. I'm sure more's come out since I became your guest." Roland looked at the dark window as beads of moisture ran along the side, pushed by the air car's flight.

"Not outright lies," Nicodemus said. "Not yet. Let me show you what we're building out here." He touched his control panel and the windows cleared.

Roland jumped back as the air car swept past a building. The sky was the color of red wine, so deep that it was almost purple, like a storm cloud pregnant with rain. Drops of water patted against the windshield. Roland looked up and saw lines of air cars stacked atop each other, their bodies lost to the thick fog, but their running lights shining through the darkness.

Their car snapped past the building, and a long line of skyscrapers stretched down a wide boulevard. The buildings' tops and bases were lost in the clouds, so Roland couldn't tell how many blocks extended down the street in the shifting curtains of rain. Out the window on Nicodemus' side of the car, the city continued.

"This is…how many people live here?" Roland tried to do a quick calculation, remembering how many residents the larger towers in Phoenix could hold. Without seeing the full extent of the city, it was entirely possible that tens of millions made their home here. If the Ibarras had a megalopolis to rival the prewar sprawl from San Diego to San Francisco or the old Beijing expanse…

"*Who* lives here is more important," Nicodemus said.

The car turned sharply into a building and floated into a garage. It came to a stop in a cradle and jets of air blew water off the exterior as the garage carried it to a curved walkway with several elevator doors.

The doors opened with a pleasant ding.

Nicodemus stepped out and motioned for Roland to follow. The light above an elevator lit up. "Hurry," Nicodemus said as he stretched out his pace and walked to the doors. "This whole garage is closed off while you're in the open. People have schedules."

"What does Ibarra tell everyone about Earth? That the place has gone to hell and we've been burning worlds to force you all out of hiding?" Roland asked as he jogged up to Nicodemus.

"Maybe I should have kept the muzzle on you." Nicodemus walked into the elevator, which opened without him having to adjust his stride. The control panel read CP, then blinked off as it began moving.

Can't even tell how many floors this place has, Roland thought.

"The people you're about to meet," Nicodemus smoothed his hair out, "they are…unwitting. You understand?"

"Not exactly." Roland frowned.

"You are my guest. Act as such."

Nicodemus faced the door, went to one knee, and opened his arms.

The doors opened and a voice squealed, "Daddy!"

A boy almost flew into the elevator and hugged Nicodemus. His hair was a shade lighter, but he had the same dark eyes and chin as his father.

"Ugh, Jonathan, you're getting so big." Nicodemus stood up, and the boy clung to his father's shoulders. "I'll need my armor to carry you soon."

"Silly," the boy said before he dropped down and ran off. "Mom! Mom! Dad brought a friend!"

Roland gave Nicodemus a sideways glance. The day had been full of surprises, but not to the point where he could ever consider the Ibarran armor a friend.

"Unwitting," Nicodemus repeated, leading Roland into the apartment. The doorway led into a living room with a beat-up couch and a floor littered with toys. The smell of cooking food came over a

low wall separating the living room from a kitchen.
He saw the silhouette of a woman in the steam as
the bang of pots and pans echoed through the
apartment.

"No! Jonathan, I told you not to touch that,"
the woman said. A baby started squalling down the
hall from a room next to the kitchen.

"I'm needed." Nicodemus pointed down a
short hallway to a dining room. "If you don't
mind."

"No problem." Roland backed down the
hallway and kicked a wooden truck with his heel.
He turned around to pick the toy up from where it
had stopped against a wall, and found it next to a
recessed chamber in the wall covered in glass.
Inside was a humanoid robot standing on a charging
mat. The robot had a matronly build to it, a standard
Rosie-22 model from Ibarra Robotics used across
Earth for menial tasks.

Given the detritus of toys and pajamas in the
hallways and a half-complete bit of crayon art on a
wall, Roland wondered if the robot was broken.

He carried the truck into the dining room, where there was a table with a fall print cloth, six chairs, and a small shrine to Saint Kallen in a corner. A plaque with a picture of four armor soldiers in their dress uniforms caught his eye. Three men and a woman stood beside a small pennant with the Iron Dragoons lance patch sewn onto it. He wasn't surprised to see a younger-looking Morrigan and Nicodemus in the photo, but he did a double take when he recognized Gideon. The third man looked to be just out of his teens and was the only one smiling in the photo.

A brass plate bore the inscription: Iron Dragoons 1/17/12 G. Nicodemus, B. Bassani, H. Gideon. B. Morrigan. TOUJOURS PRET! ALWAYS READY!

They were in the same lance together, Roland thought. *Nicodemus and Morrigan were Dragoon like me...once.*

On the walls were two paintings in rosewood frames, one of George Washington kneeling in prayer next to a horse in a snowy wood, the other—and the painting Roland chose to study further—was of the Battle of Firebase X-Ray. Armor faced off against the Ruhaald scorpion tanks and infantry besieging the outpost, a rail cannon battery near Phoenix. The focal point was of a single suit of armor leaping through the air toward one of the massive tanks, a spear held high and ready to strike. Phantom J-hooked wings of eagle feathers rose from the spear wielder's back, meant to be there in spirit.

Roland frowned, remembering his visit to Saint Kallen's tomb where the memento mori of the armor lost in the final battle with the Xaros were interred. The same wings from the painting were in three of the empty sepulchers.

"And the winged hussars arrived," Jonathan said from behind Roland. "They turned the tide at the battle and that's why Carius chose them for marty-dumb. Their names were Vladislav, Ferenz, and Adamczyk. We have to learn that at training."

"Training? Already?" Roland asked. "How old are you?"

"I'm five, but I score higher than most ten-year-olds in the VR. Can I have my truck back? Mommy said I can't eat until I clean up my mess like I was supposed to." The boy held out a hand and Roland handed him the toy. Jonathan hurried back into the hallway, the pounding of his feet stopping every few seconds as he picked something else off the floor.

Nicodemus carried in plates and silverware. Roland grabbed half and started setting his end of the table.

"My apologies," Nicodemus said. "I didn't have the chance to send a message ahead; otherwise, the bot would have had everything spic-and-span before we arrived."

"My orphanage was never clean," Roland said. "We never had a bot either. Ms. Gottfried said they were too expensive."

"We don't use ours when I'm off deployment cycle," Nicodemus said. "When I'm home, I'm home. But every family with children is issued a Rosie. Helps the parents focus on the children."

"Hello." A very pregnant woman came around the corner, carrying a baby girl on her hip that looked to be a year old. "I'm Suzzana and Alec here," she put a hand on her husband's shoulder, "didn't tell me we were having guests tonight. Forgive the mess."

"Mess? What mess?" Roland looked around, feigning confusion.

"Aren't you sweet?" Her grip on Nicodemus' shoulder turned into a pat. "Honey, get Gisele's high chair, won't you?"

Nicodemus set a fork and knife to one side of a plate and left the dining room.

Suzzana looked at the bare right shoulder of Roland's utilities—where Nicodemus bore his Templar Cross—and frowned.

"I thought everyone from the regiment would be at the feast and the vigil, unless they had family, of course," she said.

"He's still a bean head." Nicodemus brought a plastic chair and tray into the room and locked it onto one of the wooden seats. "Not ready to give the vows or bare witness just yet."

"Oh, that explains it," she said. A beeping came from the kitchen. "I sure hope that means it's done and not that it's burning." She handed the little girl off and hurried back to the kitchen, one hand on the small of her back as she went.

Roland's face flushed. He suddenly felt like an intruder, as he was not of the Ibarra Nation or a true friend to his host.

Nicodemus set the little girl into her high chair and turned around to find his son holding a small sack. He emptied the sack onto the girl's tray and she squealed as wooden blocks tumbled out.

"If you think this is complex, you should see bedtime," Nicodemus said.

"I'm not sure I should be here," Roland said.

"I invited you, didn't I? The Feast of Saint Kallen is a time for togetherness, family. The Templar traditions are new, but if we don't keep to them, they will never endure. You will join the Order someday," he said.

"Daddy, is this Bassani?" Jonathan asked.
Nicodemus' face fell. "No, son, this is
Roland Shaw. He is armor, like Bassani was."
Suzzana called for the boy and he ran off.
Roland wanted to ask about Bassani, but
Nicodemus had said "was." Past tense. Broaching
the subject at the dinner table felt wrong.

"How did you and her meet?" Roland asked.

"I went to the proccie tubes and typed in
what I wanted. Nine days later and bam."

Nicodemus watched as Roland's jaw dropped.

"Really? You think that's how it works here? I saw
her on the flight deck of the *Warsaw* when we first
arrived in system. She was one of the few
quartermasters that came with us. I never thought a
woman in a power loader would catch my eye, but
she and I pulled a twenty-hour shift to get the first
wave of builders and utility crates dirtside. It was
easier for me while in armor; she showed her iron.
Once things calmed down and I could get out of the
suit, I went and found her. Whirlwind courtship
after that."

"Are all the towers like this? Families?" Roland asked.

Jonathan carried over a tin of steaming bread and held it high for Nicodemus as his father set it onto a small beaded mat on the table. The smell of corn and butter made Roland's mouth water. The boy ran back to the kitchen, panting.

"Some," Nicodemus said. "That surprise you—that we have the procedural technology, but we still have families? That in the Ibarra Nation, men and women fight and work and that mothers focus on raising children—which is more work than you can imagine—when the tubes could create any kind of civilization we desired?"

"This is…shockingly normal," Roland said as Jonathan brought over a dish of multicolored cooked grain and hurried back to the kitchen. The little girl lunged for the new dish, but Nicodemus stopped her before she could stick a hand into the hot food.

"Human culture developed to be this." Nicodemus set a few blocks atop each other and the girl knocked them over with a giggle. "The Ibarras saw no need to try and improve on a system that works. We have children not because we need true born to be armor pilots—and I've seen enough battles that I *don't* want Jonathan to follow my footsteps, but it's what he wants—but because children are the reason for everything."

"It's hard for me to relate." Roland scratched the side of his face. "My parents died in the war. The state raised me. I don't think any of the armor on Ma—you know—are married. That normal? Like, Morrigan? She seeing anyone?"

"She was engaged," Nicodemus said. "I am something of an outlier. I'm lucky I found a strong woman that can deal with the deployments and who was willing to even look twice at me."

"You're not that hard to look at," Suzzana said as she slapped Nicodemus on the rear end and set a tray of scalloped potatoes on the table. She sat down and rubbed her pregnant belly. "And I'm spent. Get the roast, honey?"

"Are you in Daddy's lance?" Jonathan

asked.

"No, I'm still in training," Roland said.

"Do you want to be in his lance? With Aunt Morry?"

"I don't think your father needs any more help. He's one of the best soldiers I've ever seen." Roland smiled nervously. The statement was true enough, but adding that Nicodemus had dismantled Roland in suited combat could remain unstated.

"Here we go." Nicodemus brought in a tray of lamb chops. "Paidakia just like Yaya used to make."

"The tower's food combiner is on the fritz again," Suzzana said. "I had to drop your name to get all this in time. Otherwise, it would have been leftovers."

"I'll speak to the super." Nicodemus helped Jonathan into his seat and motioned for Roland to sit next to the head of the table.

"And mention the VR chambers are locked to old Las Vegas Strip. I can't take the kids for a walk down that street." Suzzana looked at Roland.

"Sorry, these buildings were built for speed, not quality. I don't complain this much normally."

"I can be intimidating if I need to be," Nicodemus said.

Roland chuckled and sat down.

"Will the guest say grace?" Jonathan asked.

"I…don't think it's my place," Roland said.

"It's my duty to say it, son," Nicodemus said. He folded his hands against the table and his family followed suit. Roland bowed his head.

"Heavenly Father…"

CHAPTER 17

The *Ardennes* burst through the Crucible gate and her fleet followed.

"Limpets away," Commander Paxton announced from her spot opposite Lettow around the tactical holo. The 14th's ships filled the holo tank as they emerged through the wormhole, many of which were new, replacements for ships lost during the battle with the Kesaht over Oricon. A moon materialized, the edge growing as the ship's scanners reached out.

"Dispatch Strike Marine teams to the command nodes. Lethal force authorized if lethal force encountered," Lettow said.

"Assault ships in the void…six of eight limpets in place. Lock down on track. All ships reporting in, Admiral Ericson and the *Normandy* coming through now," Paxton said. She'd proven capable enough since Strickland was reassigned. Losing his old operations officer was a blow, but he couldn't remain in a key position, not when he was at risk of being compromised by the Ibarras with a single message.

The moon came into focus, and Lettow frowned at the unusual surface dotted by huge craters, all of identical diameter and depth spaced neatly from each other. Moving that amount of mass was an engineering feat humanity had yet to master.

"The Pathfinders call them Z-holes," Paxton said. "Xaros scooped out what they needed to make the Crucible gates. You only see them on this end of the galaxy. Farther in, they started mining out the interior and leaving the surface pristine. No one's sure why."

"Thank you for the history lesson, XO. How

about you tell me if you found the Ibarras?" Lettow deadpanned.

"Yes, sir. Probes are away."

A few seconds later, the colony world appeared in the holo on the opposite side of the moon.

A gold-bordered comm request appeared in the holo tank, a direct line from the *Normandy*.

Lettow tapped the icon and a woman with blond hair run through with a few white strands replaced the icon.

"*Ardennes*, not to speak too soon, but our arrival is on track. The moon screened us from the target world. Should help with the shock-and-awe factor," Admiral Ericson said.

Did High Command send Admiral Valdar's old XO along to send a message…or to relieve me if I screwed up again? Lettow thought. *What I wouldn't give to have the old man around for some advice.*

"30th is through," she said. "We're set for lockdown. *Primo Victoria.*" She signed off with the

Normandy's motto.

"XO, engage limpets," Lettow said. "No need to have anyone else joining this fight."

"Aye aye," Paxton said.

In the holo tank, red pulses appeared in the Crucible. The graviton generators would create fields, making any travel through the gate impossible.

"Strike Marine Team Gold reports that control node alpha is unmanned," Paxton said. "Still waiting for updates from the rest."

"Release the *San Juan*'s destroyer squadron from formation and have them secure the Crucible," Lettow said. "We'll need IR buoys around the moon to keep comms open once we cross the horizon."

"Buoys being loaded into launch tubes now," Paxton said. "Bridge crew anticipated the need and got the techs working soon as we came through."

"A problem foreseen is a problem half-solved. Pass on my compliments," Lettow said.

The 14th and 30th accelerated around the

moon, each in an arrowhead formation with the battleships at the tip.

Lettow tapped a finger against the edge of the holo tank. Things were going smoothly—so smoothly that he worried he'd blundered into a trap.

"Hail coming through from the target planet," Paxton said.

"Comms, an attempt to get a message through the Crucible?" Lettow asked.

"Negative, Admiral," said a lieutenant in a workstation. "No IR relays detected anywhere in system. They may have something on the moon's surface we haven't found yet."

"Sir, report in from Strike Marine Team Crimson." Paxton reached into the holo tank and flicked a file toward Lettow. Camera footage of a Crucible command node came up, a domed room with several descending tiers and stairs designed for beings much taller than humans. At the bottom of the node was a blast crater. Tendrils of smoke reached through the air as the self-repair protocols of the Crucible reknit the basalt-like material of the floor.

"Team leader reports feeling a shock wave soon after entering the structure. They found the control room like this. Denethrite explosive residue detected throughout the command node. No casualties," she said.

"Was the explosion before or after we locked down the Crucible?" Lettow asked.

"It was…eighteen seconds after we engaged the limpets," she said.

"Comms detected no signal from the planet. Nothing got through…what did they blow up?"

Paxton shrugged her shoulders.

"I need better than that, XO. We have all manner of equipment bolted to our Crucibles. Find out what was in that room," Lettow said. He set a delay to open the channel with the Ibarra colony and dialed Admiral Ericson in to monitor the conversation.

A bald man with a wide face appeared in a window as several others milled around behind him.

"Hello? This is Balmaseda Governor

Thrace. Identify yourselves," he said.

Lettow stood up and clasped his hands behind his back. He looked into the camera and let his iron bearing make the first impression.

"Governor Thrace, I am Admiral Lettow of the Terran Union. Your presence here is in violation of the Hale Treaty and must be removed immediately. I've been instructed to take you, and every last illegal settler, back to Terran space. You will comply. How difficult the relocation goes depends on you."

"Now just a goddamn minute." Thrace looked over his shoulder and waved at someone. "The Ibarra Nation isn't a signatory to the Hale Treaty and we're not going to up and leave our homes because some pompous…"

Lettow looked to one side of the holo tank. Both fleets were nearly over the horizon and visible from Balmaseda.

The admiral's earpiece clicked as Paxton spoke to him.

"Planet is barely habitable," she said. "One

city on a mesa in a mountain range. Couple outlying settlements near glaciers. That must be where they're getting water."

"We're not going anywhere, Admiral," Thrace said, though his mouth wavered and his eyes betrayed just how scared he really was. This was not a man with a military background, Lettow decided.

"I am not asking you, Thrace," Lettow said. "I am telling you. I have two fleets at my disposal. Armor. Strike Marines and battalions of Rangers. Bastion is fully aware that you're here, and if I don't remove you, they'll send the Kroar or the Mendesans to deal with you. Have you ever seen a Kroar? They're seven-foot-tall hairy alligators and full carnivores. They're still angry at humans after they tried and failed to take our colony on Eire. I am the last friendly face you will ever see if you don't comply with my instructions."

"We…we're not helpless, you know." Thrace swallowed hard.

"I'm under orders to remove you without

force if possible. You fire on my ships or my soldiers and my goodwill vanishes…I don't know your background." The corner of Lettow's mouth twitched. He would bet a month's salary this Thrace was a new proccie. "But you're old enough to remember rebuilding Earth, the whole Ember War, and all the work humanity did together to fight back from the edge. I'm not here as your enemy. I am here to save you from the rest of the galaxy. Don't turn—"

The channel cut out.

"Damn it, I rehearsed that part forever." Lettow looked over at Paxton.

"Admiral, this colony hasn't been here long." Her hand tapped inside the holo tank, and a picture of the main settlement appeared. Rows of multistory buildings stretched out from four massive colony landers, each the size of a battlecruiser.

"This place is a shake and bake," Paxton said. "We did the same thing with our first out-system colonies. Drop enough people and equipment to be self-sustaining. More about planting the flag than long-term viability."

"Admiral," the lieutenant commander at the ship's tactical station stood up, "sensors are picking up rail gun batteries throughout the surrounding mountain ranges and a number buried beneath the moon's surface."

"Are they active?" Lettow asked.

"Negative, sir. Powered down at the moment," he said, "but if their tech is as good as ours, they could have rounds in the void in less than five minutes."

"*Normandy,* go to a dispersed formation." Lettow pulled the data from the tactical officer into his tank and waited as his ship's computer analyzed the number of guns and just how much damage they could do in one salvo. He grunted as the first simulation went through. Of the twenty batteries they'd detected, the colonists might have managed a hit or two through his fleets' point defense. None of their guns would have survived to make a second shot.

"Thrace isn't a fanatic," Lettow said. "At least one thing's going right for us today. Tactical. I want a full scan of the system. I don't want to find out they have macro cannons when a hypervelocity round from the Kuiper belt cuts the *Ardennes* in half."

"Aye aye."

"Low orbit to discourage a macro shot, Admiral?" Paxton asked. "They fire one on us, it'll hit the planet—massive destruction and a mini ice age for decades."

"We'll set the 30th to low orbit. Keep us in geo-synch over the settlement in case they have any surprises we've not anticipated."

"Admiral, Thrace is hailing us again," the comms officer said.

"He can wait." Lettow pulled up a menu and tapped a name. "Colonel Martel, begin landing your armor. Phase two begins now."

CHAPTER 18

"…and then I threw the dragon way up into the air and it flew away," Jonathan said.

Roland smiled and looked down at his plate. He'd had more than one serving and felt like he'd eaten a bit more than what was polite, but the lamb chops had a spice to them that Roland had never tasted before, and the grain dish was savory and had an almost-cinnamon aftertaste. Wherever this Navarre planet was, the Ibarras had made good use of the local flora.

"That's quite the story, son," Nicodemus said.

"I'm all done eating," the boy said. "Can you help me with gauss cannon targeting? Mom said you would."

"I need to take Mr. Shaw back to his

quarters," Nicodemus said.

"But Mom *said…*"

"I can get back on my own," Roland said. "Air cars are air cars. Right? The gu—people in charge of quarters won't mind."

Nicodemus looked hard at Roland, then glanced at the small shrine to Saint Kallen in the corner behind him.

Roland brushed his hand over the bare patch on his shoulder, making an implicit promise to the Saint that he wouldn't abuse Nicodemus' trust.

"Go get your gear on," the Ibarran said to his son.

Jonathan scrambled off his chair and raced away.

"Your car should still be waiting," Nicodemus said.

"Then I'll get started on dishes." Suzzana made to get up, but Nicodemus stopped her.

"We'll let the Rosie handle it," he said.

"You remember this." She pointed at Roland and then to her husband. "Spoil your pregnant wife and life will be happier for everyone."

"Yes, ma'am," Roland said, standing up. "Thank you for having me over."

"Sir," Roland said to Nicodemus as he walked toward the exit. The Ibarran joined him and grabbed him by the forearm as the door opened.

"If you think I'll go easy on you after this…" Nicodemus said.

"I didn't think you would." Roland frowned.

"Have a safe trip back." Nicodemus waited until Roland had started down the hallway before closing the door.

Roland heard muffled conversations from the other apartments as he passed. Just how many families were here? He'd imagined the Ibarrans as little more than one giant army, creating entire strike groups from their crèche farms bent on whatever Stacey Ibarra demanded from them. To know that there was a deeper dimension, that they lived lives little different from the people of Earth and the colonies…

The pair of legionnaires met him without a

word at the garage. They kept their weapons pointed away from Roland and their fingers off the trigger, but Roland could sense their alert nature. Even if he had the desire to try to escape now, he'd stand a better chance fighting armor while in his utilities and holding a butter knife.

A deep sense of uselessness and ennui came over him as the pilotless air car came up to him. There was no escape from the Ibarrans, he realized. He was nothing more than a nuisance for them now, having already given up what they wanted from him.

Resistance was useless. Without his armor, he was nothing as a fighter compared to those combat-built and -bred legionnaires.

An air car rose up and came to a gentle stop in front of him. A door opened and Roland saw a small book on the seat.

"You guys coming with me?" Roland asked a legionnaire. The soldier motioned toward the car with his rifle's muzzle.

Bolts locked the door after Roland got

inside, and the car moved off before he could sit down, the windows going dark before it moved out of sight of the legionnaires. The car turned hard and the book skittered across the seat to Roland's side.

It was the tape-covered Templar primer. Roland opened it, deciding to get some study in during the view-less trip back to his cell. He glanced at the inner cover that bore the handwritten inscription: Property of B.B.

BB...Bassani? The primer grew cold to the touch as Roland realized who it belonged to. Bassani was dead, presumably lost in battle. Roland put it down gently and turned his gaze to his reflection in the window.

I don't deserve it. I am armor, but I am a failure.

He didn't bother to keep a count during his trip. It was pointless. He crossed his arms over his chest and huddled against the door, basking in his self-pity.

After a few minutes, the screens went blank and the world outside the car was there. He turned his head just as the car passed a final skyscraper and went into the gloom. The glow from the city faded out quickly, and the air car continued unabated. The clouds darkened and rain lashed against the windows.

"Hello?" Roland rapped his fingers against the glass separating his compartment from the control systems up front. Being enveloped in the abyss wasn't unusual for an armor soldier accustomed to the womb, but being in a car on a strange planet traveling to an unknown destination brought Roland's combat instincts to life.

He looked down and saw the shadows of mountain ridges lit by travel beacons.

At least I'm going somewhere. Maybe they aren't going to use the lamest escape attempt in military history as an excuse to kill me.

A dull pyramid edged in light emerged in the distance. Roland leaned close to the windshield as the car angled down toward a hangar door that slid up one side. The structure was enormous, easily several times the size of the skyscraper he'd just come through. He saw rail cannons dotted along the pyramid, their vanes facing down as small rivers of rain ran off them.

Is this where they're holding me? This trip was longer than the flight to Nicodemus' place and with fewer turns...where is this? Roland slipped the primer into a thigh pocket as his car swooped into the hangar only a bit wider than the vehicle.

The car slowed to a stop and Roland stuck his head out, looking for the two habitual guards but found the hangar otherwise empty. A blast door slid down and locked in place with a thump that echoed through the chamber.

A doorframe lit up and Roland got out and looked around.

"Okay, then." The door slid open to a wide hallway as he approached. His boots echoed off the dark rock walls, constructed of a different material than his prison. He passed closed doors, each with foreign words carved onto the surface in neat English letters.

Roland stopped before a double door arched

with blocks, the keystone bearing a red Templar cross. The door opened down the middle and a gust of air tinted with incense wafted over him. Shadows moved in the candlelit chamber beyond. Dim light glinted off metal rings on the shadows at head height, all vanishing as those inside turned to look at Roland.

Morrigan, wearing dark chain mail, a sword belt, and a sash with a Templar cross, emerged from the darkness and grabbed him by the wrist.

"What the hell are you doing here?" she hissed.

A chill crept across his skin and Morrigan shuddered. A hooded figure walked up and light played across Stacey Ibarra's surface. A tall man with a full beard in the same dress as Morrigan followed close behind.

"He's my guest," Ibarra said. "You all don't mind if I see this part, not a problem if he joins me, is it?"

"Our invitation is to you…and to whom you choose," the man said. "He will be respectful," he put a hand on his sword hilt, "I'm sure."

"Come, Mr. Shaw." Ibarra motioned to him. "This part always fascinates me."

Roland swallowed hard and stepped into the room.

Templar, at least two dozen of them, stepped aside for Stacey and Roland as she brought him up to a ring of candles along the floor. A privacy screen hummed a few inches past the line of candles, and the barrier changed as they drew closer, opening the view into what was beyond.

He gazed down into an amphitheater where rows and rows of kneeling men and women—all in the same Templar garb, their hands gripped on their swords planted point first into the floor—faced a raised stage. The chants of prayer, prayers Roland had memorized from the primer, rose from the faithful.

Stacey tossed back her hood and the slight chill of her presence grew stronger, but was not as bone-chilling and painful as the last time he was in her presence. She gripped her sleeve with a gloved hand and wires in the coat glowed. Roland felt a bit warmer.

"They pray for hours, I'm told." Ibarra gently tilted her head from side to side, the candles' reflection twisting on her metal face. "Is it the same still on Earth for the Vigil?"

"I've not stood the Vigil yet," Roland said.

She gave him a look; even without expression, Roland felt she was perturbed.

"Those who take the final Templar rites will go to Memorial Square in Phoenix, kneel with their armor, and recite the litanies from dusk until dawn," he said. "There's more that comes afterwards, but that's revealed at the end of the Vigil."

"I love tradition," she said. "It's what makes us who we are. It's such a shame that I could never send my armor back to Earth for the rite, things being as they are. But they've made do."

"You mean this is…your Vigil?" Roland asked.

"The public part." She brought her fingers up to the side of her head and twirled them around.

"This isn't the only place to watch."

A spotlight appeared on stage and widened, bathing the wooden slats in gentle light. Toward the back, a single suit of armor knelt with a sword made of glass run through with golden lines. The armor was of an older model, one phased out not long after the Ember War ended.

"Ah…Elias," she said. "I remember him, a man singular in purpose. A true warrior, one that never wavered from what he considered to be right. His code of honor almost ruined everything…if he'd survived that last battle, he would have destroyed me the first chance he had. Still, I wish he was with us. It was his iron heart that won the war against the Xaros Masters on their world, and I bargained away my soul to win us the galaxy from the Xaros drones. But he's the one we all remember, the one with the monuments. I wouldn't have it any other way."

"What is this?" Roland asked.

"The calling," she said. "Watch. You'll understand soon. This is an exact recording from the day before the Ember War ended…well, there's some embellishment later on."

A hologram of a gray-haired soldier with a cane appeared next to the armor and walked out to the front of the stage. The holo paced along the edge, looking across the praying Templar.

"Old Colonel Carius," Ibarra said. "I remember him when I was a little girl. Grandpa used to have him over to the mansion, always asking him about the armor program, needling him for more information to make the suits work better. Carius used to say I was always too skinny, should have spent more time outside than with my nose buried in books. One day he showed up with a limp and the cane that had Chinese writing on it. He never told me how he got it, which was kind of him. No reason to give a girl nightmares."

"Armor, your world needs you," the Carius hologram said with a German accent, the words projected through speakers. "The Xaros advance on Earth—more drones than scoured Earth clean the first time they arrived, many more than we faced in the second invasion. They will reach Mars in less than a week, and no matter how hard we fight, the outcome will never be in doubt."

Carius knocked his cane tip against the floor.

"But we are not without hope," he said. "There is a way to strike the dragon in its heart. A singular hope against this coming darkness. One ship will be the sword. One ship will carry humanity's will to fight, to survive. And *I* will carry that weapon. But I cannot carry it alone."

At the edge of the stage, another hologram appeared and Roland caught his breath. Saint Kallen. He recognized her long braided hair and gentle face. She wore a shimmering gown and walked—walked—on bare feet. Her holo was ethereal…and Roland realized what Ibarra meant about an embellishment. Kallen was a quadriplegic, all pictures or statues of her he'd ever seen were of her in armor or in a wheelchair.

Carius took no notice of Kallen as she walked up beside him.

"I have fought as armor for decades," Carius said. "Many of you have stood shoulder to shoulder with me in Australia, Ceres, Mars…who will fight beside me now?"

"Take me," came from the armor.

Carius looked over his shoulder at the suit playing Elias and rapped his cane against the stage twice, then beat a fist against his heart. Roland felt the blood run from his face. Carius accepted Elias the same way the armor began pre-battle rites.

Kallen walked off the stage and slowly made her way through the still-kneeling Templar.

"Take me!" One in the back rows stood. Roland looked at the man who spoke and noted that he lacked the skull plugs of an armor soldier. Another stood and made the same offer to Carius.

Kallen stopped next to a woman and knelt beside her. The ghostly hologram reached out and touched the Templar's face. As she stood, Roland caught a glint of light off her plugs, and she shouted, "Take me!"

"I'll have you," Carius said to her.

She marched up the stairs, went to Elias, and touched the armor's leg before she vanished behind a curtain.

Across the theater, more and more Templar stood and demanded to go on the mission, a mission from which none of the armor ever returned. Carius called forth only a few, all of them armor soldiers, and only after the Kallen apparition had touched them.

Soon, every Templar in the room was on their feet.

"That's how it happened," Ibarra said. "They all volunteered. Every last armor soldier demanded to go, knowing full well it was a suicide mission."

"They're not all armor down there," Roland said.

"No, but everyone in the Nation's military keeps to the Saint. Those who've gone above and beyond the call of duty are invited to take part in this ceremony. All the new armor go through this...and whatever the final rite is that happens on the other side of the curtain."

"Do they choose to keep to the Saint, or do you program the faith into them?" Roland asked.

"If I had a heart, that would have stung," Ibarra said. "Tell me, why do you care so much about Kallen? Why bother with her? You weren't raised in the faith. No one was."

"She is an ideal." Roland watched as the hologram walked back up the stairs and went to Elias. She touched the massive sword, and the armor's helm turned and looked at her. She brought her gaze up to meet his, and she smiled. The hologram slowly faded away.

"The Saint fought to earn her plugs, kept fighting beside her lance after learning she had a disease that would only worsen if she stayed in her armor. She cared more for her lance, for humanity, for her armor, than she cared for herself. She was everything armor should be…I can only hope to follow in her shadow," Roland said.

"We left Earth so we could save it," Ibarra said. "Save us all. The Nation's purpose isn't far off from the ideal you describe. Don't be surprised that my soldiers keep to her too."

"But do you? Why don't you become Templar?"

She shook her head slowly.

"I've seen too much," she said. "Dealt with things that would scar your mind...I am not one for faith. I knew Kallen in passing. She was as kind and brave as you think she is. I saw the bond between the Iron Hearts...I leave such things for you."

She touched his arm, and he felt the ice of her being through her gloves.

"I am not one for love...or compassion," she said.

"My lady," Marshal Davoust intruded, his face flush and covered in a sheen of sweat. He passed her a data slate.

Roland felt a none-too-gentle tug on his arm and he stepped away from Ibarra and the marshal.

Morrigan drew Roland across the room while the rest of the armor clustered around the two leaders.

"What's wrong?" he asked.

"A Kesaht fleet is moving through the Crucible network," she said. Her demeanor was off. Her green eye looked on the verge of tearing up, and Roland wasn't sure if it was the ceremony or the news that had chipped away at her resolve.

"The fleet is enormous, at least four times what we saw at Oricon, and it stopped at a system a few light-years from one of our colonies," she said.

"You have colonies?"

"Then the Kesaht used the Crucible to do a point-to-point jump to Balmaseda and the colony's gone off-line. The colony's been in place for a few months, two hundred thousand people...and they don't stand a chance against a fleet that size."

Roland watched as Stacey listened to Davoust and the bearded Templar. The two men shook their heads at each other and pointed at the data slate the marshal carried.

"What will you do?" Roland asked.

"It's up to our lady," Morrigan said. "But all those civilians..."

Ibarra held up a hand and the discussion around her ceased.

"We cannot risk the enemy tracing us back to Navarre," Ibarra said. "Marshal Davoust will take the ready fleet and the *Warsaw* to evacuate as many colonists as he can."

"The *Warsaw* can bring only so many ships, my lady," Davoust said. "We'll be outnumbered and outgunned."

"Then bring our best soldiers." The throng of armor parted as she walked to the door.

A ball of ice formed in Roland's stomach as he remembered the Kesaht ship where he encountered one of their Ixio officers, as he remembered the captured humans floating in the aliens' tanks, cybernetics sunk into their skulls, their mouths open in silent screams.

"I'll go!" Roland called out. He made for Ibarra and shrugged off Morrigan as she grasped at him.

"Let me fight, Ibarra." Roland kept at her, even as one of her silver-armored guards stepped between them and put a meaty palm against his chest.

She stopped and half-turned to look at Roland as she pulled her hood back up. Her doll-like face regarded him for a moment, then she glanced over Roland's shoulder to the bearded Templar.

"General Hurson?" She left the room and the guard with his hand to Roland's chest gave him a shove that sent Roland back a step.

Roland turned around and faced Hurson and Morrigan. The man shook his head.

"Armor fights as a lance, as a company, as a squadron, as a regiment," the general said. "There is no place for a single suit."

"I've fought the Kesaht," Roland said. "I know their tactics, their—"

"No," Hurson said.

"My lance will take him." Morrigan raised her chin slightly. "We're understrength as it is. He will fight as one of us. You have my word, by my honor, and my armor."

"Nicodemus is the lance commander, not you," Hurson said.

"He has the same faith in Roland as I do," she said.

Hurson's jaw worked from side to side. "By your honor and your armor."

Morrigan beat a fist against her heart twice.

Hurson shouldered past Roland and left the room with Davoust.

"Was that a yes?" Roland asked Morrigan.

"It was. If you step out of line, the general will take my armor...and Nicodemus'. You understand what this means? You're fighting for the Ibarra Nation. Earth may never forgive you."

"I'm not doing this for Ibarra." Roland glanced at the Templar cross on Morrigan's sash. "I'm doing it for those that need me. I can't step away."

Morrigan cupped the side of Roland's face.

"There's iron in your heart. Come, you need armor."

CHAPTER 19

Gideon pulled his knees even with his waist, felt the gentle switch of the womb's amniosis, and reached through his plugs to feel his armor—the weight of full ammunition packs beneath his back armor plates, the gentle hum of his rail cannon. He tensed his shoulder and hip actuators like he was flexing muscles.

It felt good to be back inside his armor.

"Lance, send ready status, call three," Gideon said and grit his teeth. Roland was gone. "Correction, call two."

"Aignar. Green across the board. Synch optimal, trending to gold." His suit came up on

Gideon's HUD, ready for the fight.

"Cha'ril. Amber synch...suit is optimal. No issues," the Dotari said.

Gideon opened her armor's feed and concentrated on a text box next to the wire diagram of her inside the armor.

"Cha'ril, there's a medical alert on you, but it's written in Dotari. Translate."

"It's nothing, sir. Minor glandular response, so low priority that the software engineers never bothered to translate it into English. Frequent among Dotari pilots who've been out of the womb for more than a few weeks," she said.

"Did this happen when we were on the way down to New Bastion? I didn't have my feed open for you two then," Gideon said.

"Negative...but I was armored up for less than an hour. The synch bump must be what's causing the reaction. Nothing of concern."

As lance commander, he saw a private channel open between Aignar and Cha'ril. Speech data passed between them. Cha'ril's responses were short, never more than one or two words.

"Any impact on the mission?" Gideon asked.

"No, sir. Let's find the Ibarrans and ask where they've got Roland," she said.

"Iron Dragoons…to war." Gideon sent a signal to Chief Henrique and the bolts securing him inside his coffin released with a snap. He walked out and went to the reinforced lift waiting for his lance.

When the lift began moving to take them to the flight deck, Gideon opened a private channel to Aignar.

Gideon let the open static of the line pose the question.

"Nothing to add, sir," Aignar said.

"She's not acting like herself."

"She did just get sort of married. I didn't press too hard as I've had about all their culture that I can take for a while. With all the fuss they made to get Admiral Lettow involved…if there was something else we needed to know, I think they'd tell us. We may be going through trouble with the Ibarras…they're dealing with near extinction."

"You didn't go to the Templar pre-battle ceremony."

Aignar's armor shifted weight from side to side.

"There are enough full Templar aboard to perform the rite. They didn't need me there."

"Fair enough." Gideon closed the channel. The lance continued to the flight deck in silence.

****

Three tactical insertion torpedoes ripped through the skies over Balmaseda's grand mesa. As one, the torpedoes deployed retro-rockets, flaring like comets as they lost forward velocity and dipped toward the surface.

The Iron Dragoons ejected at a hundred meters above ground level and shifted their legs into treads just before they slammed into the dirt. Their torpedoes broke apart, filling the sky with chaff designed to mask their landing zone from sensors.

Aignar revved his treads in reverse, trying to slow down as he slalomed across a dry lake bed. His right side hit a rock and pitched him onto one side. Like a surfer navigating a wave barrel, he punched a fist against the ground and braced himself against flipping over, then he shoved off the ground and leveled out.

His left treads froze, then broke, leaving a trail of metal segments behind as he spun out and finally ground to a halt. He reformed back into his walker configuration and looked back at the messy path behind him.

"This was not better than the last time! In fact, I think it was worse." He banged a fist against his left leg and started running to catch up with Cha'ril and Gideon ahead of him.

"I noted at least six differences in the insertion procedure since our landing on Oricon," Cha'ril said. "The engineers must have incorporated our feedback."

"They must have missed my memo about

the acronym," Aignar said. "Or the one where I said I'd rather crash land in a Mule than—"

"Target sighted," Gideon said. An outline of several buildings nestled against a massive glacier and a mountain range appeared on Aignar's HUD.

"No weapon emplacements," Cha'ril said. "All I'm picking up are utility vehicles."

Aignar tagged movement amongst the buildings and shared it with the others.

"They know we're coming. Granted, there was nothing subtle about our arrival," he said.

"Remember the rules of engagement," Gideon said. "Lethal force authorized only if we're threatened or attacked with lethal force."

"Will they fight us?" Cha'ril asked.

"God, I hope not," Aignar said. "Miners against armor? It wouldn't be a fight—it'd be a massacre. I don't mind crushing Vish or Kesaht all day...but people?"

"Stay alert and stay aggressive," Gideon said. "We're here as an overwhelming force so there is no fighting. Ten Rangers drop in on them…they might think they've a chance in a fight. Loose V formation at two hundred meters. Weapons free."

Aignar brought his rotary cannon up onto his shoulder but didn't activate the spin. He had rounds chambered in his forearm gauss cannon, which would be overkill against an unarmored human. As they drew closer, he scanned the buildings, wary of any Ibarra armor that might be lurking within. He wouldn't get caught flat-footed again.

As they crossed into the shadow of the mountains and the tall ice cliffs of the glacier, he angled to the right of the small settlement, a half-dozen prefabricated buildings and water pumps connected to massive pipes boring into the deep-blue glacier. The pipes led around the slope of a mountain and disappeared into the shadows.

The pathways between the buildings were deserted, but Aignar saw movement around window edges.

"Come out!" Gideon bellowed through his

speakers. "We are Terran Armor Corps. You will not be harmed. Come out!"

Aignar's rotary cannon mimed the movement of his helm as he scanned the buildings. He looked over at a hauler vehicle, the metal surrounding the cab proving too thick to detect what was inside. He marked it as a danger zone and sent the warning to Cha'ril, who was much closer to the truck.

"There are eight individuals in the building directly in front of me," Gideon said. "If you do not come out with your hands up, I will rip the roof off and take you out. You have ten seconds to comply. Ten…nine…"

The door to the prefab building opened and a tall man in worker's overalls came out with his hands up, his blond hair and beard marred with dirt. Across his back was a worn-looking rifle, an underpowered civilian version of what Aignar carried back during his Ranger days.

Seven more men and women followed.

"Three in the shower unit," Aignar said,

loudly enough for the colonists to know they couldn't hide.

"Everyone out!" the blond man said. "It's no use."

Another dozen adults filed out from the rest of the work site, all looking like they'd worked long days with few breaks for months. They formed a loose gaggle behind the foreman.

"Name?" Gideon lowered his gauss cannons to one side.

"Etor. I'm the foreman on Pump 4. What the hell are you traitors doing here?" He lowered his hands to his side.

"Removing you," Gideon said. "How many at this station? You'll be taken to a transport ship in orbit."

"This is our home," Etor said. "What right do you have to come here and take us away?" The rabble behind him echoed his sentiment.

"I'm not here to explain anything. Again, how many people at this station?"

"*Putaseme!* What happens after we board

your transports? You send us back to Navarre?" a woman shouted from the crowd.

Gideon hesitated and Aignar snapped his helm at his lance commander. Aignar would have bet a month's pay that all these Ibarrans were new proccies. What would happen to them if the Omega Provision was enforced?

"My orders are to remove every person and destroy this pumping station." Gideon motioned toward the pipes dug into the glacier. "If you've got someone hiding in the mountains, they won't survive once you leave. Don't kill them out of spite."

"Do you know what we went through to build this place?" Etor asked. "Weeks of twenty-hour days. We just sent the first gallon or potable water to Balmaseda yesterday and now you're going to wreck it? Why? Spite?"

"They are in no position to negotiate," Cha'ril said.

Etor looked at her in disgust.

"That's no human in there," he said. "Is

Earth so weak they have to bring in aliens to do their dirty work?"

"Should I take that as an insult or a compliment?" she asked.

A door on the hauler burst open and a woman jumped out. She held a canvas sack bulging with denethrite explosives in one hand…and a detonator in the other.

"Loordes, stop!" Etor shouted.

Cha'ril's rotary cannon spun up.

"This is our home!" Loordes reached back with the satchel charge and swung it forward.

Cha'ril fired a single bullet and it ripped through Loordes' throwing arm just below the elbow. The satchel and the severed limb landed next to her and flopped in the dirt. As she looked at the blood spurting from her ragged stump, Loordes stumbled to one side.

Cha'ril charged forward, raised a foot in the air, and stomped down, mashing the satchel charge into the ground.

"Secure the detonator before she loses

consciousness," the Dotari armor said.

"Txortalari!" the woman slurred and fell to her side, blood gushing across her clothes and staining the earth. The Ibarrans screamed in dismay.

"My kit!" A man waved his hands in the air and pointed to an open door. "My med kit!"

"Go!" Gideon pointed at the man and tracked him with his rotary cannon as he raced to the shed and hurried to Loordes. The medic slapped the detonator out of her hand and pulled a tourniquet from his pack.

"Anyone else?" Gideon asked. "Anyone else want to be a hero?"

"She's the last one," Etor said. He looked on as the medic pressed a hypospray to her neck and she went limp. "She's…my sister. Please, sir, let me—"

Gideon motioned with a flick of his hand and Etor rushed over.

"Aignar, Dismantle the pump stations," Gideon sent over the lance's IR channel so the colonists couldn't hear. *"Cha'ril, hold your position*

267

until they move the casualty. That charge might
cause minor damage to you, but it will hurt them
more, and we aren't equipped to handle more
injuries. I'll prep a pigeon drone and get evac on
the way."

"Should I have killed her?" Cha'ril asked.
"Her intent was lethal. Restraint seemed
reasonable."

"You handled the situation better than I
would have," Gideon said. *"If this is the worst we*
have to deal with today, then I'd call it a success."

Aignar stopped next to the glacier wall and
looked up the sheer cliff. The pipes thrummed with
moving water. When he gripped a control panel
with his hand and crushed it, moans and a number
of hand gestures he'd never seen before came from
the settlers. He kicked over a battery stack and one
of the pumps ground to a halt.

"What Gideon means, Cha'ril," he said, *"is*
that this is a shit sandwich. And we've all got to
take a bite."

CHAPTER 20

"For the third time, what I'm telling you, Governor Thrace," Lettow said, keeping his expression level as he looked at the other man in the holo tank, "is that I'm dismantling your outlying stations and removing the personnel myself. Your city won't need water or power twelve hours from now and I will not leave anything behind to encourage resettlement of this planet."

"This is outrageous!" Thrace shouted. Had they actually been face-to-face, Lettow was fairly certain he'd be wiping the Ibarran's spittle away. Lettow muted the governor and glanced at the map of the high mesa with Balmaseda City.

Blue icons for the armor and mounted Ranger elements were still several miles from the city. He tapped in to their camera feeds and saw the tops of buildings and the bulk of the cargo landers at the city's center.

The 14th and 30th fleets were closing in on Balmaseda but still an hour away from taking their positions over the planet.

"Colonel Martel, what's your read?" the admiral asked.

A panel with the helm and shoulders of a suit of armor came up and Lettow was glad he didn't have to see the man inside the suit. The idea of floating in goo with plugs in one's brain sent a shiver down his spine.

"No resistance encountered. No sign of any heavy weapons," Martel said. "We shall see if a deliberate advance on the city proves to be a better move than an assault drop to seize key facilities."

"You convinced me that landers full of Rangers and armor showing up out of the blue would not minimize civilian casualties."

"We are here to remove them, but we come with peace in our hearts. Planning on the Ibarrans understanding that once they realize we're in their city but before they grab their weapons requires hope. And hope is not a method. We're ten minutes from the city's edge. Armor will lead the way. The Rangers aren't happy about that, but they aren't stupid either."

"I'm still working on the governor. He's angry but reasonable, *Ardennes* out."

Lettow unmuted Thrace.

"—but there's no proper English translation for what I just said about your mother!" Thrace took several deep breaths as he stared daggers at Lettow.

"You're done, Governor."

"Hardly! As for your father, he—"

"You. Are. Done. You have one easy choice to make, and that is how many of your people will die for your worthless pride. By now, you can see the dust rising to the south. My ground forces will be there soon and they are led by *armor*." Lettow felt a bit of pleasure when Trace flinched at the word.

"You ever seen armor fight, Governor? My father served in Australia. The only nightmares he ever had were from seeing four suits tear through a Chinese infantry battalion. I don't want that to happen. They don't want that to happen. If you're a governor, then you care about every last man, woman, and child that looks to you for leadership...and I don't think you want bloodshed either."

Lettow caught movement out of the corner of his eye. Several officers had clustered around the astrogation section and the conversation was growing heated. The admiral locked eyes with Paxton, then flicked his hands toward the disturbance. She nodded and rushed over.

"And if you do insist on spilling blood this day," Lettow said, "I know where your office is and will turn it into a smoking crater as a monument to futility and find someone else to talk to. Do we understand each other?"

Someone leaned up to Thrace's ear and

whispered to him. The governor smiled.

"I think, Admiral, that you do need to talk to someone else." Thrace's holo cut out.

"Sir…" Paxton ran over so fast she used the holo tank to stop her momentum. "There's a wormhole opening in the system—not through the Crucible. Has to be a one-way jump."

"From where? Kroar space?" Lettow zoomed the holo tank away from Balmaseda and searched for where the wormhole was forming.

"We…can't tell," she said.

In the holo tank, an alert icon popped up over Balmaseda. Lettow's brow furrowed and he zoomed back in. It was notoriously difficult to plan exit wormholes for offset jumps through Crucible gates, but there, over the northern pole, was a wormhole.

"That's impossible," Paxton said.

"Ready the alert fighters. Load forward torpedoes across the fleets," Lettow said.

Admiral Ericson appeared in the holo.

"*Ardennes,* are you seeing this?" she asked.

"I am. And were it not with my own eyes, I wouldn't believe it," he said.

The wormhole faded away. Lettow zoomed in and found a Terran battleship with a white hull and red trim. Dozens more ships appeared and the telltale flare of landing craft breaking through atmosphere appeared. They were heading straight for Balmaseda City.

"That's…I've never seen that ship before." Paxton swallowed hard. "It's not a *Warsaw* class. Similar build, but that's a good hundred yards longer from prow to stern."

In the holo, threat icons appeared over the north pole. Hundreds of them. Lettow felt ice pulse out of his heart and through his veins.

A hailing signal appeared next to the battleship.

"We've made it through worse," Admiral Ericson said.

Lettow punched the side of his holo tank and opened the channel.

A woman in her late twenties with night-black hair and wide Slavic features appeared. She bore five stars on a high collar.

"Terran ships," she said with a faint Eastern European accent, "you have violated Ibarra Nation space. As our colony is undamaged and the governor can cite only your belligerent attitude as a grievance, I am willing to be...merciful. Recall your forces. Leave through the Crucible and never return. This is your only warning."

A text message from Ericson popped up over her window: STALL. SENDING REQUEST FOR REINFORCEMENTS THROUGH CRUCIBLE.

"Since Thrace has you up-to-date, we can skip the pleasantries," Lettow said. "This colony is illegal. You have no legitimate claim to this system and I will remove it through whatever force I deem necessary. I am here under the authority of the Terran Union and New Bastion."

"An entire galaxy full of stars," the Ibarran said, shaking her head. "World upon pristine world ready to grow new civilizations, and a bunch of squabbling bureaucrats think they own them all. Who gave you this authority? What right do you have to demand anything of us?"

"Same tone, different voice from the last time I spoke to an Ibarran. You're not Admiral Faben, are you?" Lettow asked.

A smile crept across her face.

"She said you were adept as a commander, but not that clever. I agree with the latter. I'll learn the former myself. Do you think this parley will give you the chance to get word through the Crucible?"

Lettow leaned back.

A text message appeared over Ericson's face: NO RESPONSE.

"Your limpets are a good tactic," the Ibarran admiral said. "We salted the Crucible with our own when we first delivered the colonists, though I think ours will be a good deal harder to find. Is it still Terran Naval procedure to send updates back to Earth every six hours? That's a long time to go without help…"

"Wormhole detected!" the astrogation lieutenant called out. The three admirals all let surprise break through their poker faces. "Coming from the far side of the moon."

"The Crucible?" Lettow asked.

"No, the exit plane is too large," the officer said, shaking his head.

"Get me visual from the Crucible," Lettow said to Paxton.

"Our teams in three of the control nodes are off-line," she said. "Delta sent a fragment. Sending."

A screen opened in the holo tank showing the interior circumference of the Crucible. The great crown of thrones was broken, the control nodes shattered. A flash filled the screen and the screen went to static before the whole video looped again.

"Contact!" Paxton announced. A trace appeared behind an object as it slingshot around the moon and angled straight for Balmaseda. The ship's computer estimated it would impact in tens of seconds.

"What is that? The speed looks like a macro round." Lettow snapped his head toward the gunnery commander. "Get a firing solution. Don't let it through!"

"Can't be a macro, sir," Paxton said. "Mass of the object reads barely more than a few hundred pounds. No radiation returns, not a nuke."

"Chance of us hitting it at this range are near zero, sir," the gunnery officer called back. "All ships are engaging."

A curtain of fire poured out of the Terran ships tightening toward the object's projected path. Lettow knew it would take a miracle for even a lucky hit…but still let out a curse when the projectile zipped through the point defense rounds.

Lettow touched the icon for his ground commander.

"Colonel Martel, the orbital situation has changed. You've got an unknown object coming in…projected point of impact near the equator."

"We've taken antipersonnel sniper fire," Martel said. "Minor injuries to one Ranger.

Building with the sniper was reduced by gauss cannon. Say again orbital situation?"

This whole thing is falling apart, Lettow thought.

"Unknown object on rapid approach to—"

The object vanished from the plot and the channel to Martel cut out. Lettow double-tapped the icon and got an error message. He looked at Balmaseda, and the planet seemed no worse for wear...but over the equator was a swirling blue aurora.

"We've lost all contact with the surface," the communication lieutenant said. Lettow felt his heart slow as a realization hit him. He'd seen this before. On Oricon.

"Admiral," the Ibarran commander said, "the atmosphere is ionizing. It's a tactic used by the—"

"The Kesaht," Lettow said.

"New contacts coming round the moon," Paxton said. "The-the targeting computers must be off. There's no way it can be this many."

As a swarm of crescent-shaped fighters and

blocky assault ships came around the moon, a tendril broke off from the main body, on a direct course for Lettow's fleets. Larger Kesaht ships followed. Hundreds and hundreds more.

"We're getting a message from the Kesaht, Admiral," the communication officer said. "It's just three words over and over again: 'Surrender and die.'"

"It's a trap," Ericson said.

"And we triggered it." Lettow looked at the Ibarran admiral, who'd gone noticeably pale in the last few minutes.

"Their message seems directed toward us both," she said curtly.

"I agree."

"I'm here for my people. Help me get them home and I'll do the same for you," she said.

"I'm not in the habit of making agreements with people who won't give their name," Lettow said.

"I am Fleet Admiral Ivana Makarov," she said, nodding slightly.

A sneer tugged at Lettow's lips. He knew the Ibarras were using procedural technology, but he never thought they'd stoop to necromancy. An Admiral Makarov commanded the Lost 8th Fleet during the Ember War after earning distinction against the Toth incursion. The day Earth learned of the fleet's loss became a day of remembrance, with Admiral Makarov honored for her leadership and valor.

"Makarov?" Ericson asked.

"My mother gave her life to save humanity against the Xaros. I chose to follow in her footsteps. Perhaps you will bring us some of that *Breitenfeld* luck, Ericson? I can push five squadrons to you. I need the rest to keep the evacuation corridor open from the main city…"

TRUST? Appeared across Ericson's screen.

"Admiral Makarov," Lettow said, "I now consider this a joint operation in all respects. We've got…seventy minutes before the Kesaht fighters reach weapon range. We need to figure out how to keep their troops off the planet. Get your personnel off and beat their capital ships. I've got some experience with the Kesaht."

"You've had more success against them than any Ibarran commander," Makarov said. "Then again, this is the first time we've faced them with this much firepower. What would Captain Valdar say at a time like this, Ericson?"

"*Admiral* Valdar…would say, '*Gott Mit Uns*.'" Ericson said.

"Then let God be with us," Makarov said. "There are a few more surprises in the system I wasn't going to tell you about, but since we're all friends now…"

CHAPTER 21

The white noise of a wormhole jump subsided and Roland's stomach twisted into knots worse than the last three jumps the ship had made. He touched the inside of his womb and tried to activate his armor's systems. A HUD appeared in his vision, fed through his plugs and cybernetics directly into his brain.

The HUD blinked on and off for a few seconds, then collapsed into an error message. Again.

He'd been in this womb for hours with no outside contact. It felt good to feel the totality of the amniosis fluid around his body and the closeness of the armored womb after so long, but being shut off from everything else was proving tedious.

I wonder what Marc Ibarra is doing. Maybe he's lonely. This will be an interesting story once I get locked back in the cell next to him. Though he'll probably get pissed I didn't try and break him out soon as I donned my armor.

The interior of the womb lit up and Roland's eyes ached. He felt a twinge through his plugs and a camera feed opened up. He saw through the helm optics of his armor, though he couldn't move the armor at all.

He was in a launch bay. Ibarran armor techs worked around him, guiding a trolley full of gauss shells and calling out silent instructions to each other. The crews were focused, working with the same seamless efficiency that Roland knew from his maintenance team of Brazilians that tended to his armor on the *Scipio*. Sound came on a moment later and Roland heard the techs talking to each other in Basque, catching the occasional English word for armor systems and weapons.

Morrigan and Nicodemus walked into his field of view, both in their skin suits.

"You awake in there?" Nicodemus touched a screen attached to his forearm and more of Roland's systems came online. He looked around and found he was inside a drop pod.

"Been ready since we left," Roland said. He ran through a system check and found a new weapon mag locked to his back: an armor sized breech-loaded rifle with an underslung battery pack. Shells for the weapon were belted to his breastplate. He noted a sword hilt locked to a leg and was surprised Nicodemus had confidence in him to wield one in battle after Roland lost so many bouts in the dojo.

"Mauser recoilless rifle," Morrigan said. "Designed to punch through Sanheel shields with a single bullet. Haven't gone through field testing yet. It'll work wonders or we go back to the old standby." She tapped her forearm where their armor carried double barreled gauss cannons.

"We just had the final combat briefing,"

Nicodemus said. "Tried to get you in, but while Morrigan and I may trust you, the *Warsaw*'s captain does not."

"The *Warsaw* is a *Europa*-class starship. I know the crew complement and her capabilities," Roland said. "Not sure what else there is to learn."

Morrigan smirked.

"We need to suit up." Nicodemus touched his forearm screen again, then tapped his plugs. "But we can still talk," he said without his lips moving.

"That's new," Roland said as the two armor soldiers split apart and walked around the drop pod to their waiting armor.

A holo of a red-green planet dotted with a few lakes and small oceans appeared on Roland's HUD. A swarm of blue icons for the Ibarra fleet populated over the northern pole. Three spinning squares came up across the northern hemisphere.

"This is Balmaseda," Nicodemus said. "The marshal's made tight IR-beam contact with the governor and…god damn it."

The holo of the planet shrank slightly and a host of red icons appeared around the edge of the planet's innermost moon. Some of the icons formed into Kesaht claw-shaped destroyers and their capital ships shaped like blades made up of overlapping and irregularly shaped tiles. The initial reports were right; the Kesaht attack fleet was a good deal larger than what he'd encountered on Oricon.

But the Kesaht weren't what gave Nicodemus pause. Along the planet's equator, green circles appeared, then flipped over to red, then back to green, like the *Warsaw*'s computers were unsure if the new contacts were hostile or neutral.

One circle switched to a wire diagram of a human battleship, the *Ardennes*.

"The Terrans are here," Morrigan said.

"Intelligence failed us." Nicodemus' armor came online in Roland's HUD as the lance leader plugged into his armor. "How the hell did they miss Earth moving a fleet that size to…Roland. I can't bring you with us."

In the drop bay, one of the technicians put a

hand to his ear, then shook his head emphatically. Red warning lights spun up.

"This is a mark IV drop pod, right?" Roland asked. "I'm already bolted in. Crew standard for removing armor is nine minutes, then you've got to recalibrate the drop ballistics to compensate for the mass displacement. Something tells me we're going to drop before all that can happen."

"I can expect you to fight Kesaht," Nicodemus said, "not to fight Earth."

"The last time it came down to shooting another human or fighting bloodthirsty aliens, we all made the right choice," Roland said. "You expect me to believe the *Ardennes* is here helping the Kesaht?"

"The trait—Terrans are already on the ground," Morrigan said. "The data lines are a mess, but there has been some bloodshed."

Ice touched Roland's heart. This was not the way it was supposed to be.

"Any fighting since the Kesaht showed up? My—I mean, their—fleet is in a better orbital position. They must have arrived first," Roland said.

Warning sirens blared through the drop bay and the tech crews scrambled off the deck and onto raised walkways. They drew safety lines off their belts and clamped them onto red and yellow railings.

Roland felt the drop pod shake as a cage lowered from the ceiling and clamped down on the pod. A metal hatch lowered over Roland, locking his armor into the pod.

"So looks like I'm coming with you," he said.

"Son, know that I have a kill switch for your armor," Nicodemus said. "We get into a fight with the Terrans—no matter who's the aggressor—I'll shut you down. You understand? Our mission here is to get the civilians off world and to safety, not fight your people."

Your people, Roland thought. This fight would not end well for him; he was certain of that.

"I came to serve, to save the civilians," Roland said. "I'll fight as long as I'm able."

"Who are you?" Morrigan asked.

"I am armor," Roland said.

"I am fury," Nicodemus added.

"And we will not fail," Morrigan intoned.

The deck beneath the drop pods opened and wind howled through the bay as the *Warsaw* dipped into Balmaseda's upper atmosphere. The cage opened and the pod fell free.

CHAPTER 22

Gideon stood just outside the glacier station as a dry wind whipped lines of sand around him and antennae rose higher out of his helm. The array shifted position, reading through frequencies.

Behind him, Cha'ril and Aignar guarded the prisoners where they sat at a communal outdoor mess. Tarps flapped in the wind and the Ibarrans huddled against each other, covering their food trays as dust came in.

From the mortar launcher on Gideon's back, a pigeon drone shot out and flew straight up. The connection between his comms array and the drone faded out before it had gone more than a hundred yards.

"Negative contact with the fleet or Colonel Martel," Gideon said through his lance's IR net. "I'm not reading anything at all."

"Coming in weak and broken." Aignar's reply was laced with heavy static.

As Gideon walked back, prisoners shied away from the stomp of his sabatons. They'd insisted on eating together soon after the wounded Loordes was stabilized in their small infirmary, but they'd barely touched their food.

"—nic interference." Cha'ril's transmission came in as he neared. "Just like we encountered on Oricon."

"I'm not one for coincidences," Aignar said. "If the Kesaht showed up…"

"Martel anticipated the Ibarras could send reinforcements," Gideon said. "He left standing orders that any prisoners remain under effective control and we hand them off to military police for processing when we rejoin the main force."

"There's an acute lack of MPs here," Aignar

said. "It'll take us four hours to make it to the city," he said, pointing into the hazy distance.

"Should be ninety minutes but *someone* broke track. Again," Cha'ril said.

"Oh, did you stick your landing after the ballistic missile spat you out?" Aignar asked.

"Enough," Gideon said. "The disruption may be some Ibarra stratagem. Some Balmaseda atmospheric issue. We don't have enough to go on right now."

"We could ask the locals," Aignar said. "They've been talking to each other in Basque since they sat down to eat. Do they really think we wouldn't have that language translator loaded up for this mission?"

"You let on we can understand them?" Gideon asked.

"No. I've been waiting to see if anyone's planning to be a hero or idiot. Mostly they've cursed out Cha'ril and are worried about family back in the city," Aignar said.

"What is a *coño*?" Cha'ril asked.

"If we let on there's an issue, they might get bold," Gideon said.

"Hey!" Etor stood up from his table, waved at the armor, and tried to block sand from getting into his eye. "We need to go inside!"

"Denied," Gideon said through his speakers. "I expect roughnecks like you can handle a little wind."

"This can get a lot worse before you know it. I can check out the data from our weather stations, see if there's a tornado coming," the Ibarran said.

"And send a message stating how many armor are here," Gideon said. "No. I can monitor the weather just fine." He tapped the side of his helm.

Cha'ril looked up toward the glacier wall.

"I'm picking something up on audio. It sounds like…what do you call the black and yellow insects that pollinate Earth flora?"

Gideon turned up the gain on his audio receptors and heard a growing buzz emanating over the icy wall embedded in the mountain range. The prisoners looked up one by one as well, and all seemed just as confused as the armor.

A Kesaht crescent fighter roared over the edge and continued toward Balmaseda City. A loose dozen followed, then squadrons in neat four-by-three formations. Assault landers the size of Destrier transports separated the fighter squadrons like a checkerboard.

"Now we know why long-range comms are out," Aignar said, bringing his rotary cannon up onto his shoulder.

Gideon ignored the panicked shouts from the prisoners as he weighed his options. As the wave tapered off to a few straggling crescent-shaped craft, he realized the wave of fighters and landers must have numbered in the thousands.

"Hold your fire," he said. "We're not going to put a dent in them with gauss or grinders."

"A rail cannon shot will—"

"The overpressure will pulp the internal organs of the unprotected civilians, Cha'ril,"

Gideon said.

"They're not *our* humans," she said.

"Doesn't matter. They're our responsibility and—contact. Four breaking off." Gideon raised his gauss cannons as Kesaht fighters broke away from the trail edge of the formation and banked toward the outpost.

"Don't move!" Gideon thundered through his speakers. "Lance: tower shield wall."

As he brought his left arm across his body, a panel on his forearm popped open and a segmented shield opened. The ultra-dense metal unfurled into a rectangular shield that covered Gideon from his armor's shins to the shoulders.

He braced his arm with the gauss cannons mounted to it against the upper edge of the shield and backed toward the prisoners.

Etor shouted out a warning for his people to duck and cover.

Gideon fired a double shot, missing the Kesaht fighter to the far right but forcing it to do a barrel roll and break off its attack run.

Yellow energy bolts snapped out of the enemy fighters' forward cannons. The armor linked shields, forming a wall between the Kesaht and the prisoners. Gauss bullets sizzled through the air, crisscrossing with the energy bolts.

A blast hit just in front of the armor, showering them with dirt and rocks. Another bolt clipped Aignar's shield and deflected into a supply shed. Pipes exploded out and went bouncing across the sand like barrels accidentally released from a winery.

A Kesaht fighter exploded as a gauss round hit home. Another lost a wing and went twisting into the ground. The remaining two fired again and Gideon's shield took a solid hit that sent off a shower of sparks and pushed him back several yards.

As the two fighters jinked from side to side, he did a quick calculation with his ballistic computer, twisted his gauss cannon arm over, and fired a shot. Letting the recoil pull his aim to the right, he fired the second barrel. A fighter veered to one side, reacting to the flash of his first shot, and took a hit to the engines from his second bullet.

The fighter dipped down, struggled to regain altitude, then slammed into the ground belly-first…a few hundred yards ahead of Gideon. It slid forward and bounced off a boulder, ripping off a wing tip and sending it spinning forward like a giant scythe.

Gideon spun up his rotary cannon and fired at the oncoming danger. Rounds battered the wreck, but its momentum was more than enough to carry it through the armor soldier and the civilians behind him.

"Worthless scrap," Gideon said as he pulled his shield arm back and swung it into a hook as a wing sliced toward him. He connected and beat the wreck aside where it smashed against the glacier wall.

When the cockpit skittered forward, Gideon snapped around and crushed it with a stomp.

The last Kesaht fighter flew overhead, smoke trailing from its engines as it pulled up into a vertical climb. It almost cleared the cliff. Almost.

The fighter crashed against an icy outcrop and exploded into a ball of fire. Hunks of the wall broke free, several on a path to crush the civilians in the mess tent.

"Cover them!" Gideon raised his shield over the civilians as shards of ice the size of soccer balls rained down. He ignored the hits to his arms and shoulders. The sound of the ice cracking against his body was far worse than any damage it did.

An ice boulder landed a dozen yards away and broke apart with a roar of thunder.

Gideon waited for the dust to settle.

"Etor, are your people injured?" Gideon folded his shield and returned it to its housing.

Peeking over the edge of the table, the foreman raised a tentative thumbs-up.

"They'll be back." Cha'ril dumped an empty ammo canister off her back and loaded another.

"Etor, if we go overland to the city, you won't make it," Gideon said. "Give me options."

Etor stood up and gave orders to his team as

the rest emerged from under the tables.

"The pipes," he said, pointing to the man-made gap in the mountains where a shattered pipe leaked water. "The gap, I mean. We mined out enough room for expansion. Would've had another dozen stations feeding through there. It leads to a tunnel that goes to the city's utility hub."

"Room enough for us?" Gideon motioned to his lance.

"Plenty." Etor leaned to one side and pointed at a truck, the bed loaded down with equipment and pipe segments. "I can get everyone in there, but it'll take time to empty it out."

"No, it won't," Gideon said. "Get your wounded and prep to move. Leave everything else behind. Aignar."

Aignar reached into the truck bed, slammed a hand onto a pump, and pinched the metal. He tossed it behind him, then grabbed a length of pipe the size of a small car and tossed it overhead like a toddler tearing through a toy box.

Etor hurried his people toward the truck,

then looked back at his wrecked pumping station.

"This was ours," he said to Gideon.

"Balmaseda isn't pretty, but we were going to turn it into a garden. Forests, cattle, sheep. We could have made something beautiful here."

A snap of a sonic boom echoed off the mountains. To the east, the trace of a rail cannon shell from a battery nestled in the distant peaks shot toward the sky.

"That dream is gone," Gideon said. "But your people live. Nothing else matters. Keep them moving."

CHAPTER 23

Colonel Martel twisted around as a Kesaht fighter roared overhead. He let off a burst of shots with a *brrrt* of rapid fire and turned his attention away as the fighter exploded.

The Kesaht had hit the Terran column within seconds of their arrival over the mesa. Martel and his four lances of armor had reacted to the sudden reversal of fortune as best they could, but the sheer number of enemy fighters—and a wide field of Terran targets—turned the mesa into a hellscape before the first crescent fighters finished their attack run.

Smoke rose from destroyed personnel carriers. Dead Rangers littered the battlefield, most still on fire. Heat from the blaze and the blast craters left from Kesaht strafing runs played hell with his armor's sensors and he cut the IR feed. The *bam-bam-bam* of crescent-fighter bolts hitting the ground closed in behind him.

Someone shoved him out of the way and a near miss sent shrapnel of pulverized rock bouncing off his armor. Martel rolled onto his feet and saw Kesaht landers lowering into the city a bare mile away. The enemy commander obviously didn't share the same caution that Martel had when planning the operation to take the city from the Ibarras.

Missiles shot up from the streets and from rooftops, destroying more than a dozen landers that crashed with fireballs into the ground. He watched as one took a hit to the engines and veered to a side and into a building, ripping the roof off before tipping belly-up and plummeting to the ground.

"We're getting killed out here, sir!" Tongea shouted as he fired his gauss cannon at a pair of crescent fighters banking around the Terran column.

"I am well aware." Martel saw a tracked

personnel carrier next to a burning wreck and saw the name stenciled on the front bumper. The carrier's rear hatch was down and Rangers loaded casualties into the back.

Martel ran over to the carrier and waved at a soldier who was standing in a cupola and shouting into a microphone.

"Colonel Jones, keep moving!" Martel shouted. "Get into the city!"

The Ranger commander shook his head, his skull mask catching the firelight from burning vehicles.

"The Ibarras will shoot us too!" Jones yelled into his microphone, then smashed the useless thing against the top of his APC.

"There's that chance. But I can guarantee you the Kesaht won't stop—"

Jones flinched as a bolt of Kesaht fire struck his vehicle's roof. Martel had a split second before Jones' vehicle exploded and the APC's treads blew out, sweeping Martel off his feet. He landed hard enough to feel the impact inside his womb. When his helm looked up, he saw the remains of Jones and his driver mangled inside the wreckage.

"Uhlans! Odinsons! Templars!" Martel got up, the megaphones in his armor blaring. "Forward! Get them moving!" He limped forward, a blasted hunk of Jones' vehicle embedded in his knee servo.

Martel went to an undamaged personnel carrier and banged against the driver's hatch twice.

"The city. Stampede! You get me?" Martel shouted. The APC lurched forward, then continued at a slower pace. Martel kicked it in the rear hatch hard enough to leave a dent and the APC gunned ahead.

Tongea followed Martel's lead and applied physical encouragement to a pair of vehicles. Matthias and Duncan, the other armor soldiers in his lance, got the leading edge of the column moving.

Martel sidestepped out of the way of an APC that had either lost the ability to steer or wasn't afraid to run over the armor commander. A warning icon flashed on his HUD and he whirled around.

More than a dozen crescent fighters were coming right for him, flying low over the deck in three stacks.

"Action right, counter air on my signal," Martel said. His HUD wavered as his armor came online with him, forming a thin barrier between the vulnerable Rangers and the oncoming fighters.

Martel loaded gauss shells into his cannons and felt the hum of the magnet coils through the arm. Dust billowed behind the fighters as they closed in.

"Mark outer targets and shift fire to center." Martel drew a bead on a fighter bobbing up and down just above the ground. His armor made the ballistic calculation for the long-range shot—and the fighter exploded.

"Who the hell?" He looked at Tongea and the line of armor after him. The Maori shrugged. None of the rest of the armor's gauss cannons were smoking.

Martel looked back and found a half-dozen

smoking craters where the attacking fighters had been. The Kesaht had broken off their attack and were in the middle of a dogfight with black fighter craft with forward-swept wings.

A fighter roared overhead. Martel caught a Templar cross painted under the wings.

"That's not one of ours," Tongea said.

"Ibarrans. If they keep not shooting at us, our situation will be slightly less terrible," Martel said. "To the city. Follow me!"

He swung a hand overhead toward the embattled city and transformed his legs into treads, rolling forward, at the point of his lance. The rest of his armor formed into a diamond-shaped formation.

They closed on the city quickly. As he caught up to an APC, a line of broken track trailing from the left side, Martel shifted back into his walking configuration. The hatch was down, and Rangers crouched next to it, about to abandon the vehicle.

"Back inside!" Martel shouted. He ran to the front and grabbed the forward edge of the vehicle, the metal bending in his grip. Tongea herded the Rangers back up the ramp, then broke the ramp off with a quick stomp and gripped the sides.

The dozen Rangers inside held very still as the armor hefted their entire APC off the ground and began running. When a Kesaht fighter strayed too close, Tongea's rotary cannon snapped up and fired on it.

Martel twisted his helm up and all the way around to watch the skies. A dogfight raged overhead. Black Ibarran fighters and gray Terran Eagles battled the Kesaht craft. Alien landers exploded and arced toward the planet on columns of smoke and fire. In the distance, pairs of the oversized landers took off and vanished over the mountains.

Explosions popped throughout the sky, and Martel knew the battle extended well into orbit.

"Saint Kallen…witness this day," Martel said.

"She is ever with us, brother," Tongea said.

They passed a burning building and dropped

the APC next to a hastily formed motor pool in a parking lot.

Captain Sobieski, standing next to open metal doors leading underneath a mostly intact building, motioned Martel over.

Just beneath ground level were three Ibarran legionnaires, the faceplates of their armor covered with a subdued red Templar cross. A rabble of men and women in light armor and carrying gauss carbines clustered behind them.

"This is my commander," Sobieski said, the rattle of gauss fire and whoosh of missiles sounding in the distance.

"Captain Hanson," the legionnaire said, giving Martel a nod. "I've got a company of reservists that are supposed to man the walls. How many Rangers have you got?"

Martel looked back at the APCs. Just how few made it to the city hit him like a punch to the gut. The city's edge tapered down to a few low buildings and dirt. In the distance, where he'd seen the Kesaht landers, a wide plume of dust rose up.

Something big was coming.

"Maybe two hundred. Walls?" Martel asked.

As if on cue, horns blared around them. Just beyond the city's edge, a ten-foot-tall slanted metal wall rose up out of the ground. Another section rose behind that, forming covered battlements with firing positions.

"That's a neat trick," Martel said to Hanson.

"We knew this day would come," he said. "Just didn't think it would come so soon."

"Sir?" A Ranger with bloodstained armor and a cracked faceplate jogged over to Martel. "Major Whitelaw, I've got command of our Rangers after we lost Jones and the XO."

"Major, I'll leave you with Hanson to coordinate local defense," Martel said, looking into the city where a lander lifted off a few blocks away. "My armor has other priorities."

Hanson grabbed a reservist by the shoulder and shouted into the tunnel.

"We've got friendlies out here. If it's alien, shoot it. If it's human, then it's worth dying for.

Move, move, move!" He practically threw the man up the stairs and Ibarrans boiled out of the tunnel and made for the walls.

Hanson looked up at Martel and beat his fist against his chest in salute.

Martel banged his fist against his heart, and the ring carried along the wall.

"We'll man the wall, Colonel. Come running if you hear us shooting," Hanson said.

"Fight well." Martel raised his gauss cannons and took off running down a street. "Templar! With me!"

CHAPTER 24

Roland felt the slow turn of his drop pod as it fell through Balmaseda's atmosphere, his borrowed armor detecting no rise in temperature. He ran a system check on his sensor. Nothing as large as a three-suit drop pod could skirt through atmo with no friction heat.

"Stop screwing around, bean head," Morrigan said through their local IR. "You'll trigger your active scanners and spotlight us for the enemy."

"Something's off with my sensors. Did your crews not integrate my womb correctly?" Roland asked.

"I won't tell Master Chief Nieves you said that," Morrigan said as she sent him a wire diagram of their drop pod. "We're rigged for stealth. Active thermal and atmo maskers. Hull will absorb or refract any radar waves. The pod takes more time and resources to assemble than our armor, but the cost is worth getting us to the ground in one piece to fight."

"That sounds a lot better than those damned insertion torpedoes. And who are you calling a 'bean head'?"

"You. Bean head. You haven't done a combat drop yet," she said.

"What? I've done three drops—"

"Not with us, you haven't." Nicodemus popped up in Roland's HUD, a map of Balmaseda City with him. A red field bulged into the eastern part of the city. "Fortifications failed to emplace to the east. Hydraulics probably took a hit during the initial bombardment. Governor Thrace's moving what he can to stem the tide."

A line of blue traced along the enemy's

advance and unit icons popped up behind it. Roland found some relief that the Ibarrans hadn't strayed too far from Terran battle command methods.

"Our LZ's near their reserve," Nicodemus said. "We'll spearhead the counterattack. Can you do a skid stop, bean head?"

"You really should have asked me this before you loaded me into the drop pod—"

"Answer!"

Roland flinched inside his womb. He wasn't in his old lance, and the lance he was with was about to drop into the middle of a fight. That he was joking around filled him with guilt.

"Yes, sir. I'm rated excellent on skid stops and have done one in combat," Roland said.

"I'm telling him," Morrigan said. "Roland, two things you need to know. First: Nicodemus has a quantum dot communicator on his helm. Looks like a normal shortwave unit, but it has two red chevrons on it. That's how we're getting around the Kesaht jamming. If necessary, you take it and coordinate what you can with the city's defenders.

We don't have many of them."

The only reason I'd need it is if you two are dead, Roland thought.

"Second: Terrans are here," she said.

Roland's eyebrows shot up. The implications raced through his mind, and he managed one word.

"Oh."

"Good news is that we're fighting on the same side, for now," Morrigan said. "Your friends showed up intending to remove our colony and take everyone away in chains. We'll see if the truce holds long enough for us to get our people off the planet."

"I…I won't fire on them," Roland said.

"Nor do we expect you to," Nicodemus said. "Fight Kesaht. Help with the evac. What happens after that is anyone's guess."

Roland squirmed inside his womb. It was bad enough that he wore Ibarra colors on his armor, was prepared to shed blood for them…but the idea of fighting Terran forces almost made him want to throw up. He wouldn't fire on them, but to any Ranger or Strike Marine watching him down a weapon sight, he looked like any other Ibarran armor.

If they somehow identified him...

"Nicodemus, are there any Terran armor down there?" Roland asked.

"Prep for drop," Nicodemus said. "Three...two...one...mark."

The metal lid on his bay broke away and Roland saw a distant mountain range. He had a split second to note the burning buildings and fighters battling around him. The pod pushed him out and a wall of wind smacked into him. He kicked his feet down and activated the jet pack on his back.

Jets blasted, slowing him almost to a stop. To one watching on the ground, it looked like a giant angel had suddenly appeared on wings of fire.

Roland faced down a wide boulevard, wrecked and burning cars littering the road. Figures on foot milled around buildings leading all the back to a highway that extended beyond the city, where the fortifications jutted a few feet above the ground. He jettisoned the pack and fell to the road, using his momentum to propel him into a run.

A rifle shot snapped over a car, and Roland's HUD marked a Rakka foot soldier. Just behind it were three Sanheel, none of whom looked prepared for Roland's arrival.

Roland charged toward them, obliterating the Rakka and the vehicle it was using for cover with a single gauss round. Shields flared around the Sanheel, protecting them from the blast.

The three readied their long rifles as Roland closed the distance. As he brought his gauss cannons to bear, Roland swore he heard the Sanheel snort in laughter. He lowered his aim and fired at their feet.

The round blew a hole in the ground and sent one of the centaurs stumbling into another. The impact fouled the other's aim and it fired into the air.

Roland kicked a smoldering piece of the destroyed ground car at the third Sanheel. He knew it wouldn't break through the alien's shields, but the Sanheel flinched all the same, a victim of its own reflexes and instincts.

Fort Knox trained armor to *be* armor—killing machines, not simply soldiers wearing a suit. If any Sanheel tried the same trick on him, they'd receive a bullet to the face at the same time they realized how clever they weren't.

Roland grabbed the third Sanheel's rifle and thrust the weapon against its chest, snapping it in half and earning a pained grunt from the alien. Roland grabbed the stunned Sanheel by the wrist and jammed the broken end of the rifle into its face. The metal pierced the Sanheel below the chin and stopped when it hit the top of his skull.

A Sanheel thrust its rifle at Roland but he caught it by the barrel and pushed the muzzle aside just as it fired. He felt heat flare against his shoulder. The alien snarled at Roland, spittle flecking from thick lips and off needle sharp teeth.

A bayonet snapped out from the side of the rifle, the blade humming as a cutting field formed along the edge. The Sanheel struggled to push the bayonet home, but its muscles were no match for Roland's armor.

"The flesh is weak," Roland said as he twisted his upper body around on the waist actuators, doing a 360 that ripped the rifle out of the Sanheel's grasp. Roland angled the butt of the weapon around and crushed his enemy's skull when it hit home.

The final Sanheel ran off at a gallop before its companion hit the ground.

Hefting the rifle up like a javelin, Roland hurled it. The blade passed through the shields and buried itself in the alien's hindquarters. It stumbled forward and reached back to grasp at the weapon, then froze, staring at Roland.

The Sanheel's head exploded with a boom.

Roland looked behind him. Nicodemus and Morrigan carried their Mauser recoilless rifles, and smoke rose off both barrels. Seeing them in their black armor, in the middle of a combat zone, caught him off guard, and his first reaction was to see them as the enemy, no matter how much time he'd spent with them out of armor. Then he looked down at his own black arms and legs, stained with alien blood.

I am armor, he thought, *just not the same armor I was.*

"Something wrong with your Mauser, Roland?" Morrigan asked.

"I…" Roland reached to his back and unsnapped the mag locks securing his own Mauser to his armor. "I forgot I had it. Guess the field trials are a success?"

"The enemy made their push before Thrace could launch his," Nicodemus said. "We are behind enemy lines. You know what a *schwerpunkt* is?"

"A small force that's made a breakthrough," Roland replied, looking into his Mauser's breach and checking that it was loaded.

"They still teach the classics at Knox," Morrigan said.

"Time to exploit that breakthrough." Nicodemus pointed down the boulevard leading to the city. "Let's find their headquarters and pay a visit."

****

The squeal of treads over broken concrete echoed down the city street. Ranger Jerry Morris huddled against a wall, nestled in a pile of broken glass and what remained of a cooler. The soft drinks it once held had burst apart in the blast that wrecked the room, leaving a thin film of sticky sugar mist on everything. The Ranger's power armor kept him safe from minor cuts and abrasions that were part and parcel of urban combat, but knowing that he'd reek of rotting sugar in a few days gnawed at him.

He clutched his gauss rifle against his chest and quietly pulled a grenade from his belt. He took a quick glance over the windowsill and dropped back down. He couldn't see the tank, but it was close.

"Go now?" One floor up, an Ibarran woman, wearing light fatigues and a flack vest, leaned over the side of a gap in the ceiling.

"No," Morris hissed. "You wait for my signal."

A legionnaire grabbed her by the shoulder and yanked her away from the edge. Morris heard a one-sided conversation begin in Basque as the professional soldier imparted wisdom on the militia woman.

Morris looked over at Yeltzin, his squad mate, a few windows over. Yeltzin mimed a yacking mouth with his hand. In the hours since the Rangers had barely made it into the city, nothing had gone right. Comms were down. The chain of command was remade and then broken again after the next Kesaht attack hit a command post and killed half the remaining officers.

Morris's squad got separated from what remained of their platoon when Rakka overran their fighting position. A group of Ibarran defenders had pulled them into a tunnel and incorporated him and Yeltzin into their ad hoc defense team. This, he'd decided, was not in the recruitment video he'd seen back in Phoenix.

The few legionnaires had proved more than capable. The militia all seemed to have been through basic training and knew which end of the rifle to point at the enemy, but their tactical acumen fell off rapidly after that.

He heard the tank stop, then the snap and squeal of treads against pavement as it changed direction. Placing his thumb against the grenade, Morris set it to Anti-Armor Close Range. The grenade would explode into a shaped charge and send a small depleted uranium lance of metal into whatever he threw it at. Getting close enough to do the job was the hard part.

The floor bumped up, knocking debris everywhere.

Morris fumbled with his rifle and tried to scramble into the corner. A metal hatch lifted up and slammed into the floor, sending dust billowing everywhere. Glowing lights pierced through the cloud and a giant shadow rose up.

Morris thumbed his safety off, his training taking over.

"Friendly." Gideon's voice cut through the dust. The upper half of his armor became clear as the dust settled.

Morris glanced out a window again, the sound of the Kesaht tank lost in the noise of Gideon's arrival.

"Tank," Morris said.

"What did you call me?" Gideon asked.

"Kesaht tank." Morris jammed a thumb at the wall.

Gideon crawled out of the tunnel in the floor and knelt next to the blown-out gap in the building's wall.

"How many?" he asked.

"We see two up here," the legionnaire said from the second floor.

Gideon's helm and rotary cannon snapped up. The legionnaires ducked away.

"They're friendly too," Morris said. "Where did you come from?"

"Outlying pump station. I have civilian prisoners and their wounded," Gideon said. Etor climbed out of the tunnel and helped more of his people out. "Etor, this is not the utility district."

"Knew we should've taken that left," Etor grumbled.

"Prisoners?" the legionnaire said from the second floor. "You've got the wrong idea here."

"Tactical situation's been in flux," Yeltzin said to Gideon. "We've gone from controlled chaos to complete mess and back again more than once. Ibarras are evaccing their civilians through the spaceport. Colonel Martel's got us holding the line while that happens."

"And in the absence of further orders, we'll attack," Morris said.

"Where's Martel?" Gideon asked.

"Sir, I don't exactly know where the hell we are." Morris pointed to the ceiling. "Locals don't need maps and have yet to lead us astray."

Gideon looked up at the legionnaire.

"Can you get these civilians to an evac point? Got one on a stretcher," the armor said.

"I can," the Ibarran said, pointing toward the

Kesaht lines. "But we won't get far with those tanks on us, and we'll move slow with the wounded."

"I'll deal with the tank," Gideon said. "I didn't come here to babysit. Aignar." The other armor's helm popped up out of the tunnel and he lifted two civilians up. "I'll draw their fire, you attack once I have their attention. Cha'ril will transport the wounded with the locals. Link back up with us after that."

"Comms are out," Cha'ril's voice echoed out of the tunnel. "How do I find you?"

"Is the cavalry here? How many of you are down there?" Morris leaned over to peer into the tunnel.

"We'll find Colonel Martel. He'll be where the fighting's the hardest. Meet us there," Gideon said. He crawled out of the building and rose to his full height. The Ibarrans on the second floor tensed up as he looked at them.

Gideon pointed two fingers at his optics, then one finger at the Ibarrans, and took off at a trot down the street.

"Wait—how are you going to get past the tank's shields?" Morris called out.

Gideon charged the magnetic accelerators in his twin gauss cannons as his audio receptors filtered through the noise of the city and pinpointed the Kesaht tank a block away. It was moving forward slowly. Gideon ran along the street and then went prone. He spotted the tank's treads through the windows and aimed his gauss barrels at the center of his target.

He fired. The twin bolts blew through the walls and struck the tank's flank. There was a flare of blue light around the treads...and it lurched forward.

Gideon popped back onto his feet just as the tank's turret boomed. Flying bricks and glass bounced off his armor as the shell tore through the building behind him.

"Damn it!" Gideon charged through the building between him and the tank, betting his life on the tank's reloading the turret slower than he could close the distance. The tank was squat, and the hull bore tribal markings. A tangle of still-bloody bones hung from halfway down the barrel.

Suddenly, a machine gun in the upper turret opened up. Bullets beat against Gideon's armor as he veered to one side, keeping out of the way of the turret as it turned toward him. He felt each hit against his armor, heard the bang through his suit's audio and through the womb as the machine gun assaulted him.

Gideon ducked underneath the turret just as it fired again. He punched the machine-gun port and crushed the red-hot muzzle into scrap. Then, grabbing the base of the turret's tube, he swung himself onto the forward edge of the tank. Gideon lifted his right foot and his diamond-tipped anchor stabbed out of his heel. He rammed the spike into the driver's hatch and felt it hit home—into something soft.

As Gideon slammed his fingertips into the edge of a top hatch and dug into the metal seam, he heard the squeal of treads and looked up. Another tank rolled into the next intersection and brought its turret to bear.

Gideon dropped down in front of the tank he'd been standing on and ducked.

The other tank fired on its fellow Kesaht, the shell breaking through the rear armor and hitting the ammunition stored in the back of the turret. The tank exploded, sending Gideon flying into a wall that crumbled against the impact.

His HUD went red as his armor tried to parse the damage across his front. Gideon found himself in a seat made of bricks, his arms propped up in the building's wall. Bits of the destroyed tank were embedded across his chest and legs, still smoking.

The other tank rolled forward. Gideon tried to get up, but his servos locked up.

The tank aimed its barrel at him, and Gideon stared into the darkness of the muzzle as he fought to stand up.

Aignar landed on the tank, grabbed the tube, and pulled it up, the metal groaning. The tank fired, sending the round into the air and missing Gideon.

The barrel snapped in half with a crack and smoke wafted out of the stubby section still attached to the turret. Aignar impaled his improvised stake into the top of the turret, collapsing the top hatch. He tossed the tube aside, jammed his gauss cannon arm into the opening, and fired a single bullet that ricocheted through the inside of the tank.

Aignar jumped off as smoke billowed out of the turret and flames licked the edges of the hatch.

"Sir?" Aignar grabbed Gideon's hand and pulled him to his feet.

"The shields are the best thing on those hunks of junk." Gideon plucked a bit of shrapnel from his chest and dropped it. He bent a knee, then locked it out with a snap. "Close-range concussion, had to restart the actuators."

"Where to now?" Aignar asked.

Gideon pointed to tracer fire and explosions to the south of the city.

"There. Martel will be there."

CHAPTER 25

Admiral Lettow fought back a curse as the destroyer *Dempsey* exploded inside his holo tank, her death taking a number of the Kesaht fighters down with her. He rewound the last few minutes of the destroyer's life in the tank.

"Porcupine rounds proving more effective than our simulations," Paxton said. "Though I don't know what will run out first—the munitions or their fighters."

Lettow swung the holo back to the battle. His picket ships kept up a constant barrage of missiles that burst into self-guiding munitions in the middle of Kesaht fighter formations. His capital ships hung back, their batteries trained on the oncoming enemy armada, still too far away to engage with any degree of success. The enemy had fed its fighters into the meat grinder of the Terran Union's anti-void craft munitions. They'd managed to overwhelm a few destroyers at significant losses, tactics no human commander would use.

"Thirty minutes until artillery ships have range," Paxton said.

Lettow zoomed in on the Ibarra ships. Most of Makarov's fleet had taken position over the main city, her fighters and landers making constant trips between the city and ships. Two carriers and escorts had joined the Terran formation, but their captains had remained tight-lipped, sending out strikes to beat back any incursions through Lettow's screen.

A single Ibarran cargo ship remained over the northern pole, a squadron of battle cruisers guarding it.

"Ericson," the admiral said, pulling up a screen for his fellow commander.

"—said I want flechette rounds loaded. This

is combat, not a training exercise. The safety protocols are secondary to getting the goddamn munitions loaded, Gunnery." Ericson didn't yell, but the tone of her voice could have cut steel. She finally noticed the open channel with Lettow.

"*Ardennes*?"

"*Normandy,* what are the Ibarras doing? Why did Makarov leave so much of her line back with a cargo ship?" Lettow asked.

"Decent question. Better question is why we're taking it on the chin while she holds back."

"You have the fight. It's time to see how committed the Ibarras really are to this joint defense." Lettow muted Ericson but kept her line open so she could monitor his next hail.

Makarov appeared a few seconds later. He considered this young woman, who did bear a resemblance to the long-lost admiral and hero of Earth.

"Lettow, I'm impressed with how well your ships are—"

"What are you doing with that cargo ship?"

Lettow snapped. "You've got a token force with me while most of your guns are parked over the city."

"This is an evacuation." Makarov's eyes glittered. "The more ships I put to that effort, the sooner it will end."

"The void is no place for ships full of civilians, Admiral," Lettow said. "One hit to the cargo hold and they're breathing vacuum. You're young, but you're not stupid."

"Why don't I establish void superiority before conducting the evacuation, just like the manual demands? Because the Crucible is down and will be inoperable for days, that's why. I've got my own way home," she said.

"There's only one Crucible in this system." Lettow shook his head. "We need a solution to the Kesaht that are here before we worry about an exit."

"Incorrect," Makarov said. "I told you we have our own way home."

Lettow reached into the holo and zoomed in on the mysterious cargo ship. The bays were open and ship tenders with oversized engines brought long segments of dark stone stacked in the ship like cordwood.

"You have a modular gate..." Lettow said.

"Indeed. Your government has their R&D program in the works. The Ibarra Nation's had a greater need for the technology and we have a number of working prototypes," Makarov said.

"That's how your fleet escaped Oricon," Lettow said.

"And that's how you'll get your ships out," she said. "Unless you want to slug it out with the entire Kesaht armada. You hold the line until I've got the civilians away, then you've got a one-way ticket to a nearby system with a Crucible."

Lettow ran a quick simulation in the holo tank.

"The Kesaht armada will reach the planet in less than four hours. You're going to get every civilian, your fleet and mine through that gate before then?"

"No." She frowned. "As usual, the only resource we don't have enough of is time. But we can slow the Kesaht…just need a bulldog. Which is where you come in."

"Details. Now."

CHAPTER 26

A constant whine filled Major Whitelaw's ears as he came to. Feeling pain around his ankles, he rolled onto his side and found both his boots in a small fire. He crawled forward, the left side of his body stinging from the pain of a dozen lacerations.

As his hearing returned, the sound of gauss fire and shouting came through and he saw a gauss rifle jutting out from under a broken armor panel from the city's wall. Whitelaw grabbed it and pulled out half a weapon, the capacitor sparking as he tossed it aside.

"Hanson!" The major crawled onto his knees and that hurt too. The walls shook as Kesaht artillery beyond the walls kept up their barrage. "Anybody?"

The bunker he'd been in had taken a direct hit. He touched a fallen Ranger and the cracked screen on his faceplate showed a flat line for the other Ranger's heart. The snap of gauss fire came through the door that hung off the top hinge. He coughed and shouldered his way through.

Rangers and legionnaires stood on the parapet, firing over the side and ducking as Kesaht energy bolts snapped up at them.

A legionnaire grabbed Whitelaw by the shoulders. The cross on his faceplate faded away and he saw Hanson's face.

"Status," Whitelaw mumbled, tasting blood but choking it back.

"Wave attack," Hanson said, pressing an Ibarra pistol into his hand. "I've got close air sport coming in, but it won't help us."

"They teach you to quit in your legion? Rangers always…accomplish…" He leaned against the wall and felt a pain deep in his stomach, though he didn't look at the wound. Knowing how bad it was wouldn't make any difference.

"Shut up and shoot." Hanson turned Whitelaw toward the firing port. The Ibarran hefted a large gauss rifle and fired down the wall.

Whitelaw put his finger to the pistol's trigger and pulled a frag grenade off his harness. Ignoring the blood on the weapon, he flicked the pin away with his thumb, looked around the firing port, and froze.

Climbing with their bare hands, thousands of Rakka soldiers swarmed up the walls and open-topped transports disgorged more of the foot soldiers behind the tide of bodies. Sanheel officers moved amongst the Rakka still clambering to get up the walls, the Sanheel beating at the Rakka, kicking some for no reason Whitelaw could tell.

A line of Kesaht tanks in the plains beyond the walls fired, pounding the defensive positions atop the walls.

Whitelaw tossed the grenade over the edge and emptied the pistol into the oncoming wave as fast as he could pull the trigger. Accuracy meant little when it was almost impossible to miss.

"We need armor support!" Hanson ducked back as Kesaht energy bolts sprang off the parapet.

"I thought you said your armor was here." Whitelaw reached around his back and removed a thick metal rod.

"They're to the east, dealing with a breakthrough." The legionnaire touched the side of his helmet. "Still two minutes out on that air support."

"At least you have comms," Whitelaw said. "Going to have to do this the old-fashioned way."

He pulled the cap on one end of the rod back and set the color of the star cluster to red. Then he twisted the rod, feeling it click through his gloves.

Whitelaw struck the cap against the metal floor of the parapet and a red spark the size of his fist spat out and flew down the street, casting blood-colored light that shone off broken windows. Two more sparks shot off, then Whitelaw tossed it aside.

"If they saw that, my armor will come."

Whitelaw looked over and found Hanson slumped against the parapet.

"Hanson?" He gave the Ibarran a shake, and he fell back, still eyes staring up at the sky, a bloody hole in his chest. The muted sound of shouting came from the legionnaire's helmet.

Whitelaw twisted the helmet free and gently laid the dead man to one side.

"This is Shrike Team Delta, how copy?" came from the helmet.

"Delta, this is Major Whitelaw, 85th Ranger Regiment. Hanson is down. ETA?"

Whitelaw hefted the legionnaire's oversized rifle and was struggling to wield it with one hand when a Rakka jumped over the parapet and howled. A Ranger shot it in the head and threw the body off the side before it could hit the ground. Whitelaw heard a growl and swung the heavy rifle up just as another Rakka stuck its head through a firing port. One squeeze of the trigger blew it in half. The head and shoulder landed at Whitelaw's feet and he kicked it away.

"Enemy is too close!" shouted the pilot on the other end of the radio. "No way we can—"

"I know how goddamn close they are! Fire on my position, you understand? Fire on my position!"

A hairy Rakka hand reached down and grabbed Whitelaw by the wrist. He pulled against the alien, his power armor proving more than a match for the Rakka's muscles. The Rakka landed in a puddle of blood and swiped at Whitelaw.

The Ranger grabbed the alien by the throat and stared into the beady red eyes. He slammed Hanson's helmet into the Rakka's head, cracking the cybernetic implants on the side of its skull, and continued to beat the helmet against the Rakka's head over and over as the sound of jet engines closed in.

****

"Are you sure?" Martel came to a stop as he looked toward the southern wall.

"Red star cluster, I'm positive," Tongea said.

The thunderclap of bombs reverberated through the city.

"Get Matthias and Duncan." Martel pointed to where the rest of his lance was digging through a collapsed building. He looked to an elevated highway and saw the red armor of an Uhlan. A line of vehicles loaded down with civilians drove past the armor. Martel turned up the power on his IR transmitter.

"Sobieski, the battle's not going well," he sent.

The Uhlan turned around.

"Keine Schlacht, eine Rettungsaktion," Sobieski said.

"English."

"Sorry. It's not a battle—it's a retreat. Did you see that red star cluster?" Sobieski said.

"I'm moving south to support and so are you. Do you have comms with the Odinsons?"

"It's spotty. I'll relay your order."

"Move. Situation may be in doubt." Martel closed the channel and ran south, Tongea and the rest of their lance falling in behind him.

He turned a corner and found a building collapsed across the highway, the frame still largely intact, as if it had been built on its side, leading to the southern wall. A tower of smoke billowed up in the distance.

Kesaht crescent-shaped fighters fought with the Ibarra fighters with the forward-swept wings.

"Rook rook!" carried down the highway.

"Don't sound like ours," Tongea said. He stepped into the toppled building and worked his way through to the other side. Martel went through the floor next to him.

Rakka poured over the wall and through a wide gap blasted in the parapet. The aliens clustered at the bottom, chanting and banging their fists rhythmically against the ground. A larger Rakka with a half-cloak made of bones climbed onto a bus and held a human head high.

On the remains of the city's walls behind the

shaman were human corpses spiked to the wall. Ibarra legionnaires hung next to Terran Rangers.

"Rook!" the shaman shouted and the Rakka beat at the ground faster.

"*Kor gaela human!*" The shaman shook the head, then set it at its feet. Sanheel slapped at the Rakka and beat their rifle butts against their heads, but the Rakka were entranced by the shaman.

"Looks like a war dance," Tongea said.

"There's too many of them, not enough of us." Martel looked down the highway. "We need the Uhlans and Odinsons before we attack."

The shaman pointed down the highway and the Rakka tore at their faces and chests, many of them drawing blood. Rakka at the edge of the mass broke away and ran down the highway, then doubled back toward the shaman.

"We need time…let me show them my war face," Tongea said.

"What? Tongea—" Martel reached over to the Maori as he broke through the crumbling walls and into the open.

Tongea's speakers hummed as he turned them up to full volume. The Rakka went silent as the war machine approached. Tongea raised a foot and slammed it into the ground in a wide stance.

"*Ka mate!*" The words reverberated down the highway as Tongea beat his forearms against his legs with the clang of metal on metal. "*Ka mate! Ka ora! Ka ora!*"

"Sir," Duncan said, "what the hell is he doing?"

"The haka." Martel looked back and saw the rest of his armor racing toward them.

Tongea braced both arms across his chest.

"*Tenei te tangata!*" blared from his speakers. He went to one knee and pounded a fist into the road so hard it cracked the street.

A Sanheel brought its long rifle up, but Rakka mobbed it, ripping the rifle away and beating the Sanheel about the head and shoulders with it.

Tongea stomped his feet against the road and slapped his hands against his chest.

"*Nana nei I tiki!*" Tongea beat at his chest

again and again. "*Mai! Whakawhiti te ra!*"

The shaman picked the head up and shook it at Tongea.

"*Ah, upane!*" Tongea took a single step forward. "*Ka upane!*" Another step.

The Rakka swarmed toward Tongea.

"*Whiti te ra!*" Tongea slashed a thumb across his throat and beat his fists to his chest as thousands of aliens bore down on him like a tidal wave.

"*Ferrum corde!*" came from the building and ten suits of armor burst out of the wreck and charged the Rakka.

Tongea clapped his hands against the head of a blood-crazed Rakka as it jumped toward him. Its skull splattered and Tongea crushed two more aliens with a single swipe of his hand. He brought his rotary cannon up and sent the barrels spinning.

Bullets ripped through the Rakka, slaughtering them by the dozens each second. Tongea fired his gauss cannons into a Sanheel screaming at his uncontrolled soldiers and blew its chest open.

Tongea pointed over the Rakka at the shaman still on top of the bus.

"*Ka mate!*" Tongea charged toward the shaman, and Rakka scrambled out of the way. The shaman dropped the head and shrank toward the edge of the bus. Tongea grabbed him by the leg, hoisted the alien into the air, and slammed it into the ground, cracking its bones. Then Tongea slammed his heel against the shaman's head and ground it into paste.

The Rakka faltered, their battle rage suddenly gone.

The armor did not falter. They spread into a circle around the aliens and killed them with bursts from their rotary cannons, and with their fists and feet until they met each other in the center.

Purple blood stained Tongea from his knees to his boots, elbows to fingertips.

Martel looked across the field of dead, then pounded a fist against his breastplate in salute to Tongea. Tongea nodded, then looked to the east.

"More…there are more to fight," Tongea said.

"Let's find them," Martel said.

CHAPTER 27

Lettow waited as his artillery ships maneuvered between his ships and the oncoming Kesaht armada. The Kesaht battleships spread out in reaction, but not as fast as they had the last few times Lettow had feinted with his long-range ships.

"You think she's setting us up?" Ericson asked.

"Funny thing about our artillery ships," he said. "They can range Makarov's Crucible as well as the Kesaht. If she doesn't deliver, they'll destroy her gate before it's even finished. Self-repair or not, if she hangs us out to dry, she'll get to deal with everything that gets through us."

"You didn't tell her this."

"Some things are best left implied. Ready fleet maneuver in five…four…" Lettow felt the *Ardennes* shift ever so slightly as their fleet turned, sending them on a course that would cross ahead of the Kesaht armada.

"Makarov sent the first signal," Ericson said, looking away from her screen. "Activity on the moon's surface detected."

"Gunnery, engage fire plan Alpha-nine," Lettow ordered.

The artillery ships reoriented, and the long rail cannon vanes pointed toward a Kesaht battleship at the front of the formation.

Hypervelocity rounds shot out. Lettow tracked their course through the holo tank…and more rail cannon shots rose up from the moon. Dozens of rail shots converged in the Kesaht formation. Smaller enemy ships tried to set themselves between the incoming threats, but the sheer volume of fire and the close-packed formation gave the Kesaht few chances.

Two battleships broke apart along with another dozen escort ships. Lettow allowed himself a smile as two cruisers collided.

"Enemy strength decreased by eleven percent," Paxton said. She frowned as more rail cannon rounds tracked up from the moon.

"They have more batteries?" Lettow asked.

"Negative, sir," Paxton said. "Same point of origin. Their rate of fire is a hell of a lot better than our surface emplacements."

A chill went down Lettow's back. The Ibarras had significant defenses around their colony, far more guns that could put up a significant weight of fire than intelligence anticipated.

"Artillery ships, keep to the firing order, target priority on the leading ships," Lettow said.

Claw ships at the fore of the armada accelerated, reaching toward the human ships. He reached into the tank to redirect a frigate squadron, but Ericson beat him to the punch.

"Come on." Lettow tapped a finger against the edge of his holo tank. Three Kesaht battleships broke off from the main formation and changed course toward the moon. Even with the Kesaht breaking off to deal with the threat behind them, they outnumbered his two fleets by more than four-to-one.

Makarov's portrait flashed, and he touched the edge.

"Admiral, we've a slight complication," she said. "The arrival of so many fleets upset the graviton field around the planets. I've had to rework the firing solution."

"Now you realize this?" Lettow asked.

"I need you to hold them for nine minutes." Makarov swallowed hard. "That's more—twice what we planned—time under fire, but that's the only way this will work."

"Your mistake will cost lives," Lettow said. "My sailors' lives."

"If we don't do this right, we'll all die," Makarov said. "Trust me."

A timer appeared over her picture.

"Kesaht fighters breaking for the artillery

ships," Paxton said.

"My fleet will fight, Makarov." Lettow cut the line to the Ibarran admiral. "XO, have the artillery squadrons complete their next fire mission and burn back to our formation." He watched as his ships continued their intercept course toward the Kesaht advance.

At their current speeds, the Kesaht would cross the T in front of his ships, exposing the Terran ships to full broadsides from the aliens. He was bumbling into a beating, and the Kesaht commander had to see it.

"*Ardennes*," Ericson said, "I ever tell you what the older Makarov did with the *Breitenfeld* during the Toth incursion?"

"I've studied the battle," Lettow said. "She used the *Breitenfeld*'s jump drives to drop you inside their formation, then Valdar let loose laser-guided torps that tore the heart out of the Toth fleet."

"And Makarov sent her 8th Fleet into the Toth guns to hold them in place. This new one thinks and acts like her 'mother,'" Ericson said. "I just don't see how it's possible she can be who she says she is. The math is wrong."

"We'll connect the dots later," Lettow said. The *Ardennes* shuddered as her rail batteries opened fire. "We've got to sell this attack or nothing else matters."

CHAPTER 28

Roland loaded another heavy gauss round into his Mauser and fired from the hip on a Kesaht tank as its turret slewed toward him. The round tore through the shields and hit the thin armor covering the fuel cells. The tank exploded, tossing the turret straight up like a flipped coin.

He charged forward, slipping another round off the side of the large rifle and into the chamber. Around a church, the Kesaht had a built hasty barricade of electrified wires running between shield emitters. Rakka and Sanheel scrambled behind the shields, the sudden destruction of the tank outside the perimeter goading them into action

356

like a kicked hive.

"We're here for leadership," Nicodemus said. "Second emitter from the left of the tank."

Roland hefted his rifle to his shoulder and took aim, still running forward.

"Fire!"

The three Mausers let off a ripple of shots that overwhelmed the emitter. Electricity looped back through the wires, stabbing out and frying Rakka that were too close. The emitter exploded as the armor charged through the breach.

Roland locked his rifle onto his back and lowered his shoulder at a Sanheel that burst through the church doors. He crushed the alien against the stone façade, earning a crack of bones and a wet grunt as the Kesaht officer died.

A group of Rakka jumped on him, stabbing at the joints of his armor with serrated knives. Roland backhanded one off his leg, sending it on a quick but brief flight into the side of the church. He heard the whirl of a rotary cannon from Nicodemus or Morrigan and felt a tug as a Rakka on his back was shot off.

"Rook! Rook!" an alien yelled as it pulled the pin on two grenades and charged at Roland.

He kicked the Rakka and sent it barreling into another group of their infantry as they came around the corner. The grenades exploded and saved Roland the trouble of dealing with them.

"In! Go!" Nicodemus charged through a stained-glass window.

Roland heard gauss fire as he bashed down the main doors.

The inside of the church angled down and pews had been broken and pushed against the entrance. The main floor now held Kesaht equipment and holo projectors. A Sanheel in deep-purple armor stood where the pulpit had been, in front of a pile of dead human bodies that lay behind him.

The officer held an Ibarran soldier against his chest, shielding himself. The man bled from a gash down one side of his face and his chest. He was still breathing, but on the verge of bleeding to death.

Dead Rakka and a lithe Ixion were strewn among the command center. Roland crushed the broken pews like they were dried twigs as he and the rest of his new lance advanced into the church. He aimed his gauss cannons at the Sanheel's face, but one hit to the alien's shields would probably kill the soldier.

"It doesn't matter," said the purple-clad alien. "All your kind will die. What matters is whether any will serve, reduce the stain on your species by toiling for our great truth."

"I've dealt with this before," Roland said, lessening the magnetic hold of the sword locked to his left hip.

"Witness the future." The Sanheel wrapped a hand around his human shield's head and snapped his neck.

Nicodemus and Morrigan opened fire instantly, shredding the Sanheel and the dead man into a bloody mess. That neither of them attempted to spare the dead man's form told Roland just how ruthless the Ibarran armor had become.

"Don't wreck the equipment," Nicodemus said, going to a blood-splattered holo tank and holding up a hand. His wrist opened and a scanner node extended out. "They're communicating through their own interference. Maybe we can learn how."

"Perimeter." Morrigan pointed at the other side of the church and Roland stepped around the equipment. The church walls had been pierced by bullets, and most of the stained-glass windows along the sides were shattered. The sound of the raging battle filtered through. The muffled *crump* of explosions, snap of Rakka weapons, and roar of fighters locked in combat made him feel like they would never leave the city.

One window remained mostly intact, depicting an older suit of armor pinning a Xaros Master to the ground with a glass and gold sword. The Xaros looked like a demon of fire and obsidian, grasping up at the armor as it died.

Roland caught movement out another

window, a group of Rakka moving away from the command center.

"They're not coming for us?" Roland asked.

"Maybe they know when they can't win," Morrigan said.

"Got this one." Nicodemus turned his scanner to a barrel-shaped object with a crown of crystals.

A soft ululation sounded over Roland's head. He jerked his cannons up, but there was nothing in the rafters. Sunlight filtered through cracks in the ceiling and the wooden beams rattled in tune with distant explosions.

"Did you hear that?" Roland asked.

"Brave meat. Foolish meat," hissed from the front of the church. Roland scanned through his visuals filters but found nothing.

"Heroes die. They always die," echoed around them.

Nicodemus snapped his hand back into place and drew his sword. The blade extended from the hilt and gleamed as light from the Kesaht equipment reflected off the razor-sharp edge. He backed toward the center of the room, Morrigan and Roland following his lead.

"The last one demands true born." The ululation returned, louder this time. "These are always true born. Give yourself to him. Honor yourselves."

"We give nothing," Nicodemus said. "Come and claim us."

A ribbon of light deformed along the wall just above the broken windows. The deformity leaped at Roland, and he had just enough time to throw a punch as it slammed into him. His fist connected, and a stealth field collapsed as the impact shoved him into Morrigan's back.

A Toth warrior, clad in bulky crystal armor, latched clawed feet against Roland's waist and legs. The reptilian reared up, raised its arms to the side, and struck at either side of Roland's helm. Roland got his arms up and blocked the blows. The Toth pressed his arms in, grasping for his optics. Roland's actuators strained against the alien's strength and found he couldn't overpower this foe.

Inside the Toth's multifaceted faceplate, Roland saw a forked tongue press against the crystal.

Roland raised his arms up, then slammed his upper body toward the ground. The Toth took the brunt of the impact and Roland got his cannon arm free. He fired a double shot into the Toth's chest, cracking the armor. The Toth released its hold on Roland's waist and legs and attempted to squirm away.

Roland extended his fingers and drove them into the broken armor like a dagger. As the strike punctured the crystal and his hand invaded the flesh beneath, the Toth let off a high-pitched scream. Roland gripped a handful of organs in the alien's chest cavity and ripped his hand out. Yellow blood bubbled out of the wound and Roland tossed a beating heart aside.

Roland looked aside and saw Morrigan lying on her back, a Toth warrior bent over her clawing at her breastplate. She was still fighting, knocking aside blows as best she could.

Roland drew his sword, brought the hilt back to his hip as the blade extended—ready to ram the weapon into the Toth so focused on Morrigan—and caught a blur of motion to his side just as he struck at the Toth. A glint of light passed in front of his helm and a blow jarred his sword out of his hand.

A Toth with a crystal-edged halberd jabbed the spike on his weapon at Roland. The tip struck his chest and pushed into the armor, glancing off his womb. Roland's HUD went berserk with warnings as he brought a hand up and chopped at the haft.

The halberd broke, but the axe head and spike remained embedded in his chest.

The Toth swung the other end of his weapon, tipped with a spiked mace head, against Roland's lower back. The impact rattled him inside his womb. He sent an impulse for his gauss cannons to reload and swung a hasty fist at the Toth. The snap of two gauss rounds loading into place echoed through the church.

The warrior ducked the blow and brought the mace down toward Roland's head. Roland caught the Toth by the wrist and punched at it with his other hand. The Toth brought its foreleg up, grabbed the gauss cannon arm, and used all its strength to push Roland's aim away…and straight toward the Toth still beating on Morrigan.

Roland fired and blew an arm off the Toth over his lance mate.

There was a flash of crystal and the Toth still grappling with Roland whipped its tail up and struck him in the helm. His faceplate cracked and his vision swam as his armor tried to compensate for the damage. He ducked his helm down as the next strike dented the black armor and broke antennae loose.

The Toth grabbed his wrist with another foot and stretched his arms out. Roland felt the strain on his servos as the alien tried to tear him apart.

"I'll have you, meat!" the alien hissed. "I'll feast on your—"

A sword point burst through its face from

behind and it went limp. Roland shrugged the corpse off just as Morrigan set a boot against the Toth's back and ripped her sword free. Nicodemus kicked at a pile of three dead warriors at his feet.

"Thanks," she said.

"Same," Roland responded as he reached for his sword hilt and missed, grabbing at air. "I can't tell if it's my servos or optics that are off." He tried again, but his fingers refused to grasp.

Nicodemus picked up Roland's sword, returned the blade to the hilt, and slapped it against the mag lock.

"It's both," he said. "Your armor will compensate for the damage. Give it a minute."

"No more speculation," Morrigan said. "The Toth are alive, and they're behind the Kesaht."

"Lady Ibarra will need proof to show Earth and the rest of the galaxy." Nicodemus ripped a hand and forearm off a Toth warrior and shook out the yellow blood.

"The Toth…" Roland looked over one of the crystal-armored bodies, wondering just how they designed their exoskeletons to match his strength. "What does this mean?"

"There will be no peace between us and the Kesaht," Nicodemus said. "Not now. Not ever. The Toth twisted them into their servants. Made them fanatics. And the only way to deal with the true believer is to kill them. No middle ground. No compromise."

"I'm oddly comfortable with that," Morrigan said.

The ground shook, a low rumble that reverberated through the church.

"That wasn't an explosion," Roland said.

The rumble returned and a shadow passed over the street outside. Roland went to the stained-glass image of the armor slaying the Xaros Master and saw, several blocks away, the top of a walker moving between buildings. The design was more delicate than anything he'd seen from the Kesaht before: a cone-shaped head and spindly vanes extending up from the shoulders. It stopped in an intersection, and Roland saw it had large crystals mounted to the side of its egg-shaped torso instead of arms. Thick legs extended down from hip actuators beneath the torso. The opal-blue surface gleamed in the sunlight.

"I've not seen one of those before," Roland said. "Is it new? It looks new."

Shields flared around the walker as gauss bullets struck home. Panels in the top of the torso opened and missiles fired, arcing up and away. It swung to one side and the crystals lit up. Roland dimmed his optics as the crystals let off a torrent of energy that obliterated a residential building. It continued on, heading for the spaceport.

"It's new." Nicodemus lifted his chin. "Command says the Mausers aren't getting through. Every time we shoot at it, it responds with missiles and it slags another building. Air support can't get near it."

"Then we hit it with rail cannons," Roland said.

"Shields are too strong," Nicodemus said. "Look at this."

He sent video of the walker under fire. Ley lines of energy appeared along the shields as they flared.

"The emitters must be there," Morrigan said, highlighting spots on the walker's torso.

"They have to drop the shields to get the missiles through," Roland said. "You saw the way they arced. We'd have to come in from the top."

"Here." Nicodemus brought up a map of the city and tagged several buildings along the most direct route from the walker's location to the spaceport. "Another lance can poke the bear for us. It's up to us to take it down. Let's move."

****

Roland ran down an alley, his boots crushing fallen masonry. Emerging out the other side, he saw the high walls around the spaceport. Turrets let off ripples of fire, punctuated by tracers as they pushed back against any Kesaht fighter that got too close.

He slid under a highway overpass and ran beneath it toward the target buildings, three tall residential structures along a highway.

Nicodemus' location pinged on his HUD, just ahead of Roland.

"The governor's got a little more than half the population to safety," Nicodemus said. "They can't risk another big hauler so long as this walker's out here."

"Getting off this rock is one thing," Roland said. "How'll you get back to Navarre? Smashing the Crucible is pretty standard practice for any planetary assault. Could be days before it self-repairs."

"How about you worry about the walker and let the squids worry about the wormholes?" Morrigan asked.

Light flared over the overpass like a lightning strike. Roland caught a glimpse of the Kesaht walker between buildings and heard the rumble of a collapsing structure in the distance.

"You two up tower A," Nicodemus said.

"I'll go B. I'll signal the other lances once we're in place."

The stomp of the walker's advance echoed around them as Roland ran through a chain-link fence and a playground. Toys and small carts littered the area, testament to a sudden evacuation and parents leaving with upset children. Looking at a doll and stuffed bear left in a puddle, he hoped whoever left them behind was already safely away in orbit.

"Grip the outer frame." Morrigan sent Roland a blueprint overlay for the building.

"Got it." Roland jumped up, punched into the building's façade, and found the metal skeleton. He braced his feet against the wall and began climbing, punching through the concrete and lifting himself higher.

Morrigan laughed, a sound that froze Roland in his tracks.

"What was that?" He looked where she was climbing a dozen yards away.

"Just remembered an old TV show my

grandfather used to watch. It was ridiculous," she said. "Keep moving. If the walker gets past us, we'll be silhouetted against the skyline so well, we deserve to get shot."

"Right." Roland tested a foot against a windowsill and broke a segment of the wall away. It tumbled down and shattered against the parking lot.

The walker stopped. Through the glass on the other side of the building, Roland saw the walker's helm turn toward them.

Roland pressed himself against the metal bar just beneath the concrete outer wall. Rays of light shot through the cracked glass windows...and the walker began moving again.

"I would slap the back of your head for getting that thing's attention," Morrigan said, resuming her climb. "But the frame must've masked us and now it won't suspect an attack from here. Quick thinking."

"I'm making this up as I go along," Roland said, pulling himself over the edge of the roof and lying facedown next to Morrigan. Both had their palms pressed against the roof as the snap of heavy gauss weapons echoed in the distance.

"Get ready," Nicodemus called out from the top of the next building over.

Like a sudden dawn, light grew from the walker's crystal cannons.

"What about the missiles?" Roland asked.

The walker's cannons fired, sending off a wave of heat that sent steam and smoke roiling off the roof.

Nicodemus' building rocked from side to side, then collapsed in on itself with a cloud of pulverized concrete dust. Roland watched in horror as it fell, floor by floor.

"Nicodemus?" Morrigan lifted her head up.

Kesaht missiles shot up and roared directly overhead.

"Now! Now's our chance!" Roland popped up and sprinted toward the edge. Morrigan followed a step behind.

He leapt off the roof and fell through the smoke of a passing missile. The walker's head and shoulders were a few stories below. Roland wished he'd kept his jet pack as he hurtled toward the walker, knowing that just a little push would send him to a decent landing.

Instead, his heels clipped the edge of the walker's shields and pitched him forward. He belly-flopped against the walker's hull and started sliding down. He slammed a hand against the blue surface, but the metal didn't yield to his armor's strength. Roland slid toward the edge faster and faster.

He flailed against the hull, then two fingers gripped an open missile port that whirred as it brought up a new munition and launched it with a rocket flare. Ignoring the damage as the heat threatened to fuse his knuckles solid, Roland swung a foot up and hooked it on to the port's edge and hauled himself up. He grabbed the edge with his other hand as another missile launched, scorching his armor and sending static through his HUD.

Part of him felt embarrassed, taking this abuse, but it was better than falling.

"Roland! Take my hand." Morrigan reached

down from the shoulder and pulled Roland up.

Roland steadied himself as the walker began moving. He looked back at Nicodemus' wrecked building, then to Morrigan.

"Now what?" he asked.

"We're not here for the view," Morrigan said, going to the walker's head. The glass panes of its "face" were turned toward the spaceport. She punched the back of its head, leaving a divot in the blue metal. She struck again and again, whaling on it like it was a punching bag.

The walker stopped and the head spun around. An Ixio sat in the cockpit, mouth agape as Morrigan hammered a fist against the glass.

"Roland! The emitter!" she shouted.

Roland pulled his Mauser off his back and went prone on the walker's shoulder. He looked over the edge...and saw nothing but the torso's smooth surface.

"I can't see it!" he shouted.

Across the highway, gauss fire opened up, peppering the walker's shields. Motes of energy flowed off the hull…and Roland spied a focal point. He fired his Mauser and blew off a fragment the size of the car hood.

The walker swung around, turning its back to the direction of gauss fire.

"Get the other emitter!" Morrigan kept one hand gripped against the glass edge of the cockpit while she pounded the other against a crack in the glass. The Ixio inside shouted and waved its spindly arms about.

"They have to shoot—" Missile fire from the opposite shoulder cut him off. He spun around and crawled toward the other side, nearly slipping off as the walker lumbered forward.

A line of light formed a square between him and Morrigan on the hull. A hatch popped up and an Ixio stood there, holding a rifle that pulsed with blue light. The alien hefted the weapon out of the hatch and aimed it at Morrigan.

Roland slapped a hand around the Ixio's skinny neck and flung it away from the walker. It struck the inner shield wall and vanished in a snap of electricity. Roland jammed a foot against the hatch before it could close and stood over the opening.

A pair of Ixio looked up at him from a compartment inside the walker. Roland loaded a round into the Mauser and calmly pointed it into the opening.

"Soft hearts," Roland said, firing the high-powered shell into the walker, which tore through the deck plating. The explosion sent a gout of flame through the hatch, and cracks and smoke broke along the upper side of the walker's shell, like a creature within was trying to break out.

"Do you think that took out the emitter?" Morrigan asked.

"I'll just keep shooting it until—"

Three rail cannon shells tore across the city and struck the walker dead center, the impact and lines of ignited air preceding the booms by several seconds. The hypervelocity shells punched clear through the walker and ripped into the tower behind it. The walker tipped back and broke in half.

Roland and Morrigan went into free fall, their arc taking them toward the blasted-out tower. Roland snapped his anchor spike from his heel and struggled to keep his head and shoulders high as he fell.

He slammed one hand home against a metal spur and stabbed his anchor into the concrete. He slid down the side of the building, ripping loose masonry as he went. Turning around, he reached for Morrigan, whose fall was a few feet short of ever reaching the wall.

Roland snatched her by the forearm and she swung like a pendulum into the building. Roland felt the wall quiver as he fought to hold the weight of two suits of armor.

The walker collapsed against the base of the building, fire spreading through the broken hull, the weapon crystals shattering into small hills of glass.

"Roland, you got me?" Morrigan asked.

"Nope."

The wall broke free and they fell a hundred feet to a slope of debris. Roland landed hard, the impact sending static across his HUD and straining his hip and knee actuators. He skidded down the slope, knocking loose an avalanche of concrete fragments and dust. Morrigan beat him down, making her descent look like child's play as Roland stumbled into the street beside her.

"Well," he said, "that could've—"

Morrigan grabbed him by the shoulder and pulled him forward just before a multi-ton section of the fallen façade rumbled through where he'd been standing.

Roland tapped the side of his helm.

"I think my audio receptors were damaged," he said.

"You think?" Morrigan looked to the second building where Nicodemus had been. "I've got his emergency beacon. Come on!"

Roland followed her into the wreckage, a tangled mass of metal beams and the remnants of the lives the colonists had inside. Morrigan began tearing through a pile of beams mixed with the couches and beds of a family apartment. Roland pushed aside an elevator, his servos squealing with effort.

"Nico!" she shouted through her speakers. "You're not dying like this! You hear me! This isn't how she said you'd go!"

Roland tore open a metal casing for the elevator shaft.

"There's a void in here," he said. "This where his beacon is?"

"No," Morrigan said, shaking her helm. "Back there." She pointed to a field of rubble. "No, it's bumping around in the mess." She turned around. "I'm not...I can't leave him. But there are so many civilians left."

"The Saint never wept for him," Roland said. "That's what you meant a second ago, right? She never wept, so he's not going to die in his armor."

Morrigan touched the Templar cross on her armor.

"Then have faith, Morrigan. If he's—"

A fist punched through the rubble next to a

metal beam. Roland lifted it aside and found Nicodemus' dust-covered armor. His helm was cracked, a deep dent in the forehead.

"Nico! Are you okay?" Morrigan helped him to his feet.

"Of course I am. Why wouldn't I be?" Nicodemus' helm twisted to one side and snapped against the servos. He slapped the palm of one hand against his helm and it popped back into place. The lance commander looked over the remains of the walker.

"Good...you two did good," Nicodemus said as he pulled his feet out of the rubble.

"Was that a compliment?" Roland asked. "How much of that building fell on you?"

Nicodemus gave Roland a short punch to the shoulder.

"The last transport is almost ready," Nicodemus said as a light on the side of his quantum communicator pulsed on and off. "Full evacuation coming...not enough birds to get the crunchies out...Kesaht are pushing on the spaceport. They need us."

Nicodemus made for the highway leading to the walled spaceport, dust sloughing off him with each footfall.

"Bean head," the lance commander said, "you're doing better than I thought you would. Morrigan?"

"He's iron," she said.

"Sorry, what?" Roland asked.

"We'll fight beside you any day, Roland." Nicodemus beat a fist against his chest.

Roland slowed down as something stirred in his heart, a feeling he hadn't felt in a long time. Pride.

****

Gideon's rail cannons snapped with electricity, the forward tips glowing red-hot from the shot. The Kesaht walker lay broken against a building, fires fluttering around it.

Aignar brought his rail vanes up and slid

them down his back where they locked into their housing. His anchor came loose from the road, taking a chunk of asphalt with it, so he stomped his heel down and knocked it clear.

"You think the Ibarra armor survived?" he asked.

"It doesn't matter to me," Gideon said as he unlimbered from his firing position and pulled his anchor from the ground.

"Their tactics were unorthodox," Cha'ril said. "One of them stopped their fall against the building and caught the other. Do you think they planned their escape that way? Too many things could have gone wrong. The angle of the walker's fall. If it exploded instead of—"

"If it's stupid but it works, it isn't stupid," Aignar said. "That thing was about to fire on the spaceport and they opened a chink in the armor for us."

Gideon looked down the highway and saw a lance of Ibarra armor running toward the spaceport.

That you, Nicodemus? Gideon wondered.

Are you even here?

"Sir," Cha'ril said, pointing down the highway, opposite the direction the Ibarra armor were going. A red-armored Uhlan raised a spear over his head, traced a circle in the air with the tip, then pointed to the east.

"Regroup," Gideon growled. "More Kesaht to deal with before the traitors."

CHAPTER 29

Lettow clutched the side of his holo tank as his ship lurched from another hit. Lights flickered and a damage report flashed on a panel.

"XO, get fighters to the *Normandy*," Lettow said, reaching into the tank, but the icons sputtered each time he tried to touch them. "She's venting atmo, and that means deep structure damage."

"All squadrons are engaged," Paxton said. "Every fighter we have is in a dogfight. We've got nothing to send."

"Admiral, the Kesaht are hailing us." The communication's lieutenant waved at the command deck.

Lettow looked at the timer; still six minutes left.

He patched Makarov and Ericson into the hail. Makarov came up instantly. Ericson's visor was cracked, a patch job of tape over the left side of her helmet. Tiny spurts of air leaked out through her seals.

"Ericson, you're venting," Lettow said. She put a hand to her helmet, then exhaled long and hard, fogging the inside of her faceplate. Lettow froze as she ripped her helmet off with a puff of air as she exposed herself to the raw vacuum of a ship under combat conditions. She slapped on an emergency helm and fastened the seals around her jaw and the back of her head.

"That's better," she said. "Valdar used to make us do that drill every day."

Lettow opened the channel to the Kesaht.

A tusked Sanheel in red and gold armor filled the holo tank.

"Humans…" it rumbled, "I know one. Let-tow."

"Primus Gor'thig," Lettow said. "I remember you and your ship blowing up over Oricon."

"Death is little more than a setback for the Kesaht," Gor'thig said. Lettow couldn't help but glance at Makarov. "You've fought well, but you are outgunned and outmaneuvered. Surrender now and I will not kill you in the void. Your crews born of abomination will labor under our command until their final day. Your true born will meet a different, greater fate."

"Die free or live as slaves. You don't know humans very well, do you?" Lettow asked.

"This battle is over. The Kesaht are victorious. Surrender now or there will be no mercy," Gor'thig said.

"You're right," Makarov said. "This battle is over. I won it nine minutes ago."

"Doppler hit!" Paxton shouted. In the holo tank, macro cannon rounds appeared, all vectored toward the Kesaht ships battling the Terran fleets. Ericson waved goodbye to Gor'thig.

The bedrock of any system's defenses, macro cannons were massive cannons that could propel multi-ton shells to several percentages of the speed of light and lay fire to most any spot in the solar system—and a few more besides, if using planets to slingshot a munition.

With any such system, time was a key factor. As fast as the shells were, they took time to reach their target—time in which the target could change course. And even the slightest variance in a munition's ballistic calculations could cause a miss by thousands of miles.

To bring the Kesaht fleet into a designated kill box, then flood that kill box with simultaneous strikes from the system's macro cannons, was a tall order. But baiting Gor'thig with a poor maneuver by the Terran fleet had brought the aliens to the right place at the right time for the defenders.

Macro cannon shells whipped past the Terran fleet and tore through three Kesaht cruisers before pulverizing Gor'thig's battleship. The ship exploded into an expanding fireball that winked out in seconds, leaving a cloud of tiny fragments behind. More shells smashed into the Kesaht, turning their armada into a sky full of fireballs and shattered hull plating.

"Some claw ships survived," Paxton said. "We'll pick them off before they can regroup."

"The remaining ships near the moon are moving into low orbit," Makarov said. "Smart. I can't risk a macro hit on the moon. It could knock enough of the surface away to threaten the planet…but then again…"

"Are all your systems this well defended, Admiral Makarov?" Lettow asked.

"Attack another and you'll find out," she said.

"What do we do about the surviving Kesaht ships?" Ericson asked.

"We attack before they can damage the Crucible any further," Lettow said. He reached into the holo tank and selected the least damaged ships in the two fleets.

"I told you I'd get you to a…where?"

Makarov looked to one side, then back to Lettow and narrowed her gaze.

"Contacts," Paxton said, flinging the Crucible moon into the middle of the holo tank. Blue icons of friendly ships appeared over the horizon. Lettow froze his channel with Makarov.

"Admiral Lettow." A Terran admiral with five stars on his collar appeared. "High Command decided to send in the fleet reserve through an offset jump when you didn't check in. Good thing we brought pioneers to repair the Crucible."

"Fleet Admiral Hastings." Lettow swallowed hard. "The situation—"

"Looks to be well in hand," Hastings said. "I see the Ibarras stole the one-time gates from us too. Your artillery ships have the range. Take it out before they can escape."

"Admiral, after the Kesaht arrived, we agreed to terms with the Ibarras—"

"And the Kesaht are dealt with. I've more than enough ships to make quick work of what they've got left. We sent you here to do a job,

Lettow. Is there a problem?"

Lettow thought hard, searching for some way to de-escalate the situation.

"The Ibarras still have their macro cannons, sir. The—"

"Yes, we know where they all are now. Far out system. Shouldn't be too hard to mitigate the risk. How long until you have a firing solution?" Hastings' tone hinted that he was quickly running out of patience.

"Stand by." Lettow put the channel on hold. He looked up at Paxton and locked eyes with her.

"I'll go speak with gunnery." She winked. "Should be awhile until we can fire, what with all the…jamming, or something."

Lettow looked at Ericson's holo.

"My system's going on the fritz," she said. "I have to shut it down. Send text if there's anything pressing." She shut down her perfectly fine connection.

Lettow touched Makarov's portrait and the young woman came up.

"Makarov…how long until you can jump out?" Lettow asked.

"Just like that?" she asked. "You gain the upper hand and our deal is gone? I should have known you—"

"Not my decision. We all work for someone and Fleet Admiral Hastings sees things differently than I do. I'm trying to help you, but I need to know how long until you can jump."

"Fifteen minutes," she said.

"Best I can give you is ten." Lettow clenched his jaw as anger flashed across her face. "Ten minutes of bad computation data. Hastings isn't an idiot. If I try to stall longer than that, he'll relieve me of command and send orders direct to the artillery ships and you won't have three minutes before you're trapped here with him. Now get everyone out that you can."

"And what of those I leave behind?" she asked.

"Prisoners of war. Treated as best as I can manage."

She bit down on a knuckle, then pointed at Lettow.

"You...I can forgive for this. But now...I will never trust you—or any other Terran—again. Any harm that comes to my people I will revisit on you tenfold, you understand me?"

"Get out of here, Makarov." Lettow gave her a quick salute. "Don't take this personally, but I hope we never see each other again, because it won't be as friends."

"Best not, for your sake." She cut the channel.

"Gunnery," Lettow called across the bridge, "time on that firing solution?"

CHAPTER 30

The rotary gun on Roland's shoulder ripped through an open-topped Rakka transport, and sparks flew as the bullets punched through the thin metal and out the other side, slaughtering the aliens within. The weapon snapped toward another transport where Rakka leaped over the sides and kept spinning.

"Out of rotary ammo," Roland said and ran to the transport, jamming his hands beneath the tracks and flipping it over. Rakka went flying through the air and the transport burst through the wall of an administrative building.

An alien shot Roland in the back of the

helm, the hit cracking an antennae array and scrambling Roland's HUD. He twisted around, grabbed the Rakka by the leg, and used it as a club to crush two other Rakka while a third tried to run. Roland hurled the mangled mess of his club and splattered the two against a wall.

"Duck!" Nicodemus shouted over his speakers.

Roland fell to one knee, just as a Kesaht tank tumbled through the air right where his head and shoulders had been. The tank hit the remains of a hasty barricade put up by the Ibarran defenders and flattened two Sanheel. Looking back at the source of the flying tank, he saw Nicodemus and Morrigan finishing off the last of the Rakka.

Beyond the barricade was the spaceport, separated from the city by a chasm. Three causeways crossed over the expanse that stretched from a few dozen yards in width toward the far edge of the spaceport to almost a quarter mile wide at the causeway nearest to Roland.

Rakka and Sanheel advanced down the

causeway toward a fighting position manned by legionnaires. Remnants of Kesaht tanks and their dead littered the battlefield. This wasn't their first push on the spaceport, but it would be their last if they broke through the final line of defenses.

"They're attacking," Roland said. "How do you want to—"

A spike hit the ground near Roland's leg and bounced off his shin. Sanheel in the bottom floor of a nearby building stabbed their rifles through windows and fired on the black-clad armor.

Roland swung to the side and drew his Mauser as a spike ricocheted off his breastplate, leaving a long gash. Firing his heavy cannon, he blew out a support beam and the building collapsed, pancaking several floors onto the Sanheel attackers.

"Damn it," Morrigan said as she pulled a spike out of her left knee servo. Nicodemus tugged a spike out of his shield and tossed it aside.

"They must really want us alive," Morrigan said. "Stupid decision if they think we'll ever—"

"Watch out!" Roland yelled as he caught a

flash from the upper floors of the building behind her. He reloaded a shell as the report of Sanheel rifles broke through the air.

Nicodemus lunged toward Morrigan, his shield stretching over her. A spike struck it dead center. The next shot chipped off the edge and pierced Morrigan's back. Her armor locked up, then pitched forward like a toppled statue.

Roland fired into the building, blowing out windows and disintegrating entire floors. He put two more rounds into the enemy position before he looked to Morrigan.

Amniosis fluid leaked out of the tear in her armor. Nicodemus had one hand at the base of her helm's neck servos.

"Morrigan?" Roland asked.

"She's alive," Nicodemus said. "Hurt, but alive. Get to the bridge. The last transport isn't away yet." He pulled Morrigan's sword hilt off her leg and tossed it to Roland.

He caught it and held his arm steady.

"She needs—"

"Who are you here for!" Nicodemus roared. "For her or for your oath as a Templar?"

"For the innocent," Roland said, looking back at the spaceport where the Kesaht advance had broken through the first line of defenses around the chasm. "For us all."

"Save them." Nicodemus pointed toward the bridge, and Roland saw three Kesaht spikes embedded in Nicodemus' arm, hip, and lower back.

Roland brought Morrigan's hilt up to his helm in salute, then ran toward the battle, transforming his legs into treads and accelerating forward. At least a dozen Sanheel were charging down the causeway, their shields flaring as the fighting position fired on them.

Where the causeway met the road stretching along the outer edge of the chasm was a burnt-out Kesaht tank. Roland drove toward the tank and slapped a new round into his Mauser.

Rakka huddled next to the tank, looked up just in time to see Roland as he drove right over them, and used the tank as a ramp. Roland let his momentum carry his treads over his head as he sailed through the air. He fired his Mauser on a Sanheel at the back of the pack and hit it where its upper body met the hindquarters.

Roland slapped in another round, transformed his treads back into legs, and got off another shot that punched a Sanheel into the chasm. Then he swung himself upright and landed in the middle of the officer pack.

Roland bashed the barrel of his Mauser into the face of an alien and dropped the weapon. He grabbed his sword hilt off his thigh and hit his forearm against the same Sanheel's neck while he hooked the bottom of his sword behind its head.

Roland pulled the alien off-balance and used it as a shield between him and another alien as it lunged at him with the crackling bayonet at the end of its rifle. The alien ran his companion through. Roland jabbed the edge of his blade at the alien—that looked horrified at what it had just done to a friend—and cut a deep gash through its throat.

A blow to his back knocked Roland forward.

He rolled over the bayonetted alien, slapped a hand against a Sanheel fumbling with its rifle, and shoved forward, sending it through the railings on the side of the causeway and plummeting to its death. Drawing Morrigan's sword, he lunged to one side as a Sanheel reared up to strike him with its front hooves. Roland stabbed it in the belly and twisted the blade, then cut across and disemboweled his attacker.

He then brought both swords over his head and launched a twin slash down on his next target. The Sanheel tried to block with its rifle, but the blades broke through and hacked into its shoulders.

Roland ignored its screams, put a boot to its chest, and kicked it free.

The remaining Sanheel formed a circle around Roland, their rifles held high and bayonets pointed at him.

"You want them, you alien filth? You have to go through me! You understand!" Roland yelled.

A Sanheel lunged at him. Roland parried the strike and sent a riposte up the barrel, severing the attacker's hands at the wrists, then he ducked and made a blind swipe with his other blade through the air, connecting with a stab from behind and breaking the muzzle.

A bayonet rammed into his left arm just above the elbow. Sympathetic pain arced through Roland's body. The Sanheel wrenched the bayonet from side to side, its mouth open and bellowing.

Roland jerked away, but the enemy's blade was wedged tight.

A Sanheel ran at Roland from the other side, rifle braced against its side. Roland reversed the grip on his other sword and swung the flat of his blade into the rifle, deflecting it to one side and into his already stricken arm.

The impact ripped Roland's left arm off. His HUD pulsed with damage reports and he felt his connection to his armor lessen as the suit tried to prevent his nervous system from overloading and sending him over the red line.

Roland kicked the charging Sanheel into the other one and they mashed against the railings, the metal creaking and bending as their combined bulk proved too much for the rails. They broke through and tipped over the side. One managed to grab the edge of the road, its hand holding on for a second, then it slipped away.

Roland raised his good arm over his head, the blade angled down toward the three remaining Sanheel.

"You go through me," Roland said.

"I will carry your shell back to the savior," the Sanheel in the middle said and aimed its rifle at Roland.

Gauss shots snapped from the fighting position, igniting the Sanheel's shields. It whirled back toward the source of the attack and fired its rifle, blowing away a corner of the barricade. One alien swung its rifle toward the fighting position; the other aimed at Roland.

Roland bent his arm and threw his sword. It hit with a thump and buried in the alien's chest. Roland picked up the other sword from his severed arm and charged. The blade cleaved a Sanheel's head, and he left the weapon there and tackled the last one, landing on top of the alien and punching it in the face, cracking the orbit around one eye.

"Through me!" Roland brought his fist up again and struck with all the force his armor could muster. The blow split the Sanheel's skull and cracked the road beneath as the sound of distant gauss fire and fighter engines drifted over the causeway.

Roland stood up and shuffled toward the sword buried in his enemy's head, pressing what remained of his other arm against his side. He ripped the sword free and looked down the causeway where alien dead littered the road.

A team of legionaries peeked over the fighting position.

Roland motioned toward the spaceport.

"Get out of here," he said.

"It's too late for that, sir," a legionnaire said.

The causeway rumbled and a transport lifted over the walls, angling up and roaring toward the sky. Gray Eagles and black Shrikes formed an escort as the transport made its escape.

"You could have made it," Roland said.

The legionnaire shook her head. "If they got through you, they'd have to get through us."

The air rumbled and a Mule in Ibarra colors flew overhead. The rear ramp was down and a crewman waved to Roland from the cargo bay. Roland scanned through his comms frequencies, but his damaged antennae found nothing.

One of the legionnaires had a hand to the side of her helmet.

"Tell them there are two armor soldiers just to the south of here," Roland said. "Both damaged and in need of extraction. Nicodemus and Morrigan."

The legionnaire did a double take, then nodded. The Mule banked away.

"Pilot's got eyes on them," the legionnaire said. "Said he can take two suits, not three."

"Get them out of here. We'll hold here for pickup." Roland looked down at his wrecked arm. "You got a name?"

"Loiola, sir…what?" She cocked her head to one side. "Roger." She took her helmet off and red hair spilled down one side of her face. Setting the helmet down on the top of the barricade, the open end angled toward Roland, she touched the control screen on her forearm.

"Roland?" Nicodemus' voice came from the helmet's internal speakers.

"Yes, sir. Transport's away. Morrigan?"

"We're loaded." The Mule rose up from where Roland had left them behind and it roared on the same path the last transport took, afterburners glaring in the sky. "Admiral Makarov's ordered a full and immediate retreat. Ours is the last Mule off Balmaseda."

Loiola tightened the grip on her rifle.

"You had a deal with Lady Ibarra," Nicodemus said. "Now she's honoring her end. I'm transmitting our Kesaht data to your armor and you can go home."

Roland looked up at the Mule as the afterburners cut out and it vanished into the sky. A data line on his HUD flashed as a small file transferred over.

"Was that the plan all along?" Roland asked. "Leave me behind once this was done?"

"Lady Ibarra told me to give you the choice to stay with us or go back. The war made the choice for you. I am Alec Nicodemus, *ferrum corde.*"

"I am Sinéad Morrigan." Her words were tinged with static as the distance between them grew. "*Ferrum corde.*"

"Take our names with you, Roland," Nicodemus said. "—ght well…Templar." The speakers cut off. Looking to the sky, Roland asked himself if he would have returned to the Ibarras if he had the chance. After several long seconds…he still didn't have an answer.

"What was that about, sir?" Loiola asked.

"I don't know," Roland said.

"Contact." One of the legionnaires pointed down the bridge where armor advanced down the causeway. Red Uhlans followed the white-clad Templars of Colonel Martel's lance.

"Sir, what do we do?" Loiola asked.

Roland looked down at Morrigan's sword in his hand. He flipped a switch on the hilt and locked it against his leg.

"It's over," Roland said. Reaching up to his rotary cannon, he unlocked it from the mount, tossed it aside, then discarded his gauss cannons with a flick of his arm.

The Terran armor stopped a few dozen yards away, but Martel and Tongea continued forward. The colonel looked Roland over, studying the damage to his suit.

"Governor Thrace has ordered all Ibarra forces to lay down their arms," Martel said, "and surrender. I'll have your name."

"I am armor."

Martel stepped back and looked at Tongea. If Martel didn't recognize his voice, Tongea certainly would. Roland dipped his head in shame and slouched down to one knee, studying his black armor and the alien blood staining it.

"What have I done?" Roland asked. "What

have I done?"

"Why are you here?" Tongea asked.

"Because I am armor." Roland looked up. "Because I could not let others go to war while I chose to stay behind."

"Then you are our brother," Martel said. "Stand. The righteous will never be shaken. And they will be known with honor."

Roland got to his feet.

"Will everyone see it that way, sir?" Roland asked.

"No." Martel placed a hand on Roland's shoulder. "But who we are will never change."

CHAPTER 31

Roland examined the manacles around his wrists and the chain connecting them to a hook embedded in a metal table.

"Let's go over what you thought you saw in that church," Commander Kutcher said as he leaned back in his seat opposite Roland. "You encountered some sort of genetic variant of a Sanheel—"

"They were Toth." Roland sighed. "How many times do I have to tell you what they were?"

"And how many times do I have to ask you if you're a xenobiologist?" Kutcher slapped a palm to the table. "You were trained in the Armor Corps, not as a Path Finder. Just because you might have come across what could be another part of the Kesaht doesn't mean what you saw were Toth."

"I told you where the bodies are," Roland said. "Go to that church and find them. Have an actual xeno specialist get an answer that you'll accept. I told you what they were, what they said to us. They didn't move like Sanheel, weren't armed like Sanheel, and they didn't fight like Sanheel. Why? Because they weren't Sanheel. They were Toth."

"How convenient that church was destroyed in the fighting and your armor only had the last few minutes of video logs before Colonel Martel found you." Kutcher crossed his arms over his chest. "Convenient, no?"

"It was a battlefield, not a parade ground. Things tend to get damaged," Roland said.

"Hardly. Forensics says the data was erased through a nonlocal command. Your Ibarra friends didn't want us to see what's behind their curtains," he said.

"Nicodemus must have sent the command

when he transferred the Kesaht data. You have looked that over, haven't you?" Roland raised an eyebrow.

"What I'm more interested in is what you told the Ibarras." Kutcher shifted in his seat.

"All they wanted from me was what I knew about the Ixio...Ibarra made the connection to the Toth from that. Killing their warriors on Balmaseda turned theory into known fact. And since you haven't answered whether you've seen the data they gave me and since you're not that interested in anything I learned from them about the Kesaht, I assume that you did indeed get that data...sir."

Kutcher's lip twitched.

"Tell me again about the cell where you and Marc Ibarra were held..."

CHAPTER 32

President Garret reached over his desk and touched a screen, clicking off the holo of Roland's interrogation. Ambassador Ibanez, General Laran, and the Keeper sat across from him.

"He's telling the truth," Garret said. "At least, that's what the head of every intelligence agency assures me. They've had him interrogated by their best, monitored his biometric readings with every answer…everything checks out and that is pissing me off."

"We're better off with uncomfortable truths than pleasing lies," Keeper said, her metal shell shifting colors.

"The Toth!" Garret stood and threw his hands in the air. "The one species with a vendetta against Earth is out for blood. There's no common ground. No way we can make them see reason. Could you imagine someone suggesting we bury the hatchet with the Xaros? No!"

"They're a problem," Ibanez said. "But the Toth overlords stayed in the background. Bastion thinks the Kesaht are a new aggressive species, not one with any particular agenda. Believe me, I'm not going to get in front of the galaxy and use 'the Toth want revenge' as a bargaining chip." She looked down at the bottle of water in her hand and rolled her eyes.

"And what of Bastion?" Keeper asked. "We took over eight thousand Ibarrans prisoner on Balmaseda. Have you seen the medical scans? Almost all of them are post–Hale Treaty procedurals. By the Omega Provision, they should all be…destroyed."

"Bastion knows," Ibanez said. "The Ruhaald observers made sure to broadcast that we brought

Ibarra's people back with us. They don't have the med-scan results, though. Damn sure they'll want them after the Haesh come back and confirm that the bodies the Vish had are violations of the treaty."

"Will Bastion push for full enforcement?" Garret asked.

"Tough to say." Ibanez frowned. "With the Kesaht attack and our siding with the Ibarras, every last conspiracy theory you can imagine is floating around those domes. *We've been in league with the Ibarras this whole time…The humans always do the right thing like on Takeni…The Kesaht are another tool of the Xaros come to finish us off.* I've heard it all. The next conference is in five days."

"And nothing from the Ibarras after they vanished through their mobile gate?" Garret sat back down in his seat and laced his fingers behind his head.

"Almost nothing." Keeper held up a palm and her shell morphed into a black box with leather straps on the edges. "The quantum communicator we used to speak with Marc Ibarra has switched on

414

and off a few times. There's no answer when I use it, but I think they might want to talk."

"She's waiting," Garret said. "Stacey Ibarra's waiting to see what we do about the prisoners. We bend to Bastion on the Omega Provision, she'll be our enemy forever. We push back, she might become an ally."

"Then who do we want on our side?" General Laran finally spoke up. "Her or Bastion?"

"Most every adult in the Union remembers when Bastion sent the Naroosha and Ruhaald to take the Crucible away from us," Keeper said.

"That was the old Bastion," Garret said. "The new incarnation's much more reasonable."

"It's full of the same players," Keeper said. "Let's not forget that."

"If we choose Bastion over Ibarra, we've got a worse problem." Laran stood up and walked to the back of the president's office, light glinting off the plugs at the base of her skull. "There was a good deal of…fraternization between our forces and the Ibarrans on Balmaseda. Because their legionnaires keep to Saint Kallen and fought beside our Rangers, many now see them as much less of an enemy." She pointed to the holo emitter where they'd watched Roland's interrogation.

"And video of his fight on the bridge has gone viral. His identity isn't known beyond the Armor Corps, but the rank and file are calling him the Black Knight." She rubbed a temple. "If we push against the Ibarras, the Templar could mutiny—not just the armor, but also the sailors and Rangers that keep to that creed."

"Are you just going to throw this problem in my lap and skip out of here, Laran?" Garret asked.

"The problem could be the solution," she said. "The investigation into Roland is ongoing."

"What is there to investigate?" Keeper asked. "He went to fight the Kesaht. We just had two fleets stand shoulder to shoulder with the Ibarras. Are all of them under suspicion too?"

"Admiral Lettow made that decision *after* he arrived," Laran said. "Roland put on their colors before he ever arrived in system. He could have done so knowing he'd fight his own. Treason. Cut and dried."

"But all the intel types say that he's telling—" Ibanez stopped talking when the president raised a hand.

"Continue," Garret said.

"The investigation isn't final," Laran said. "It can conclude whatever we need it to."

"Tossing one person into a deep dark prison hole on Charon doesn't do much for us," Garret said.

"We release him," Laran said. "The Templar's Vigil is in a few days. The Templar will officially induct him into their ranks, and they'll do so knowing full well what he did with the Ibarras."

"And then we charge Roland with treason," Garret said.

"Now wait just a damn minute—" Keeper stood up, her surface roiling with fractals.

"It will stain the Templars," Laran said. "If they try to protect him, their guilt will only be more obvious to everyone. Who would stand beside a traitor—especially after the thorough and above-board investigation?"

"I haven't trusted the Templar since so many of them left with Ibarra. Can you neutralize them without too much…trouble?" Garret asked.

"I'll need a few weeks to get everything ready," Laran said.

"You're talking about framing the Templar," Keeper said. "They've been nothing but loyal to us—to humanity—since they were founded. You can't do this."

"If they embrace a traitor, then they aren't loyal, Keeper," Laran said. "Don't let your history cloud your judgment. We need the Terran Union to be a union. Tolerating a splinter with its own agenda will only weaken us in the middle of this crisis."

"She's right." Garret let out a long breath. "We'll let Roland back into the Corps. After that, we'll let the Templar decide where their loyalties really lie."

CHAPTER 33

The white tunic almost gleamed beneath the lights. Roland ran his hand over the stitched Templar cross and adjusted his sword belt again. The weight of the empty scabbard on his hip made him feel like he was forgetting something.

He looked up at the clock in the small dressing room: almost sunset.

Someone knocked on the door. Roland went over the ritual words in his head and put one hand on top of his empty scabbard. He opened the door, expecting to find his escort. Instead, there was Aignar in civilian clothes.

"Well look at you," Aignar said.

Roland hugged his friend and got a pat on the shoulder from a metal hand.

"Aignar! I heard you were on Balmaseda. They've kept me locked away until this morning and—and why aren't you dressed? You should be ready for the Vigil," Roland said.

"The cross suits you, Roland. It doesn't suit me, not anymore," Aignar said. "My son's in Phoenix. He wants to spend time with me. I'd rather be his father than a Templar. That's all there is to it."

"Oh...I see," Roland said.

"Besides, all I could do at fellowship was sit around and read. You got to spar with swords and drink punch. I saw you on Balmaseda. Saw you with the Ibarra armor. That was us that speared the walker."

"I appreciate your aim." Roland ran a hand down his tunic, suddenly self-conscious. "I didn't know you'd be there. They told me about the Kesaht, and that's why I—"

"You don't have to justify yourself to me. If

I had to choose between sitting on my ass or cracking Kesaht skulls, I would've hitched a ride too. Cha'ril sees it the same way," Aignar said.

"Where is she? She doing better since she almost redlined?"

"She's with her husband—"

"Husband?"

"Well, not a husband husband, but it's about the same thing."

"Husband? Cha'ril?"

"Boy, they have kept you in the dark since Martel found you on that bridge. Look, I'm on a three-day pass. They let you loose after the Vigil, give me a call. My boy would love to meet the Black Knight—won't shut up about you—and Armor Corps eat for free at every Standish-owned restaurant in the city. You know someone at Deco's that can get us a table?"

"Black Knight?"

The squeak of an opening door carried down the hallway. Aignar looked to one side and went noticeably pale.

"Glad you're back with us," Aignar said. "See you soon." He left, the metal feet in his boots making his footfalls heavier than the person coming down the hallway.

Gideon stopped once he saw Roland. He stared at the tunic and cross, his eyes alive with anger, and one side of his mouth curled with disgust.

Roland clicked his heels together and ran his hands down the crease in his pants. He stood up straight and said, "Sir."

Gideon walked closer, his face fighting back whatever rage boiled in his heart.

"You…" Gideon put a fist up next to Roland's jaw. "You were with them. Nicodemus and Morrigan and—" He brought his hand back down.

"Bassani, the fourth of your old lance, was killed in action," Roland said quietly. "I don't know when exactly. They never told me."

Gideon turned his face to one side and squeezed his eyes shut.

"He died in his armor," Roland said.

"He would have…" Gideon took a quick breath and composed himself. "Colonel Martel holds you at no fault. Captain Sobieski holds you at no fault." He reached into a pocket, pulled out the Iron Dragoons patch, and dropped it at Roland's feet.

"I am not Martel or Sobieski and it doesn't take a felt cross to make one loyal." Gideon turned on a heel and marched away. "I will see you on Mars."

Roland picked up the patch and ran his thumbs over the stitched symbol of a *fleur-de-lis* over a palm frond. He sat down in the dressing room, staring at the Iron Dragoons' symbol, their heritage.

"Some men need their hate," Tongea said from the open door. He wore the same uniform as Roland.

"Sir," Roland said and bolted to his feet. "This initiate stands ready to—"

Tongea raised a hand.

"Not yet," Tongea said. "You've got a splinter in your heart. I can see it. You know why you were selected to stand the Vigil?"

Roland slid the Iron Dragoons patch under his tunic and put it into a breast pocket.

"If an initiate has shown enough dedication and aptitude, then…that's all I thought there was to it," Roland said.

"We don't put everything in the primer." Tongea smiled, the tribal tattoos on his face almost seeming to crack with the effort. "Two Templar must endorse you. They give you their names to carry to the Vigil."

"That's why…that's why Nicodemus and Morrigan said that before they got off planet." Roland's eyes darted from side to side. "But they're not Templar. Not our Templar."

"What part of the oath says 'Terran Union' or 'Ibarra Nation'?"

"None of it."

"That's right. The Templar are Templar. They deemed you worthy. We don't question their word. Honor's not here, son," Tongea said as he touched Roland's tunic over the pocket with the patch. He moved his finger to Roland's heart, then put his hand to the side of Roland's face.

Roland thought back to the Ibarra ceremony, where the hologram of Saint Kallen touched the armor being inducted to their order.

"You're judged by your actions. Not your convictions or beliefs," Tongea said. "You take the cross and the final oath, it means you've already been measured. Already found worthy. One sees you're Templar, it means you'll pay the ultimate price for humanity. That you live by an ideal that the future must be fought for, no matter what it costs you. That's who you are."

Roland raised his chin.

"The Vigil honors those that came before," Roland said.

"And through the Vigil, you are what is honored," Tongea said. "If you're ready, I'll have your name."

"I am armor."

"Whose name do you carry?"

"Alec Nicodemus. Sinéad Morrigan."

"I know their quality and their oaths. Come with me, armor."

****

Sunset gleamed off the armor. The metal was polished to a silver sheen, all the weapons stripped away but for a ceremonial sword almost as tall as Roland, the blade clutched in the armor's hands and held tip down, the hilt locked just in front of the helm's optics.

Roland looked up at the armor, a factory-fresh unit assigned to him at the last second. His Ibarra armor had been taken away and sent to Intelligence. If he ever got it back, he was sure it would come in many small pieces.

The Corps may learn something useful. At least they got the Mauser. If we can bring a better weapon to the fight against the Kesaht, then something good came out of that fight, he thought.

Ranks of armor stood motionless to Roland's sides and behind him. Every Templar in system and not on an active deployment was here, as was the tradition. Hundreds of suits and soldiers stood in silence around him. Across a parade field was Memorial Square and the statues of the Iron Hearts, Carius' Templars, and Winged Hussars, who all died in the final battle with the Xaros.

Most of the soldiers bore a sword in their scabbard—full Templars. Roland and the rest of the initiates filled the first rank.

Tongea grabbed Roland's elbow from behind, passed a small disk into his hand, then touched his own plugs. Roland pressed the disk home and felt a hum through his plugs. He'd used the mime relays at Fort Knox before earning his full plugs on Mars.

A double pulse through the disk signaled that the new armor next to him was keyed in. Roland lifted his left foot slightly, and the armor mimicked him.

Tongea cleared his throat loudly and Roland

put his foot down quickly.

Colonel Martel walked across the front of the formation, his battle-scarred armor keeping pace behind him. He stopped ahead of Roland and faced the Templar. The colonel made the sign of the cross, then did an about-face.

"Forward," Martel sounded, "march!"

Roland stepped forward and his linked armor followed. In the distance, a drum sounded for the Templar to keep pace. Roland felt the world close in as he approached the Memorial. For years he'd walked past it to and from work, never giving the place much thought. Now...now he wished he could remember what it was to wander around the statues in ignorance again, feel what it was like to live without the burden of wars and the weight of his decision.

Childhood is over, he thought.

Dust and gravel creaked underfoot as they crossed the parade field. Martel looked over a shoulder and called a halt.

The colonel raised a hand up and slowly

moved it to grip his hilt. Roland reached through his armor and could almost feel the blade against his palms. Martel drew his sword and held it high, reflecting light from the ever-burning flame at the center of the memorial, then he flipped the sword down and gripped the hilt with both hands.

Roland raised the sword in his armor's hands, and, as one, the Templar drove their swords into the ground with a clash of metal on stone. Roland put his right hand on the sword and went to one knee, and his armor mirrored him.

Armor and soldier knelt together.

Roland lowered his head, and he heard the whine of servos from his armor as it did the same. A few minutes later, he smelled incense as Chaplain Krohe walked through the ranks with a censor.

Martel's armor pounded its sword into the ground twice. Roland held his hand against his blade as he made his armor raise the weapon and drove it back into the ground.

"*Sancti spiritus adsit nobis gratia,*" the Templar intoned. "*Kallen, ferrum corde, perducat nos ad portam salutis. Amen.*"

Roland took a deep breath, concentrating on the aroma. Now began the hard part. The Templar would recite the litany, the collected psalms and prayers of the order, all of which Roland had memorized from Bassani's primer during his time in the Ibarra prison cell. Once the litany was complete, the Templar would chant the *Da Pacem Domine* until sunrise.

Roland closed his eyes and joined in with the brother and sister Templar around him.

"Domine, Jesu Christe, sancta pater, aeterne Deus…"

****

Roland heard the sound of boots against the ground. He looked up, and Colonel Martel and Chaplain Krohe stood in front of him. Roland continued his chant, his throat sore from hours of recitation.

Krohe handed a sword to Martel. The

colonel examined it, running a thumb around the seal within the round pommel, and then Martel drove the sword into the ground in front of Roland. Martel grabbed Roland's arm, not touching the ceremonial sword the armor held and pressed his hand to the new sword's hilt.

The colonel backed up, raised one hand, and struck it against the armor's blade, which cut into Roland's palm. Roland did not flinch, continuing his chant as blood dripped down the sword. Once the first drop reached the earth, Martel removed Roland's bleeding hand and pressed it to the hilt of his new sword.

"Roland Shaw," the colonel said, "find those worthy to carry your name here. The Templar know you."

Martel nodded to Roland and moved away.

Roland ignored the throbbing pain in his hand. His voice trailed away as he felt someone else approach. He looked up, but there was no one there. The sun's early light broke around the statues, and his gaze went to the Iron Heart, Elias.

A touch went down the side of his face and Roland's eyes welled with tears.

I'm Templar, he thought. He looked down at the red cross on his tunic and felt the press of his Iron Dragoons patch beneath.

I am Templar.

CHAPTER 34

Marc Ibarra paced back and forth in his cell, twisted light from the privacy screen reflecting off his metal body.

"We've been in worse spots, Jimmy," he said, wagging a finger at the drawer where he kept the dead Qa'Resh probe. "Remember all those years under my tower while the Xaros picked the planet clean? I don't. You made me sleep through all that. Something about me going insane after so long. Well, that's not going to happen here!"

He raised his finger higher, then froze. He tucked the hand behind his back.

"I'm talking to you again. That's not what a sane person does. We talk to ourselves. Wait—no we don't."

The privacy screen snapped off and Marc

found himself looking at the closed vault door. He whirled around to Roland's cell...and found Stacey sitting on the cot, the door open. She held Bassani's primer in her lap and was gently flipping through the pages.

"Hello, Grandfather," she said.

"Stacey...I-I-you're here! Because you want to be, I assume. To talk. Not because there's been another coup and we get to stare at each other and think about our life choices," Marc said.

She set the primer aside and looked up at him, any emotions she might be feeling hidden behind her doll-like face.

"You never gave me the chance to explain," Marc said. "I kept the back channel open to Earth to feed them misinformation! That's how it works. If you'd known then, maybe something would've slipped up and then the whole situation would—"

"Stop." Stacey stood up and took a step toward the bars between them. "Lies. All lies with you. Forever and always. You built your empire on a lie that you were this amazing inventor. You raised me on a lie, that I was born just a little different by accident." She ran the tips of her silver fingers down the length of her other hand. "You built the fleet that would survive the Xaros invasion on a lie. We lied to them all to win the war…and that lie brought us the Toth.

"Our debts are called due. Old sins require absolution. Yours and mine."

Marc went to the bars and reached out to her. She stood firm.

"We created Navarre to save humanity," she said, "then you betrayed it all."

"I was only trying to help—"

"Lies!"

"What do you want from me, Stacey? An apology? To beg for my freedom? I know what I've done through the years. If my soul went to the great beyond after my body died, I'm confident it's in hell. But you know why I did it—for all of humanity, to ensure a future…not extinction."

"You thought we couldn't create that future?" She lifted her arms to her sides. "We have the procedural technology. A clean slate. Whatever future we chose to design."

"The galaxy would never let us have that," he said. "I thought it might, but for once in my life, I was naive. The procedurals are too dangerous *because* they're a clean slate. What have you done since you cast me out?"

"You lacked conviction. You lacked faith in me. Having you down here has given me breathing room…so to speak. The great plan continues…but I have built my empire on the truth. The nation knows the threat. They know what they are and why we fight. You should see them, Grandfather. The truth has set us all free."

She stepped out of the cell and ran her fingers along the bars as she walked toward the vault door.

"What did you do to Roland? Did you kill him?" Marc asked.

Stacey stopped and wrapped her fingers around a bar.

"Ah, my little poisoned seed," she said. "I

let him go home, armed with the deadliest weapon I could give him. Something you could never harness." She looked him in the eye, and Marc felt a sorrow well up inside him. The Stacey he had known was so far gone. Was there anything left of her?

"The truth." Marc's shoulders slumped.

"Wrong!" She said the word like it was a triumph. "The truth was the method, but not the weapon. I showed him who we are. Showed him a path that would take him back to Earth and his Templar with the weapon—and he went willingly. Roland is back on Earth and he's already spread the weapon…doubt. The Terrans know that we're not so different from them, that we have the same heroes. Our children cry the same as theirs. Widows weep for slain soldiers. The Ibarra Nation is more like Earth than any ally from Bastion."

"If our armor realize what you've done—"

"The armor are not loyal to me or to you," she said. "I've known this for years. They are loyal to their creed, to humanity's continued future. So long as I embody that future, they will follow me. Roland is doubt on Earth, but on Navarre, he was certainty—certainty that the Terran Union can be shown the light and brought over."

"You don't know Garret like I do," Marc said. "He put that careerist Laran in charge of their Armor Corps after we…oh no…"

"Oh yes, Grandfather. You taught me well. Divide and conquer. The longer Roland is allowed to walk around, the more doubt will spread. Eventually, Earth will be forced to act and then…"

"Rebellion," Marc said. "You're using him as a pawn. This game won't go the way you think it will, Stacey. Don't do this to him—he's a good kid."

"Now you care. You didn't care about me when you first sent me to Bastion. I didn't learn the truth until I realized that this—" She struck the bars hard enough to send them ringing. "—this is what I was."

Marc backed away.

"That's why you put him down here—to get

just the right information for him to feed back to Earth. Well played, Stacey. I'm impressed. Did you come down here just to gloat?"

"No…" She picked up a data slate from the floor. "I need your help. The political situation between Earth and Bastion is proving difficult to manage. I need your help with another project while I deal with the bigger picture." She slipped the corner of the data slate through the bars and asked, "Interested? Or do you want to keep reading the classics?"

Marc looked at the slate and the promise of new information, news from beyond his miserable little cell. If he still had a mouth, it would water.

"I'm…you have my attention." He reached for the slate, but Stacey yanked it away.

"I need an old friend and his ship," Stacey said. "Admiral Valdar and the *Breitenfeld*. You'll help me, won't you?" She tapped the slate against the bars.

Marc hesitated, then took it from her.

EPILOGUE

Tomenakai and the rest of the Kesaht Grand Council waited as Bale watched several video screens of footage from the battle on Balmaseda. Ruhaald text lined the edge of each screen, shifting with new data as the fighting continued.

The Ixion and Sanheel risen of the Grand Council stood uneasily as the ends of Bale's nervous system twitched. The Savior was difficult to read, as he'd ascended from his body many years before.

"Survivors?" Bale asked.

"The Kesaht held true to the cause and died fighting. Any that were trapped in disabled ships killed themselves before they could be taken by the humans, Master," Tomenakai said. That the Grand Council had chosen him, a disgraced Ixion whose immortalis implants had been deactivated for failure. Senior Kesaht leaders all had the implants, which kept their minds alive for centuries, jumping from body to body.

"Though, the risen commander of our colossus unit was lost when Gor'thig's flagship was destroyed," Tomenakai added.

"Gor'thig was a fool," Bale said. "He should not have damaged the Crucible so quickly. Then he allowed himself to be drawn in to the human's trap. He will not be missed."

"The human's use of the macro cannons was a new tactic," Tomenakai said. "Why our Vishrakath allies did not share that the cursed ones had this technology is of question to the Grand Council."

"The Vishrakath are spineless! Weak!" Bale raised one of the mechanical limbs beneath his tank and crushed a holo projector. "They want others to bleed for their schemes while they grow in power. This will not be their galaxy! Do you all understand that? Every race will join our great unity then we will have true peace."

"The Vishrakath have asked as to the investigation of their missing envoys," Tomenakai lowered his gaze.

"The explosion on their vessel was most unfortunate. Send off our findings and whatever organic matter remains," the ends of Bale's nerves twitched slightly.

"The losses we suffered on Balmaseda are…significant," Tomenakai said.

"And replaceable," Bale said. "We will continue the war against the cursed humans until the Vishrakath finally deliver the rest of the galaxy into the fight against Earth and the Ibarras, just as they promised. Then we will sweep across their worlds and wipe them out. All of them."

THE END
The story continues in *A House Divided!*

FROM THE AUTHOR

Richard Fox is the author of The Ember War Saga, and several other military history, thriller and space opera novels.

He lives in fabulous Las Vegas with his incredible wife and two boys, amazing children bent on anarchy.

He graduated from the United States Military Academy (West Point) much to his surprise and spent ten years on active duty in the United States Army. He deployed on two combat tours to Iraq and received the Combat Action Badge, Bronze Star and Presidential Unit Citation.

Sign up for his mailing list over at www.richardfoxauthor.com to stay up to date on new releases and get exclusive Ember War short stories. You can contact him at Richard@richardfoxauthor.com

Lightning Source UK Ltd.
Milton Keynes UK
UKHW021009211122
412567UK00012B/2421

9 781096 802808